NO NEWS IS GO[...]

A high society wedding is just [...]
something turns up missing. [...]

TV reporter Jenny McKay c[...]
heiress—and uncovers a stash of family secrets, high profile
lowlifes, political scandal, and unanswered questions. It's a
story that turns her celebrity segment "South Street Confidential" into the hottest spot on the nightly news.

And it's pulling her in a little too deep . . .

BROADCAST CLUES
A Jenny McKay Mystery
by Dick Belsky,
Former Metropolitan Editor of the *New York Post*

"NOT ONLY IS THIS BOOK TOUGH TO PUT DOWN, YOU
END UP HOPING BELSKY IS WORKING
ON A SEQUEL."
—*Associated Press*

"SEX, MAYHEM, GOSSIP, HEADLINES,
EXCLUSIVES, TV DIRT, AND SOCIETY JUICE . . .
A FLAVORFUL READ!"
—*New York Post*

"ENGAGING."
—*Kirkus Reviews*

"AN EXCELLENT STORY . . . A FINE STORYTELLER."
—*The Cedar Rapids Gazette*

"VIVIDLY RE-CREATES THE GRITTY, DOG-EAT-DOG
WORLD OF TV NEWS . . . A RIVETING
THRILLER PENNED BY A NEWS PRO."
—*Star Magazine*

"A LIVELY TALE . . . FIRST-RATE!"
—*The [Cleveland] Plain Dealer*

"WONDERFULLY FUNNY . . . A TERRIFIC BOOK.
PLEASE LET US HAVE MORE OF JENNY McKAY!"
—*KMB Newsletter*

BROADCAST CLUES

DICK BELSKY

Published in hardcover as *South Street Confidential*

JOVE BOOKS, NEW YORK

This Jove Book contains the revised
text of the original hardcover edition.
It has been completely reset in a typeface
designed for easy reading and was printed
from new film.

BROADCAST CLUES

A Jove Book / published by arrangement with
St. Martin's Press, Inc.

PRINTING HISTORY
Jove edition / June 1993

ISBN: 0-515-11153-8

Jove Books are published by The Berkley Publishing Group,
200 Madison Avenue, New York, New York 10016.
The name "JOVE" and the "J" logo
are trademarks belonging to Jove Publications, Inc.

PRINTED IN THE UNITED STATES OF AMERICA

10 9 8 7 6 5 4 3 2 1

Television seems particularly useful to (a person) who can be charming but lack ideas.

Print is for ideas. Newspapermen write not about people but policies. . . . They do not care what a man sounds like; only how he thinks. . . .

The television celebrity is a vessel. An inoffensive container in which someone else's knowledge, insight, compassion, or wit can be presented.

And we respond like the child on Christmas morning who ignores the gift to play with the wrapping paper.
— Joe McGinniss,
The Selling of the President

I know it's true . . . I saw it on TV.
— John Fogerty song

For Laura

PROLOGUE

Prologue

By the time Kathy Kerrigan was twenty-five years old, the memory of what happened that day by the water was pretty much a blur.

She still thought about it sometimes. On birthdays. Anniversaries. Sometimes late at night, when she lay awake listening to the sounds of Manhattan traffic below and the clink of ice cubes as her mother poured another drink in the next room. But the picture was never a clear one. The memories flitted into her mind only in brief snatches, coming and going like some fickle friend who never stayed long enough for you to get to know him.

Until the TV show.

For maybe the one thousandth time, she put the tape of it into the video recorder and watched it unfold on the screen in front of her. The image was only there for a few seconds. He was older, of course, weighed a bit more, and looked different. And then he was gone, melting back into the past again as suddenly as he had appeared. Viewing it all, in freeze frame, slow motion, and all the other technological wonders of the 90s, only made it seem more unreal, like one of her dreams.

1

But still . . .

In five days, Kathy Kerrigan was supposed to get married. It would be the social wedding of the year. She and Brad planned to exchange their vows at St. Patrick's Cathedral, then host a lavish reception at Tavern on the Green and finally head off for a month-long European honeymoon. The beginning of a wonderful new life for the two of them. A chance, finally, to bury the memories of the past.

But, as she sat there, with the past staring back at her from the TV screen, Kathy knew that some memories simply cannot be buried.

There was no choice for her—she had to go back.

Back to the time when she was a little girl again.

Back down the tangled trail of memories she hoped would somehow lead to the answers of what really happened that day twenty years before that had changed her life so irrevocably.

And back to wherever that trail might lead her.

1

It's 6 P.M.—Do You Know Where Your Life Is?

A lot of people have done a lot of damn important things after turning forty.

Samuel Morse was fifty-three when he first sent the words "What hath God wrought" over the telegraph. Raymond Chandler didn't write his first novel until he was fifty. And Winston Churchill was considered a has-been and a failure when he was finally elected Prime Minister of England at the age of sixty-four.

On the other hand, Thomas Edison got a patent for his first invention when he was twenty-one and figured out the electric light bulb by the time he was thirty-two. Truman Capote published his first fiction when he was nineteen. Chopin was seven when he composed his first piano concerto. For that matter, the Beatles were twenty-five when they did *Sgt. Pepper*, and they were finished by the time they hit thirty.

But, all in all, getting old isn't the worst thing in the world. It's nature's way. Everybody does it. And, as someone once observed, it's a helluva lot better than the alternative.

I turned forty yesterday.

Now I'm not one of those women who normally gets all

hung up over every birthday or little wrinkle on her face, but this is major trauma time. The big forty. Cellulite city. Mid-life crisisville. And it couldn't have come at a worse time. I'm on a new diet (the pair of Calvin Klein jeans I bought at Bloomingdale's last month won't zip up anymore); back in the dating game (my boyfriend and I just broke up); looking for a Manhattan apartment that I can afford, which is sort of like Diogenes hunting for an honest man; and I'm having a lot of problems at work. Basically then, in a matter of days, I've lost my youth, my figure, my home, my love life, and maybe my job.

I'm having a tough week.

But maybe I should start from the beginning.

My name is Jenny McKay and I work for TV station WTBK. I'm a reporter on the six o'clock news. That's not exactly the same as working for the "Dan Rather Report." WTBK is a kind of joke around New York, the seventh-ranked station in a seven-station ratings race. It's located in a big old warehouse building on South Street down by the East River, near Chinatown, while everyone else has plush offices in places like Rockefeller Center. Our place on South Street is cramped, badly needs painting, and the air-conditioning usually doesn't work. When that happens the only air we get is from a rusty fan perched near an open window overlooking a coffee shop next door, and by eleven or so you can always tell what the specials of the day are going to be. As they used to say in those Smith-Barney ads on TV, we got where we were the old-fashioned way—we earned it. We don't spend much money, we don't take much in. But it's a living.

I was sitting in the newsroom trying to deal with all these weighty issues, as well as the weighty issue of how to deal with a cottage cheese and fruit lunch, when a voice startled me.

"Hi, love," it said.

I looked up to find a guy I'd never seen before standing by my desk. He seemed to be in his early thirties, with thinning, closely cropped hair, and wearing corduroy slacks, a champagne shirt, and a cardigan sweater wrapped around his shoulders. I have never in my life met anyone who wore a sweater wrapped around his shoulders that I liked. I wasn't about to start now.

"The name's McKay," I said evenly. "Jenny McKay. Ms. Mckay is what I prefer. Or Miss McKay, if you like. But never *love.*"

"Sure, sure." He grinned. "I can relate to that." He plopped down in a chair next to my desk and looked around the newsroom.

"Boy, you sure don't spend a lot on overhead here, do you?" he said.

"You here on some sort of business?" I asked wearily. "Or are you just an interior decorator making a house call?"

Still grinning, he stuck out his hand.

"Bob Carstairs," he said. "I'm working with Edward Cafferty."

Edward Cafferty was the station's owner.

"Good for you," I said.

"Your boss back there said I should talk to you." He pointed toward the office of Joe Gergen, the news director.

"Gergen sent you to me."

He nodded.

I picked up the phone in front of me and dialed Gergen's extension.

"There's a guy sitting next to me now," I said. "Someone named Carstairs. Says he works for Cafferty. Did you send him out here?"

"That's right."

"Why?"

"Listen to him. He's got a story idea for you."

"I've already got a story. You assigned me to cover the opening of the circus this morning. It starts in forty minutes and—"

"Oh yeah, I forgot about that. Well, I'll get Travers to do it."

"Travers! He's the goddamn weatherman, for chrissakes!"

"We all have to pitch in here, Jenny. Travers'll do the circus. You talk to Carstairs."

"Christ!" I muttered.

"And Jenny . . ."

"Yeah?"

"Remember he was hired by Edward Cafferty. The guy who owns this station. Be nice to him."

"I'm always nice."

"Sure," he said and hung up. I think he was being sarcastic. I turned back to Carstairs.

"Okay, so what do you have?"

"I've come up with an idea for a new segment to run regularly on the six o'clock news," he said. "It'll be about the world of gossip and celebrities and the New York fast lane. We'll call it 'South Street Confidential.'"

"Sounds nifty," I told him.

"Do you know who Kathy Kerrigan is?" he asked.

I nodded. "Sure, she's one of the beautiful people around town, some sort of an heiress or something."

"That's as good a description as any, I guess," Carstairs said. "Her family runs The Kerrigan Corp., which owns about half the free world. Oil, financial institutions, manufacturing— you name it, The Kerrigan Corp. is involved."

"Isn't she related to the senator too? Jonathan Wincott, our esteemed senator from New York?"

"That's her stepfather. He married Kathy's mother, Audrey, about fifteen years ago."

I nodded. The names seemed vaguely familiar to me from the gossip columns, but that's about all.

"So what's the story?" I asked.

"She's getting married," Carstairs said.

"Kathy Kerrigan?"

"That's right." He took out a clipping from *The New York Times* and handed it to me. It was an announcement of the marriage of Kathleen Mary Kerrigan to someone named Bradley Jeffries. There was a picture of her with a caption underneath saying "Betrothed." I laid the clip down on the desk in front of me.

"And you want me to be the bridesmaid?" I asked.

"No," Carstairs said, "I want you to cover it."

I stared at him. "Cover it? Like in cover a story?"

He nodded.

"Are you sure you don't have me confused with Rona Barrett?"

"It's a good story, Miss McKay," he sighed. "A lot of our viewers will care about it. Our studies have shown that people have an insatiable appetite to learn more about the rich and famous."

"Oh yeah? Who did the study—Robin Leach?"

He stood up.

"Do the story, Miss McKay. Cover the wedding. Cover all the wedding preparations. Make it come alive for our viewers."

A few minutes later I was in Gergen's office.

"Who cares about a stupid society wedding?" I told him.

"Bob Carstairs does. And Cafferty has hired him as a special consultant to give us advice, boost our ratings, and improve our general competitive situation in the tri-state market. Anyway, that's what the press release that's coming out later today says. And he answers directly to Cafferty. So if he says it's a good story, it's a good story." Gergen paused and looked at me. "You could use a good story, Jenny."

"What's that supposed to mean?"

I knew the answer. My contract with the station was up next month, and there were rumblings that it might not be renewed. Gergen had warned me about it the day before. Something about my personality quotient and interaction with the rest of the WTBK "action news" team not being good enough. Personality quotient, can you believe it? Damn, a few years ago I was a real journalist, writing life-style features for a paper called the *Trib*. Then it folded, and I wound up at a magazine. When it went under, I worked at the *Greenwich News*—a weekly like *The Village Voice*—until it died. Three strikes and out, I was unemployed. Finally Gergen, my old managing editor at the *Trib*, came through with this TV job. I'd given it a shot, but I just didn't seem cut out for the work.

"It's the same business I told you about the other day," Gergen said now. "They're on my case about you upstairs. They say you're still not relating to the others on-screen."

"What does that mean?"

"Well, take last night, for instance, when Cassie made that joke to you on the air."

Cassie White was one of our two anchor people. She was a twenty-five-year-old blonde hotshot from Boston who made no secret of the fact she planned to have an important job at one of the big networks by the time she was thirty.

"Yeah?" I said.

"You'd just finished reporting on a celebrity pie-baking contest. Cassie said to you: 'Boy, it must have really taken a lot of crust to cover an assignment like that.' But you didn't laugh. You didn't give her a quip back. Why not?"

"Because it wasn't funny."

"Who gives a crap? It's just show business."

"I see, I thought it was journalism."

"Don't start with me, Jenny. You know what I mean."

I didn't say anything.

"Listen," Gergen said, "do me a favor, do yourself a favor. Bust your ass on the Kathy Kerrigan wedding story. Go up and talk to the family now. Maybe we can get some kind of an advance on the air tonight."

I went back to my desk. Carstairs was nowhere around. Larry Travers, the weatherman, was getting ready to go cover the circus. Travers was a middle-aged black man who always seemed unhappy.

"The circus," he muttered. "The fucking circus, can you believe it? What the hell do I know about the circus? Hell, I hate the circus. I'm a meteorologist, not an elephant and clown reporter. They've got absolutely no respect here for my profession."

"You said it," I told him. "I mean you almost never see Storm Field covering elephants."

"That's goddamn right."

"Of course, he makes about five hundred grand a year too," I pointed out.

Travers grunted something unintelligible.

I walked back to my desk and sat down. In my mail there was a late birthday card from a guy I knew who did PR for the telephone company. There was a smiling woman on front and the words "A lot of people think it's not so bad turning 40." Then inside it said "Of course, most of them are in old age homes." I ripped the card into little pieces, threw it away, and sat there brooding.

I was getting too old for these hassles. Most women my age were mothers. Some of them even grandmothers. I needed to get my life together and settle down—find a new man, maybe a new career too. It still wasn't too late for me to go to law school or get a graduate business degree. Maybe I'd even leave the city, find a little farm someplace.

I thought about something Tony, my ex-boyfriend, said to me the week before he left.

"Life's passing you by, Jenny."

At the time we were lying in bed after making love.

"Thanks," I told him. "I saw skyrockets too."

"I'm sorry, but all you think about is that damned job. Chasing fires, murders, politicians, and God knows what else twenty-four hours a day. Even when we're making love, your mind seems a million miles away."

"I'm just going through a difficult phase of my career," I said defensively. "It'll pass."

"When? You're going to be forty next week."

"I know I'm going to be goddamn forty," I snapped.

"So is this the way you're going to be all your life?" he asked.

I shook my head now thinking about it. What an asshole Tony was. I was better off without him.

I got up and walked to the ladies' room at the end of the corridor.

When I got there, I stared at myself in the mirror. The face looking back at me didn't look like a forty-year-old woman. Okay, there were a few gray hairs speckled through the brown ones. And a wrinkle here and there. But what's wrong with being forty? Linda Evans is over forty. So is Raquel Welch. And Candice Bergen too.

Hey, Mary Tyler More is now past fifty.

On the other hand, all Mary Tyler Moore's success on TV came when she was Laura Petrie in her twenties and Mary Richards in her thirties. By the time Mary was forty, her situation comedies were bombs. Hmmm.

I looked at myself again. I noticed more gray in my hair this time. And the wrinkles seemed deeper. I looked tired, as if I needed to sleep for about a week.

Damn!

Maybe Tony was right.

Maybe that's why he rode off into the sunset.

Maybe all work and no play does make Jenny a dull lay.

2
The Vast Wasteland

I grew up watching TV news back in the 60s.

You remember the 60s. John F. Kennedy. The Beatles. Haight-Ashbury. I dated a guy then named Tommy Kane who played guitar and sang protest songs and thought he was going to be the next Bob Dylan. I was going to write a Great American Novel that would change the world.

A lot has changed since then. Now JFK, Jr., dates movie stars. John Lennon is dead. And San Francisco is better known for earthquakes. The last I heard Tommy was teaching music and auto shop at a high school in Clifton, New Jersey, and I'm covering society weddings for TV. Life goes on.

The people who gave you the news seemed different back then.

Cronkite. Huntley and Brinkley. Howard K. Smith. John Chancellor. Not guys who worry about what sweater to wear. Or who remind you of the William Hurt character in *Broadcast News*.

I think it all began coming apart in the 70s with the advent of what is known as "happy news." Suddenly we got talking mannequin heads for news anchors. Wisecracking newscasters.

Weathermen who dressed up in silly outfits to give the forecast. Sportscasters more interested in doing their schtick than in giving the scores. It no longer mattered what you knew or had to say, only how you looked.

Now, as we make our way through the 1990s, this has been combined with a new phenomenon: tabloid TV. As in the *National Enquirer* or some of the British newspapers, suddenly anything goes. Juicy gossip about the stars. Relatives of murder victims weeping over open coffins. Grotesque stories about two-headed babies and dying children. Exorcists. Astrologers. Bizarre sexual practices. Any pretense of journalism has gone out the window, and the TV news show has become the equivalent of something you glance at while standing in the supermarket checkout line.

And along with the news we've gotten the pseudo news shows. Oprah. Sally Jesse Raphael. Geraldo. Maury Povich. ''A Current Affair.'' ''Hard Copy.'' The lines between news and entertainment and exploitation have become totally blurred. Where does it all stop?

Now I don't mean to suggest I have a solution to any of this. On the contrary, I'm part of the problem.

I was in a Channel Six mobile van riding uptown to Kathy Kerrigan's place. We took the FDR to the Upper East Side, then 59th Street west until we got to Central Park and the Hilldale House, where she lived. It was the end of June, and New York was already in the middle of its first major heat wave. The temperature was in the nineties, and there were warnings it could hit one hundred before the end of the day. All over the city kids were playing under open fire hydrants, air conditioners were going full blast, and the unlucky ones who didn't have them were sitting on front stoops in their T-shirts.

The Hilldale House is one of those fancy buildings on Central Park South. Snooty doorman. Chandeliered lobby. Terraces overlooking the park. The kind of place you read about whenever Princess Radziwell has a birthday or Diane Von Furstenberg throws a dinner party.

My camera crew and I walked through the marble lobby to where a doorman—in immaculate black uniform, highly shined shoes, and white gloves—was monitoring an elaborate TV security system.

"Is there something I can do for you?" he asked coolly.

We were weighed down with equipment. Besides me and my microphone, there were Alan Sanders, carrying a ton of video stuff, and Artie Jacobson, my sound man. It was hot outside, and we were all sweating.

"Yeah," I told him. "How do we find Kathy Kerrigan?"

"Ms. Kerrigan or her family don't see anyone without an appointment," he said stiffly.

"Tell them we're with WTBK. Channel Six. We'd like to do a Six segment on her wedding."

"Did you call to make arrangements?"

"No," I said. I'd thought about it, but sometimes I find it's just better to show up on someone's doorstep. The element of surprise.

"Well, then I don't see how . . ."

Sanders groaned. "C'mon, Pops," he said. "There's no time for this. We're not here to shoot porn movies of the chick. Just point us to the apartment, okay?"

Sanders is a twenty-three-year-old black hotshot who's good, but gets me in trouble sometimes with his mouth.

The doorman's face turned red with anger.

"Hey, hey," I interceded, "there's no problem here. We just want to give them some publicity. How about you get them on the house phone for us and see what they say?"

The doorman finally agreed. He picked up the phone, said something into it, and listened for a second. Then he sighed and handed me the receiver. A woman's voice came over the line.

"Kathy Kerrigan?" I asked.

There was a long pause.

"Uh . . . no . . . she's not here."

"Is this her mother?"

"Yes. This is Audrey Wincott." Her voice sounded a little funny—like she was slurring her words. Or maybe it was just a bad connection.

"My name is Jenny McKay," I said. "I'm with 'Channel Six News.' We'd like to talk to you and Kathy about her wedding. Could we come up and do that?"

Now another sound came over the line. She seemed to be crying.

"Mrs. Wincott, are you all right?"

"She's gone," she sobbed. "She disappeared."

"Disappeared? You mean like missing?"

"Yes. Oh, I don't know what to do. Could you help me . . . ?"

My mind was racing. Damn, this could be a real story. Heiress disappears on the eve of her wedding.

"Just tell your doorman to let us in," I said.

A few seconds later, after talking again to Mrs. Wincott, he turned to us and said grimly: "It's penthouse apartment A. Take the express elevator on the left all the way to the top floor."

We gathered up our gear and headed in that direction.

"Thanks a lot," I smiled sweetly over my shoulder. "Have a nice day."

On the way up, I glared at Sanders.

"That was real cute back there. You almost screwed up this interview before it began."

"Look, it makes me nervous to wait around in lobbies of buildings like this."

"Why's that?"

"Because I don't like being arrested."

"I don't get you."

"I'm black, remember?"

"So?"

"Well, if you lived in a building like this, and you saw a young black dude walking through it with a lot of expensive video equipment, what would you think?"

I smiled. "I see your point."

Jacobson just leaned against the wall of the elevator and worked on a crossword puzzle as we rode to the top floor. He did crossword puzzles all day long wherever he was.

"Who gives a fuck?" he muttered. "It's a shit assignment anyway."

They were all shit assignments to Jacobson. He was fifty-four, and nothing excited him anymore. To hear him tell it, nothing ever had. We used to play this game on long stakeouts:

try to find some assignment—just once in his career—that had gotten his adrenaline going. No one ever won. Murders. Big fires. Elections. Vietnam. They were all the same old boring shit as far as he was concerned. Once I thought I had him. "How about the Kennedy assassination?" I asked. "That's the biggest story of our lives. Even you couldn't have acted jaded about that. C'mon, didn't you get just a little excited when John F. Kennedy was killed that Friday afternoon back in 1963?" Jacobson barely looked up from the crossword puzzle he was doing. "It didn't happen on my shift." He shrugged and went back to his puzzle.

The elevator doors opened and we stepped out into the plushly carpeted hallway. Sanders rolled his eyes at the surroundings.

"Lawdy, Miz Jenny, you white folks sure do live nice," he said. "Wait'll I get back to Harlem and tell my mama about this."

I grunted. "Do me a favor and drop the depressed minority routine," I told him. "I happen to know you grew up in Larchmont and your father's a corporate lawyer who makes two hundred and fifty grand a year."

A woman was waiting for us at the door of penthouse apartment A.

"Miss McKay?" she said. "I'm Audrey Wincott."

Audrey Wincott was probably about fifty, but she seemed to be trying hard to look thirty-five. She had bright red hair that hung down in bangs over her forehead. Looking at the skin around her eyes I figured her for at least one facelift already. There was a drink in her hand. She led us to a velvet couch in the middle of a huge living room with a view of Central Park.

"Here's the way we'll do it," I told Mrs. Wincott. "I'm going to ask you some questions first, without any camera, to get some idea of where we should head in the interview. Then we'll turn the lights on, get the camera rolling, and do it for the six o'clock news. Okay?"

Mrs. Wincott nodded. I wasn't totally sure she understood what I was saying.

We sat down on the couch.

"Tell me a little bit about your daughter."

"Well, Kathy is twenty-five. She's quite attractive and intelligent—she received her masters in literature from Harvard last year. Since then she's been living at home."

"And you don't have any idea where she is now?"

She shook her head.

"When's the last time you saw her?"

"Two days ago. She left the apartment about two o'clock."

"Where was she going?"

"Out."

"That covers a lot of territory," Sanders chipped in.

I glared at him.

"I don't know where she went," she said quietly.

"Has she ever done anything like this before?" I asked. "Disappeared, that is?"

Mrs. Wincott didn't say anything. Instead she drank what was left in her glass, walked over to a bar by the window, and poured herself another.

"Your daughter, Mrs. Wincott," I said, "has she ever gone off like this without telling you?"

She sat down again on the couch and twisted the glass nervously in her hands.

"I'm going to be honest with you, Miss McKay. We're not a particularly close family sometimes. Certainly not as close as I would like . . ."

"Oh?"

"Yes. It was not that unusual for Kathy and me to go a few days without talking to each other. She's a very headstrong girl."

"What about her relationship with her father?"

"Her stepfather. The senator is not Kathy's real father. He died a number of years ago."

"Right. So anyway, how did they get along?"

"Kathy and her stepfather or Kathy and her real father?"

"Both."

"Kathy idolized her father. She was crushed by his death, which happened when she was very young. Because of that, I guess, she's never been close to my second husband, Jonathan. They don't communicate too much."

I looked down at what I'd written in my notebook.

"Her marriage is supposed to be this weekend," I said. "Do you think maybe she just got cold feet?"

Mrs. Wincott shrugged.

"Could she have run off somewhere with another guy?" I blurted out. I paused then, realizing that it probably sounded insensitive. "These things happen sometimes," I said quietly.

"I just don't know."

"And her fiancé. What's his name again?"

"Brad Jeffries. He works for Kerrigan Oil."

"Is it possible he might know more about it?"

She shook her head. "No, he's just as mystified as we are."

"How about your husband? Can I talk to the senator?"

She stood up and walked over to the bar and poured herself another refill. "Well, he's in Washington now. I suppose when he comes back . . ."

"Have you reported her missing to the police?" I asked.

"No. Tom told me not to."

"Tom?"

"Tom Sewell. He's our family attorney. He's also been a lifelong friend as well as sort of a substitute father for Kathy. Anyway, he said she was just off on her own somewhere and would be back soon."

"But you're not so sure."

"Well, I've been getting more worried as the days go by. So when you came here today . . . well, I just decided on my own that something had to be done."

I looked down at my notes again.

"One more question before we get started for real," I said. "You told me Kathy left the apartment about two P.M. What did she do before then?"

"Well, that morning she'd gone to see Tom Sewell."

"Your lawyer?"

She nodded.

"Why?"

"Kathy said she wanted to ask him some questions about her father."

"You mean the senator?"

"No, her real father."

"The one who died. Why was she asking about him?"

Audrey Wincott shrugged. "I don't know."

"Did you ask her?"

"Of course. But she just got very agitated. . . . As I told you, Kathy and I don't communicate very well sometimes."

It took thirty minutes for Sanders, Jacobson, and me to set up the equipment and tape the interview. It went pretty well, I thought.

Afterward, Audrey Wincott walked us to the door.

"Miss McKay, I'm so glad you came this morning."

"Well, I'm . . ."

"You do think this will help, don't you?" she asked. "I mean I know I haven't always been a very good mother to Kathy. But I do love her."

I wasn't sure what to say.

"Tell her on TV that I want another chance to patch it up," she said.

"I'll do my best."

"God bless you," she said, grasping my hand with one of hers. The other hand still held a drink.

A few minutes later, as we rode in the elevator, Sanders looked at me and rolled his eyes. "She's a real piece of work, huh?"

"Yeah, the lady's got herself a real drinking problem," Jacobson muttered. "The way she's going, I figure she should be good and stewed by lunchtime."

I shrugged. "You guys are too cynical."

"Like you're not." Sanders snorted.

"I believed her," I said. "I really think she is worried about her daughter."

Jacobson just shook his head. "The day you start believing people," he said, "is the day you should get into some other line of work."

"Maybe you're right," I said.

We rode the elevator the rest of the way to the ground floor in silence, then walked through the marbled lobby of the Hilldale House and into the hot sunshine outside.

The doorman didn't bother to say good-bye.

As we started to head back to the station we got a call on the car phone in our van. A gunman had taken hostages during a bank robbery at Park Avenue and 33rd St. Gergen wanted to divert us there. No problem, we told him.

Only there was. Somewhere in the 40s we got stuck in a massive traffic jam that turned much of Midtown into a giant parking lot. According to the WINS-Radio traffic reporter, it was all because of a huge water main that had burst and flooded 42nd Street. There was no way in and no way out.

Eventually Sanders called the office to tell them about our situation. When he hung up there was an annoyed expression on his face.

"Well," he announced, "we're not going to be the lead item on the six o'clock news tonight, that's for sure."

"What do you mean?" I asked.

"They want us to forget about the Park Avenue bank and get some footage of this traffic mess. Angry motorists, harried traffic cops—that sort of thing."

"So what's the lead story?"

"The hostage thing."

"Is it still going on?" I asked.

"No, it's over."

"And?"

"It seems the gunman wanted to talk to a member of the media before he surrendered. Guess who got there first and volunteered?"

"Don't tell me. . . ."

"That's right, Cassie White. She walked out of the building with the guy, right into the hands of the cops. Another WTBK exclusive under her belt."

"Christ," I muttered.

Covering the traffic jam wasn't as easy as it sounded. First, we had to abandon the van for a while in the middle of the street, which infuriated everyone behind us. Then, a lot of the drivers—who'd been stewing in cars under the broiling sun for more than an hour—seemed to enjoy taking out their frustrations against us. I lost count of how many times people shut windows in my face or gave me the finger. The heat was really bad, too. By the time we got enough interviews I was soaked with perspiration and my blouse was sticking to my back.

Then, when we got back to our van, we discovered that someone had urinated down the side of it.

Eventually we managed to edge our way out of the mess and make it over to the East Side, but the urine smell lingered during the entire hot ride back to the office.

I love New York in June, how about you?

3
South Street Confidential

ANNOUNCER: It's the News at Six on Six—with the WTBK team of newsbreakers!

Here's Conroy Jackson and Cassie White at the anchor desk, Bill Hanrahan on sports, Larry Travers with the weather, and Jenny McKay with a new celebrity segment.

While the announcer was doing this voice-over, a pulsating theme song nearly drowned him out. There was no real melody to it, just the pounding that was supposed to connote an air of urgency. I sometimes wonder who wrote it. Probably the same guy who writes "Heartbeat of America" for Chevy.

We sat on the news set waiting for the theme music to stop. My hair was perfectly coiffed by the makeup people. I was wearing a heavily starched white blouse, a sky blue scarf around my neck, and a navy blue blazer with the WTBK emblem on the front pocket. It was times like this when I really missed newspapers where you could dress any way you wanted. When I had worked at the *Trib*, I sometimes showed up wearing a T-shirt, baggy pants, and sandals. It didn't matter how you looked so long as your work was good. Here your looks were all that mattered. The only thing you could get away with was from the waist down, which was always out of the camera's line of sight. Today I was wearing a pair of blue jeans. My own little rebellion.

ANNOUNCER: And now, here's Conroy and Cassie with tonight's news.

The red light on the camera flashed and the two of them smiled.

JACKSON: A tense hostage situation is over in Midtown after a four-and-a-half hour siege. Our Cassie White was there and she not only covered the story, she was the story! Cassie?

WHITE: Thank you, Conroy. It began at 10:15 this morning when a gunman walked into the First National Savings Bank at Park Avenue and Thirty-third Street. When it was over a bank manager was dead, the gunman in custody, and twenty employees and customers were just thankful it didn't turn out worse.

It took six minutes for her to do the segment. At least five of those minutes were devoted to recounting how she volunteered to go in and talk to the gunman, and then convinced him to surrender to police. There was videotape of her walking out of the building with the guy into the hands of waiting police.

JACKSON: Well, it sounds like a very frightening experience. We're all proud of you, Cassie.

WHITE: Thank you. But my only regret is I couldn't stop the one death that resulted from this tragedy. That's something I'll never forget. My heartfelt sympathy—and the sympathy of all here at WTBK ''News''—goes out to the family of bank manager Walter Heller who died at the gunman's hands.

The screen dissolved to a picture of the slain bank employee, then back to Cassie. She had a solemn look on her face.

The camera zoomed in for a closeup of that. If she could have managed to work up a tear trickling down her cheek I'm sure she would have. But there wasn't time. There was more news to do.

The second story of the night was about a derailment at Grand Central Station. Then there was a press conference by the mayor and a corruption trial going on at the federal courthouse. After that they got to me.

WHITE: Well, as you probably know, the big social event in town this week is supposed to be the society wedding of Kathy Kerrigan, heiress to the Kerrigan fortune and daughter of Senator Jonathan Wincott, at St. Patrick's Cathedral. Everyone who is someone has been invited. But now our Jenny McKay has learned that there could be a startling no-show to the big event: Kathy herself. Jenny?

She turned to me and smiled sweetly. I smiled back. Friendly. Pals. We're just one big happy family here at WTBK News.

McKAY: The invitations are all sent out, the caterer's ready to go, and the honeymoon reservations have been made. Everything's ready for the big wedding at St. Patrick's Cathedral between Kathy Kerrigan and Brad Jeffries, an executive in her father's financial empire. Everything except one thing:
   No one can find the bride!

While I was talking, a logo with the words *South Street Confidential* appeared on the screen behind me. Then the video went to a view of the outside of the Hilldale House.

McKAY: WTBK has learned that Kathy Kerrigan has dropped out of sight ever since leaving her family's fifteenth-floor penthouse apartment here on Central Park South. She simply went out the door and never came back. Since then nothing—no calls, no telegrams, no communication of any kind.

Now there's no indication of any foul play. In fact, the police haven't even been called in on the matter, since the family was concerned about embarrassing publicity. But this morning I spoke with Kathy's mother, Audrey Wincott, who has become increasingly worried over her daughter's disappearance.

The video cut to a scene of Mrs. Wincott in the living room.

MRS. WINCOTT: I last saw Kathy two days ago. She went out in the morning and came back around lunchtime, then went out again at approximately two in the afternoon. When she didn't come back that evening, I wasn't that concerned. I figured she'd just gotten involved doing something. But the next morning I discovered her bed hadn't been slept in. I called around to a lot of people— friends, her fiancé, business associates—and no one had seen her.

McKAY: Did she give you any indication at all as to where she was going?

MRS. WINCOTT: No. None at all. She just left very suddenly.

McKAY: What about the plans for the wedding? What's happening there?

MRS. WINCOTT: They're on hold for the time being. A lot of time and money is involved. But I'm not concerned about that. All I care about now is Kathy.

McKAY: Do you think something might have happened to her? Do you have any reason to think her disappearance might not be voluntary?

MRS. WINCOTT: Well, we didn't think so. At least not at first. But now . . . well, I just don't know.

McKAY: If Kathy's out there somewhere watching this right now, Mrs. Wincott, is there a message you want to convey to her?

MRS. WINCOTT: I'd just like to say, "Kathy, honey, we miss you. Come home and let's talk. Whatever the problem is, we can work it out. Please honey, come home now."

The camera came back to me live in the studio.

McKAY: A couple of other notes of interest here. Financial experts tell me the Kerrigan family fortune is worth upwards of six hundred million dollars. As for the wedding itself, well the estimates are that it was going to cost somewhere in the neighborhood of one hundred thousand dollars. But, for the time being anyway, that wedding could be off. And the whereabouts of Kathy Kerrigan remain unknown.

I turned toward Cassie and Conroy and smiled.

McKAY: Cassie?

WHITE: Thank you, Jenny, for that report. [She turned to her co-anchor.] Whew! Six hundred million dollars. That's a lot of money.

JACKSON: It sure is. That's even more than you make, isn't it, Cassie?

WHITE: [chuckling] A little, but not as much as you get, right?

They both laughed now.

JACKSON: Well, speaking of millionaires, Queens has a new one today. He's Anthony Pressarrio, a twenty-two-year-old chef at Tasty Pizza on Queens Boulevard, who today received a three-million-dollar check from the New York State Lottery . . .

I made a face off-camera. God, I thought, if the two of them get any cuter I'm going to puke.

Later, after the show was over, Gergen called me into his office.

"Not bad," he said. "Not bad at all. Politics. Money. A missing girl. That ought to be good for the ratings."

"Since when did we care about ratings?" I asked.

"That's not funny," Gergen told me. "Especially not now. Cafferty's brought in Bob Carstairs because he doesn't think we have to be last in the ratings. He thinks we can turn it around. Maybe he's right. This guy Carstairs has quite a track record. His last station was in Sacramento. He turned it around in less than a year."

"Sacramento?" I thought for a second. "Isn't that the station where the anchorman did the live on-the-air seance to try to communicate with Elvis's spirit?"

"Yeah, that's it," Gergen·said. He grimaced noticeably. "They got a sixty share that night."

Sometimes I thought Gergen was as much out of place in TV as I was. For fifteen years he'd been the managing editor of the New York *Trib*. He was hard-driving, decisive, tough, and colorful—all the things a good newspaper editor needed to be. Sort of like Humphrey Bogart in *Deadline U.S.A.* or Cary Grant in *His Girl Friday*. But now he acted different, unsure of himself at times, often just going through the motions. He seemed to have lost something over the years. Hell, maybe we all did.

"You're going to follow up on this Kerrigan girl tomorrow, right?" he asked.

"Yeah. I thought I'd try the fiancé, the stepfather, and this friend of the family Mrs. Wincott mentioned to me. A lawyer named Thomas Sewell."

Gergen nodded. "We're going to put you on 'South Street Confidential' full time," he said.

"What are you talking about?"

"I want you to do more celebrity interviews, gossip on clubs around town, star chatter, who's sleeping with whom. It'll be a three-minute segment every night."

"Why me?"

"Why not? It's a good assignment. Carstairs gives this stuff a really high priority."

"But I'm no celebrity reporter," I told him.

"You are now."

"I'm a hard-news reporter," I insisted. "A damn good hard-news reporter."

"You're not that good a hard-news reporter," he said. "At least not on TV."

"What's that supposed to mean?"

"It means that 'South Street Confidential' could be the life raft that saves you, Jenny. Go for it."

"Is that a warning?"

"Let's just call it good advice."

Cassie White walked by the open door. Gergen saw her and motioned for her to come in.

"I've got something to say to you," he told her.

She smiled. "I know. The hostage arrest was a helluva piece, wasn't it?"

"That wasn't what I was going to say," he said.

"But I thought—"

"Cassie, that was a damn fool thing you did today. You could have gotten yourself killed."

She appeared stunned. "Well, I was just trying to get the story," she stammered.

"No, that went beyond getting a story. You've got to use common sense out there on the street. This isn't a game. You were lucky this time. The next time you might not be."

Cassie stared at him.

"And this isn't the first time either," Gergen continued. "Last week, you went skydiving out of a plane without any formal instruction. The week before you climbed into a bear cage at the Zoo to show it could be unsafe for children."

"I'll do anything it takes to get me out . . . I mean get the story."

"Get you out of here? You mean to a better job?"

"Hey, sure, I'd love to go to a network someday. Is that such a crime?"

"Not at all. It's very admirable. I'm just concerned with how you do it."

"I'll do it my way," Cassie said.

I cleared my throat. "Didn't Frank Sinatra say that first?"

Cassie glared at me.

"You want me to waste my life away here?" she asked Gergen. "To become just another mediocrity? To wind up like her?" She pointed in my direction.

"Thanks." I smiled. "I admire your work, too."

"Just try to be a little more careful, Cassie, okay?" Gergen said.

She didn't say anything. Just whirled around and stalked out of the room.

"Nice lady," I said after she'd left.

"Aw, she's all right." Gergen shrugged. "She's just young and full of ambition."

"That's not all she's full of," I told him.

4

Liz and Suzy
and Me

Celebrity news works like this.

There are maybe thirty people—thirty-five tops—that anyone in the gossip world writes about.

You know the names as well as I do. Sylvester. Burt. Liza. Most of these people have not done anything important in years. Some of them never did. But this doesn't stop the gossip mavens chronicling their every movement—from lunching at Tavern on the Green to shopping at Tiffany's to partying at Nell's or the Limelight.

Now the people who are actually accomplishing great things are not in the gossip columns. That's because no one knows who they are yet. Eventually people will find out and they too will take their place alongside Sylvester and Burt and Liza. By that time, though, they probably won't be doing anything important either. As you can see it's somewhat of a vicious circle.

It is important to understand that the people who write about this sort of thing for a living—Liz Smith or Suzy—don't always go to parties and restaurants and such to cover events. A lot of the time they just sit home and get calls and handouts from press agents, which they then print verbatim in their columns.

Occasionally, this can cause some embarrassment, such as the time one gossip writer wrote about a big party where she said caviar was served and a host of other luminaries attended. As it turned out, an enterprising reporter from another paper actually went to the party, where he found out that none of those people was there and the food being served was jumbo shrimp. This caused quite a stir for a while in New York gossip circles.

Here's the way it usually goes in one of those columns: A press agent for someone—let's call him Joe No-Talent—calls up Liz or Suzy or ''Page Six'' or the ''New York Intelligencer'' and gives them a news tip. The next day an item appears something like this:

Joe No-Talent was lunching at Tavern on the Green yesterday and told friends he's fielding offers from Hollywood, which wants to turn his hot new book into a screenplay. He hopes to get Jack Nicholson and Meryl Streep to play the leads. Steven Spielberg may direct.

Now there is no movie deal in the works. No contract with Jack Nicholson or Meryl Streep. No overtures made to Steven Spielberg. Maybe even no book. Just a press agent planting a rumor, hoping it will make his client sound hot to some Hollywood mogul who will leap to his phone to try to beat Spielberg to the punch. And it's all perfectly acceptable in the world of celebrity gossip.

Often the items seem to read like one big inside joke. I can read an entire column and not know most of the people the writer is talking about, but the writer obviously does. And she assumes her readers do too.

It goes something like this:

Oh, by the way, darlings, Sly Stallone showed up at Nell's with a very special friend on his arm, who he introduced to Duke and Lady Astor, Nan Kempner and Diane Von Furstenberg. Not to mention Prince Albert and the Countess del Christo. Cornelia Guest, Sly's ex, was there, too, but she DIDN'T meet the prospective new Mrs. Stallone. Instead she occupied herself with Prince Von Errickson, a relationship that is still very much on the front burner. But then you already knew that, didn't you, darlings?

Or else:

Flash: Betty Bimbo, who was so terrific opposite Liza Minnelli in her last picture, has quietly married Gary Goldigger in a quiet ceremony last week in the south of France. All very quietly, shhhhhhhhhh.

Not only is this news to you, dear readers, it's also news to several rejected suitors who have crossed Betty's path in recent weeks. They are going to be devastated when they read this. No names, please. You know who you are.

That's the kind of stuff they say people go for. Me, I'd prefer root canal. Go figure.

But it was a world I was going to have to enter if I wanted to continue making a living. Another day, another dollar.

I left the office about 7:30 and went straight home. Home—for the moment anyway—was a one-bedroom apartment on Washington Place in the Village, with a view overlooking Sixth Avenue. I unlocked the three locks I'd had installed on the door six months ago after a woman was murdered on the first floor, pushed open the door, and said: "Yoo-hoo. I'm home, Hobo!"

There was a loud bark. Hobo is my dachshund, a black-and-tan miniature who eats like a Great Dane. At the sound of my voice, he got up from the couch where he'd been sleeping, shook himself, and wagged his tail furiously. He licked my face for a few seconds, then ran over to his leash and began pushing it around to show he wanted to go for a walk.

It was never my idea to have a dog in New York City. It just sort of happened. Tony, my ex, came home one day carrying the dog. Tony said he'd seen him wandering around on the street, obviously lost and almost being hit by cars, so he picked him up. Tony was like that, always kind to animals. Rotten to people, but kind to animals.

We checked everywhere—Bide-A-Wee, ASPCA, want ads. No one had ever heard of him. No one wanted him. So we decided to keep him and I came up with the name of Hobo. It seemed to fit.

Tony was an actor. A few years ago, he'd landed a regular spot on one of the daytime soaps that gave him some pretty good money and regular exposure. That's when I met him, and I was sort of swept off my feet. He was glib, successful, and good-looking in a swarthy kind of way—like DeNiro or Pacino. Only about six months ago, his character on the soap suffered a brain tumor and died an agonizing death. So did Tony's TV career and, as a result, our relationship. He couldn't find another job in New York and we had to live on my salary from the TV station. It was enough, but the tension level between us kept getting higher and higher.

He hated the fact that I had a well-paying job and he didn't and constantly complained about the amount of time I spent at work.

On my part, I wasn't exactly thrilled that he spent most of his days sleeping or watching TV and then wanted to go out and party all night.

Let's put it this way—our life wasn't exactly a picture of domestic bliss.

Then about a week ago, I came home after work one day and found the apartment empty. No Tony, none of his clothes, nothing. Just Hobo. There was a note from Tony about how he needed a new start, maybe in Hollywood, and he was sorry about leaving like this but. . . . Well, I won't bore you with the rest of the crap.

The bottom line is he wound up with everything and I got the dog. Man's best friend, I thought to myself as I looked down at him now, waiting eagerly by his dog dish.

Well, what the hell, I needed a friend these days.

I walked Hobo, then picked up the *Times*, sat down at the kitchen table, and turned to the apartment ads. Why not, I figured. I was already depressed, why not be good and depressed.

Two days after Tony left, I got a notice on official-looking stationery from our landlord. It said the primary tenant in the house—Tony, who'd signed the lease—had moved out and the apartment now reverted back to the owner. As an unauthorized tenant, I was required to vacate the premises within thirty days.

No problem, I thought to myself at the time. I'll just get a new place. That night I went apartment hunting in New York for the first time in years.

The first place I looked at was a second-floor walk-up at Third Avenue and 25th Street.

It was dark and dingy, the paint was peeling, and the view from the only window was blocked by a Single Room Occupancy hotel across the street. There was a sign on the apartment door indicating the previous tenant had been something called Princess Leanna's Fortune-Telling and Leisure Lounge, which, I was told, departed in the middle of the night with creditors in hot pursuit. I wasn't exactly sure what kind of business Princess Leanna was running, but while I was looking at the place one of her leftover customers showed up. The guy kept banging on the door and, when I opened it, he told me he wanted to be my love slave. I had a feeling—call it a crazy hunch—that Princess Leanna was doing more than reading tea leaves.

The next place I went to came with a classified ad that said: "Spacious four-room apartment—large living room, master bedroom, country kitchen, and family dining area. Gramercy Park view."

It turned out to be your traditional boxcar-designed living room, with a medium-size closet masquerading as a bedroom, and a tiny kitchenette with a built-in breakfast counter and two stools, in case I ever had a friend over. You could see Gramercy Park from the window, but only if you stood on your toes on a chair and used a high-powered telescope. The rent was $1,500 a month.

"There's a lot of people in Manhattan who would kill for this apartment," the real estate agent said as he showed it to me.

He was right, too. When I looked at it, I wanted to kill him.

All the other places I called about were already taken. That's another trick of the trade. You've got to get to see places *before* the ads actually appear in the *Times* or *The Village Voice*. All over New York people desperately bribe newsstand dealers to get an advance copy of the Sunday real estate section, which is delivered during the week before the rest of the paper. If you wait until the paper actually comes out, it's already too late.

Actually looking for an apartment in Manhattan is a lot like the Woody Allen joke from *Annie Hall* about the two old women eating in the Catskills. The one where they complain that the food is awful, and besides that, the portions are too small. Well, I guess that's how I feel about the Manhattan real estate market. The apartments are all dumps and there aren't enough of them.

I walked over to the cupboard with Hobo following on my heels.

"So what do we feel like tonight?" I asked him. "The Mighty Dog beef and bacon or the chicken and liver?"

Hobo barked loudly.

"Yeah, I think the beef and bacon's a good choice too. That's what I'd go for if I were you."

I opened the can and at the same time pondered my dinner. What did I want? Well, that was easy. What I wanted was a nice juicy steak or a pizza with the works or maybe some nice chocolate cream pie for dessert. But I was committed to my new diet. Well, I wasn't that committed. I'd only started it that day when I found my extra poundage had gone into double digits for the first time. But I had to give it a shot so I'd been good. A grapefruit with some cottage cheese on the side for breakfast and a yogurt and cottage cheese for lunch. The only noticeable effect so far was that I was acquiring a deep and passionate loathing for cottage cheese.

I reached into the refrigerator and took out a Stouffer's Lean Cuisine dinner. One of those diet specials. It looks real good on the package except there're only about three mouthfuls inside. I thought about eating maybe twenty of them—sort of popping them like Lifesavers—but I figured that would defeat the purpose. So I just took one, a cheese cannelloni in tomato sauce, and put it in the oven.

While I was waiting I clicked on the TV. There was a news

special on NBC. Maria Shriver was interviewing Henry Kissinger about nuclear disarmament. Now I figured Maria Shriver knew as much about nuclear disarmament as I did. But there she was on national TV talking about it.

She's got a regular gig on the network doing interviews. Plus she's also filled in as a cohost on "Today" with Bryant Gumbel. And NBC probably gives her a limo ride to work every day, a personal hairdresser, and a complete fashion wardrobe.

What a sweet deal.

"How come I can't get a job like that?" I said aloud to the TV. "I mean what's Maria Shriver got that I don't have?"

The answer was obvious to me even before I said it.

"The Kennedy millions and Arnold Schwarzenegger."

I switched over to see what was on the other networks. A tearjerker TV movie starring Meredith Baxter and one of those sappy programs where people show embarrassing home videos. Finally I clicked over to MTV, where they were showing an old Pat Benatar video. I danced around the living room to that while I waited for the cannelloni. Actually Maria Shriver looked a little like Pat Benatar, if you thought about it. Most people don't think about things like that. But I do.

When my dinner was ready I took it to a table in the living room and sat it down. Then I put Hobo's dish on the floor next to me. We both started eating.

"What do you think, Hobo?" I asked as he wolfed his food.

He gave me a short yip.

"Yeah, me too," I said.

Hobo finished his meal without another bark.

He's never been big on dinner conversation.

5
Power
Politics

Thomas Sewell sat at a table at 21, chewed thoughtfully, and talked to me about Kathy Kerrigan.

"This is really a lot of fuss about nothing, you know," the Wincott family lawyer said. "Audrey was very wrong to get you involved at all, I told her that. Kathy's in no harm, I'm sure."

When I'd called Sewell's office earlier, he absolutely refused to be interviewed on camera for a story. I persisted though, and he finally offered this compromise: we'd have lunch at 21 together and he'd talk to me about Kathy. But nothing we discussed would be for attribution.

Since I hadn't anything to lose, I agreed. Besides, it was a good excuse to cheat on my diet. So here we were in the wood-paneled dining room, munching on sautéed brook trout and the Crêpes Soufflés "21," while black-jacketed waiters moved quietly around us taking orders from board chairmen, pols, and celebrities.

The invitation had been only for me, so Jacobson and Sanders were eating at a Burger King a few blocks away.

I didn't figure that was going to help our working relationship any.

"What can you tell me about her disappearance?" I said.

"I really don't think we should use the word *disappear*," he
replied, patting his mouth carefully with a white linen napkin.
"It connotes some sort of mystery or foul play. There's
nothing like that. We just haven't heard from her in a day or
two."

"Her mother thinks it's unusual."

Sewell spread his hands in resignation. "Their relationship—
Audrey's and Kathy's—well, let's just say it leaves a lot to be
desired."

"So what do you think happened to Kathy?"

"My honest opinion? Strictly off the record?"

"Sure."

"I think Kathy's just trying out her wings for a few days,"
he said with a big smile. "Checking out the rest of the world.
Maybe the impending marriage and all the responsibilities that
go with it spooked her. I don't know. In some ways she's a
very immature girl, and I think she's just mixed up right now."

"How do you mean mixed up?"

"Trying to find herself. Get her head together, as the young
people say." He smiled again. He looked like the type who
smiled a lot.

After we had finished our meal, a waiter came over and
asked us if we wanted coffee. Sewell said that we did.

"I hope your lunch was all right," he said, as the waiter took
up our plates.

"Yeah, great," I told him.

The truth was the fish was a bit overdone and the sauce had
too much salt in it. But I didn't want to hurt his feelings. Not
at these prices, especially since he was picking up the tab. Hell,
maybe the chef just had a tough night last night. It happens to
all of us.

"So as I told you before," he said, "there's really no story
here for you. No evidence of anything wrong. Mrs. Wincott
simply overreacted by implying to you there was. I think she
realizes that now. I would hope you could just let all of this
drop. It's really just a private family matter, nothing more."

I poured some milk into my coffee, paused at the Sweet 'n Low for a second, then reached for the sugar. What the hell, why not live dangerously? "Tell me about the Wincott money," I said.

"What do you mean?" Sewell asked. He wasn't smiling anymore.

"I mean how much there is. I hear about six hundred million dollars."

"I really don't see what that has to do with anything."

"Maybe it does and maybe it doesn't. I've always found that whenever there's a lot of money mixed up in something—well, the money's usually involved somewhere."

Sewell fidgeted nervously with his coffee.

"It's a matter of public record that the overall family fortune is somewhere in the neighborhood of six hundred million dollars," he said.

I nodded.

"That, of course, includes all aspects of the Kerrigan holdings, which are still controlled in name by Thomas Kerrigan, Audrey's father-in-law."

"Thomas Kerrigan? You mean 'King' Kerrigan?"

Sewell nodded. "You remember him, I see."

"Who wouldn't?" He got the nickname because he was such a kingmaker during the 50s and 60s. Elected mayors, congressmen, senators, maybe even a few presidents. Controlled a huge chunk of American industry. The guy was right up there with the Rockefellers and the Kennedys. "I didn't realize he was still alive."

"Very much so. He's pretty much retired, though. Lives by himself in New England on a big estate, and hardly anyone ever hears from him directly anymore. He's probably pushing eighty by now."

I wanted to get him back on the topic of Kathy.

"I understand you talked to her the day she disappeared."

"Yes . . . yes, I guess I did. She came to my office that morning."

"And asked you questions about her long-dead father?"

He looked at me sharply. "Who told you that?"

"Mrs. Wincott."

Sewell sighed.

"So did you?" I asked.

"Did we . . . ?"

"Talk about her real father?"

"Yes, that came up in the conversation."

"What did she want to know?"

"Nothing specific. We just reminisced a bit about Michael. Kathy still has never really gotten over losing him. She was very close to him when she was little. And I guess I knew him as well as anyone. He was almost like a brother."

"Did she tell you why she was bringing it up again now?"

"No."

"And you didn't think it was a little bit unusual?"

Sewell spread his hands in resignation. "Kathy's a little bit unusual sometimes."

"But to just come into your office and start talking about her long-dead father . . ."

"Miss McKay," Sewell said, "you're looking for a story, and there's no story here."

I shrugged.

"I really wish I could persuade you of that," he said.

"But the fact that she came to your office for no reason at all and brought up her father . . ."

"She's come to me many times over the years. We've talked about a lot of things. Her father. Things that were bothering her. Like I said before, her relationship with her mother is not the best. And she's never seemed to accept the senator as her father. So sometimes when she's upset and wants to talk, she comes to me. I'm not just her family lawyer. I'm a friend, too."

"How about Senator Wincott?" I asked. "How does he feel about all this?"

"Why involve him?"

"Because he's her father."

"Stepfather."

"Well, he's the closest thing she's got to a father." I paused. "Is he running for anything these days?"

Sewell shook his head. "His term still has four years to run . . ."

"I've heard talk of him having some presidential aspirations. Anything to that?"

"Such speculation is always flattering," Sewell said. "But that's what it is—speculation."

"I don't suppose it helps to have a lot of publicity about a dipsy daughter who drops out of sight on the eve of her big society wedding."

"No one likes their dirty laundry aired in public," Sewell agreed.

"You think I can talk to him?" I asked.

"The senator?"

"Yeah. He is Kathy's stepfather."

He shrugged. "I'll see what I can do."

I finished my coffee and thought about everything for a minute.

"How did he die?"

"Who?"

"Michael Kerrigan, Kathy's real father. How did he die? I was just wondering."

"It was a boating accident. It happened at the Kerrigan summer house in Nantucket. A terrible tragedy."

"How old was Kathy?"

"About five. Well, actually she'd just turned six. She was there and saw him just before it happened. I guess that's why she's never been completely able to get it out of her mind."

"Was there ever any suggestion that it was anything more than an accident?"

Sewell stared at me. "What in the world are you talking about?"

"I don't know; maybe Kathy discovered something about how her father died. Something that put a whole new light on it. That could account for her strange behavior."

"Miss McKay, the record is very clear. Michael Kerrigan died when his sailboat overturned off the coast of Nantucket in the summer of 1973. He was alone in the boat at the time. It was a drowning, pure and simple."

"Then you don't think there's any possibility that it might be linked somehow to Kathy's disappearance?"

"No," Sewell said evenly. "I don't think there's any possibility of that at all."

After I left 21, I walked over to the Burger King and met up with Sanders and Jacobson.

"So how was lunch?" Sanders asked.

"Not bad."

"You didn't bring us a doggie bag?"

"Not cool at 21," I said. "Actually very gauche. You understand, right?"

"Yes'm, Miz McKay," he said. "Don't you worry none about us hired help."

"C'mon, you guys had a good meal here, didn't you?"

Jacobson belched loudly.

"How about I spring for the Maalox and we call it even?"

"It's a deal," he said and stood up. "C'mon, let's go."

"Where to?"

"We've got an assignment."

It turns out that we'd gotten an anonymous tip Madonna had walked into a video store on the Upper West Side an hour or so ago and bought a bunch of tapes to watch. Carstairs thought if I could find out what they were it would make a great segment for "South Street Confidential"—Madonna's home video guide. Hey, I just get paid to do what I'm told.

The video store owner was a curly-haired guy, wearing a flannel shirt and jeans, and with a mustache that turned up at the ends and made him look a little like Elliot Gould. He didn't seem surprised when we told him what we wanted. In fact, it quickly became apparent he'd been our anonymous tipster. He used the name of the store in every sentence and spelled out his last name three different times. There was a bill with Madonna's signature on it and the notation that she'd paid in full with cash. The movies she'd bought were *Basic Instinct, Thelma and Louise,* and *All About Eve*. I took down the information and did an on-camera interview with the owner.

As we were packing up, I said to him, "Doesn't this bother you?"

"What do you mean?"

"Calling us up like this and invading the woman's privacy. I know it's not much, but it really is invading her privacy. All she did was come in here because she wanted to see some movies in the privacy of her own home. Why does the public have a right to know that information? How would you feel if you were her? Doesn't that bother you just a little bit?''

"No.''

I shook my head.

"Why? Does it bother you?'' he asked.

"Yeah, it does.''

"Well, don't bust my chops about it. You're doing the same thing.''

"I know,'' I said. "That's why it bothers me.''

That night on the six o'clock newscast I started out the "South Street Confidential'' segment with a follow-up on the Kathy Kerrigan story.

McKAY: You remember we told you yesterday about how heiress Kathy Kerrigan has suddenly gotten cold feet on the eve of her big wedding at St. Patrick's Cathedral. Well, now a new development in that story: Sources close to the family have confirmed to us that only hours before she dropped out of sight, Kathy was seemingly obsessed with finding out information about the death of her father twenty years ago. Why was she doing this instead of preparing for her wedding? Is there any connection between this and her sudden disappearance? No one knows the answers to these questions. The only thing we know for sure is that the groom is still waiting at the altar. Stay tuned for more on this one.

Then I went into the Madonna piece.

McKAY: Okay, so you're the Material Girl. And you want to see a good movie to get your mind off all those pesky photographers outside. So what do you watch? Well, certainly not *Shanghai Surprise*. Actually Madonna's tastes run more to recent box-office hits such as *Basic Instinct* and *Thelma and Louise* along with an old Bette Davis classic. That's the word from the One-Stop Video Store on Broadway and Seventy-ninth where they were all whispering "Who's that girl?" this morning when you-know-who walked in and . . .

When I was finished and the camera was off me, I looked toward the side of the studio and saw Carstairs watching me. He was nodding his head in approval and smiling. When he caught my glance, he gave me a big thumbs-up sign. I stuck my finger in my mouth like Joan Rivers does to pretend she's barfing.

I was just grateful Edward R. Murrow wasn't alive to see this one.

6

It's Money
That Matters

There was a meeting called for the entire staff in the newsroom the next morning.

"What's this all about?" Sanders asked me as we sat waiting for it to start.

"Maybe they're going to tell us what a good job we're doing and there're raises all around."

Sanders chuckled. "Hardly. The latest ratings report came out, I heard, and Gergen spent all day yesterday with our new programming whiz."

"Good news with the ratings?" I asked innocently.

"Hardly."

"We're still seventh, right?"

"Only because there's no eighth. If we went any further down, we'd have less people watching us than one of those public access cable channels where the people read poetry and Bible passages."

"Uh-huh," I said. "It sounds like it's going to be another great day."

Bill Hanrahan, the WTBK sportscaster, slipped into the chair next to me.

"Jenny, babe, how you doin'? You're looking good."

Hanrahan thought he was God's gift to women. He came on to every woman in the office.

"I'm sorry I can't say the same," I said.

"Cute. You're really a cute lady, Jenny."

I picked up a newspaper and tried to pretend I was reading it.

"You know, I've been thinking, Jenny," he said, "now that you've broken up with that actor boyfriend of yours, maybe you and I should have dinner some night."

I stared down at the paper and didn't answer him.

Hanrahan was persistent. "So what do you think about dinner with me? Help us get to know each other a little better. Would you like that, babe?"

"I'd rather be tied to a stake under a broiling sun with red ants crawling all over my body," I said.

He smiled. "Well, that could be fun, too."

"Get out of here!" I shouted.

Hanrahan laughed again, then moved over to the other side of the room.

"Maybe some other time," he said.

"Christ, what a zoo this place is," I muttered to Sanders.

Gergen came in with Carstairs a few minutes later.

"I have spent most of the past twenty-four hours going over the ratings report," Gergen said. "It was no fun. No fun at all."

He went through it with us. It was as bad as I had figured. The only show rated lower was "Sermonette."

"I want to look at the bright side of this," he said. "The bright side is we have no place to go but up."

"Now Bob Carstairs, whom most of you have already met, has come up with some ideas to try to turn things around. I don't want to say they come out of desperation, because that would be too optimistic. Let's just say we should consider them very seriously if we all want to continue working here. Bob?"

Carstairs stood up and looked around at us.

"There's no mystery about what's wrong with this show," he said. "We're too set in our ways, too passive—we accept the fact that we're the bottom of the ratings barrel. Well, no more.''

He took out a sheet of paper.

"Now for one thing I want to step up the jokes and quips on the air, kid around a lot more than you've been doing—so it looks like we're all one big, happy family. The viewers go for that.''

I grimaced noticeably.

"Problem, Miss McKay?''

"No, nothing,'' I said.

"Anyway the idea is that after every news item on the show, the reporter does a little humorous repartee with one of the anchors. I know we're already doing some of that, but not enough. Let's entertain the viewer, make him want to watch us as personalities.''

"Yeah, don't bore him with the news,'' someone behind me muttered.

"You people all know as well as I do that demographic sweeps show viewers like that sort of camaraderie,'' Carstairs said defensively. "A lot of stations do it—a lot of successful stations. It's what people want. So what's so bad about that?''

"Maybe we should put on a top hat and carry a cane and do a little dance routine while we're out there covering a fire or a press conference,'' I suggested. "The viewers ought to love that.''

Conroy Jackson cleared his throat nervously.

"Am I to understand that we anchors have to go out there every night and ad lib funny material?'' he asked. "Without any help or rehearsal?''

Sanders leaned over to me and whispered: "Conroy's plenty worried. The guy couldn't ad lib a fart at a bean dinner.''

I giggled. Conroy Jackson was one of those anchormen who looked good on camera, but was as dumb as they came. If there was ever a real-life version of Ted Baxter on the old Mary Tyler Moore show, he was it. He needed a teleprompter to remember his name.

"Don't worry, Conroy.'' Gergen sighed. "You'll have help with the ad libs. They'll be written in advance and given to you well before air time. All right?''

Jackson nodded, obviously relieved.

"Now, for the next thing," Carstairs continued. "We'll be starting a new contest everyone should be aware of. On the show each night, one of you will call a number at random in the viewing area. Anyone who answers on the other end with the words, 'I watch the news on WTBK, at six and ten each and every day,' wins one hundred dollars."

"You're kidding," I said.

"No. . . ."

"C'mon, that's the kind of tacky thing top forty radio stations do. Not TV news shows."

"So? It works for radio stations, doesn't it? We've got to do *something*."

"In all this discussion about how to improve our news show," I asked Carstairs and Gergen, "did anyone ever mention the word *news*?"

"As a matter of fact, Miss McKay," he said, "I was just coming to that. We're not doing enough of the kind of stories we need to do to keep the viewer interested in watching our show. We have to capture the public's fancy, make them want to watch us instead of another station. Give them a reason to tune in to us.

"Therefore, we need to do more things that stir people's emotions—tug at their hearts, move them, arouse their feelings in some way. I don't want reviews of French films and PBS specials or long stories about the city budget deficit. I want to see more medical stories, human interest stories, stories about people who've accomplished things against great odds. . . ."

"Are we talking about things like coma babies and kids who need liver transplants?" someone asked.

"There's nothing wrong with coma baby and liver transplant stories."

"It sounds a lot like tabloid journalism. Sort of like a *National Enquirer* of the air."

"I'll point out that the *National Enquirer* sells millions of copies," Carstairs said. "Keep that in mind. Also, we can't have too many celebrities," he continued. "The more the better. And the bigger the celebrity the better. Big names on the news translate into big ratings.

"We need to be on top of what's hot in New York. On the cutting edge of the entertainment and social worlds. The idea is to give our viewers a first-hand peek into the world of parties, clubs, and celebrity gossip."

He paused and looked at me.

"That's why I think we've made an important first step with our 'South Street Confidential' segment Jenny here has done the past two days. This is an example of the kind of thing we'll be doing a lot more of and—"

Cassie White was trying furiously to get the attention of Gergen and Carstairs.

"Uh-oh," Sanders said to me. "Watch your back on this one. Little Miss Ambition suddenly smells an opportunity."

"Yes, Cassie, what is it?" Gergen asked.

"Well, I was just thinking about what you said. I have some awfully good contacts in the entertainment and celebrity fields. I know a lot of the 'in' places around town. Now I'm not saying that Jenny hasn't done an adequate job the last few nights. But since you're putting so much emphasis on this area, I thought you might want to—"

"Feel that, Jenny?" Sanders chuckled. "There goes the knife."

"—put someone with a little more—well, sophistication in these matters on it."

"That's very generous of you, Cassie," Gergen said. "But I think Jenny should be able to handle it herself."

Cassie scowled.

After the meeting was concluded, Carstairs came over and said he wanted to talk to me alone. I followed him into his office, which was in the process of being set up. Thus far it consisted mainly of a big teak desk, a couple of chairs, and a plaque on the wall: BROADCASTING ACHIEVEMENT AWARD TO Robert Carstairs WHO TOOK KTSF FROM WORST TO FIRST IN SAN FRANCISCO IN JUST SIX MONTHS. WELL DONE, BOB. Carstairs was wearing another sweater tied around his shoulders, and this was June. Obviously it was a fashion statement of some kind. He sat down behind his desk.

"Miss McKay, you seem very cynical."

"Who, me? Nah, I was just overcome by emotion from your

stirring little talk back there. What was it you said? 'We need to be on top of what's hot in New York. On the cutting edge.' Beautiful.''

He sighed. "I understand you were a newspaper reporter before you came here. Is this part of your newspaper reporter's persona?''

I didn't say anything.

"I want to talk to you about some things," he said, gesturing toward one of the chairs in front of his desk. "Sit down for a minute.''

I sat down. He gazed across the desk at me.

"Miss McKay, I can make you a star—if you want to be one.''

"Just like that?''

"Just like that," he said.

"Sort of like Lana Turner being discovered at a soda fountain in a drug store, huh?''

"They don't have soda fountains in drug stores anymore.''

"I know, but the concept's sort of the same, right?''

"If you'd like to think of it that way.''

"Why me?'' I asked.

"Why not? You're what I've got to work with. If you don't work out, I'll get someone else. It's up to you.''

"And what do I have to do?''

"Just what I tell you.''

From a desk drawer he took out a folder that had my name on it.

"Your contract with the station is up next month," he said. "There's some question about whether or not it will be renewed.''

"I'm aware of that.''

"One of the problems is that your Q rating is very low.''

"My personality quotient?''

"That's right. Your personality is not coming across to the viewers.''

"Maybe I need a personality transplant.''

He looked at me. "You need coaching, Miss McKay. Your on-air delivery is poor, you don't make good eye contact with the camera, your elocution needs work—you don't sell yourself properly. You don't seem comfortable when the red light is on. I can work with you on that. I've done it before with other people and it seems to work."

"Anything else?"

"Yes, your appearance. Your hair looks like a rat's nest. Cut it. Your makeup isn't applied properly, get one of our professional people to help you with it. And take more care with your clothes. I noticed last night that your WTBK blazer seemed to have some kind of a fresh stain on the lapel. Did you spill something on it before you went on the air?"

"Yeah, probably cottage cheese. I'm on this diet and—"

"It didn't look like cottage cheese. It looked like chocolate fudge."

"Well, one or the other. Cottage cheese and chocolate fudge, they both look the same."

I thought about suggesting I wear the blazer tied around my shoulders next time, but I decided against it.

"Can I ask you a question?"

"Go ahead," he said.

"What's going on? For years this station had no ratings, and no one seemed to care. Why the change?"

"Andrew Cafferty."

"Who?"

"Andrew Cafferty. He's the son of Edward Cafferty, the station's owner. His father is in the process of retiring and recently turned much of the operation of the station over to him."

"So?"

"Andrew looked at the books and was appalled. He's tired of losing money. So he called me in to fix things. We'll be spending a million dollars here in the next six months to try to turn this station around. If it works, we'll make ten times that in additional ad spot price increases."

I stood up.

"Think about the things I've said, Miss McKay," he said. "It's up to you."

"I will."

"I hope I didn't hurt your feelings with any of my comments. But I find it best in these situations to be direct."

''No problem.'' I started to walk out, then turned around at the door. ''There is one thing though.''

''What's that.''

''I don't feel very much like Lana Turner anymore.''

I left his office and went to the ladies' room. I looked at myself in the mirror for a long time. Then I took a comb out of my purse and tried fixing my hair a new way. Without bangs. With bangs. With the back pinned up. None of it seemed to be an improvement. Finally I gave up, left it the way it was when I started, and walked back to my desk in the WTBK newsroom.

A rat's nest?

7
Wanna Die Before
I Get Old

The phone was ringing when I got to my desk.

I grabbed it, leaned back with my feet up, and said, "I watch the news on WTBK, at six and ten each and every day."

There was a pause on the other end.

"Jenny McKay?"

"Sorry, just practicing. I figured I might be able to pick up a quick hundred bucks. Yeah, this is McKay."

"I'm afraid I don't understand."

"Me neither. Who's this?"

"My name is Dave Paxton. I work in Senator Wincott's office."

I put my feet down and sat up straight. "Hi, how are you?"

"Tom Sewell called me yesterday. Said you wanted to talk to the senator."

"That's right. It's about his daughter."

Paxton cleared his throat. "Well, I'm not sure that's possible. You see, that's a very private matter and Senator Wincott feels it doesn't need to be discussed in public. You can understand that, can't you?"

"Not really. But maybe I would if I talked to the senator directly about it. Could you set up an appointment for me?"

"You mean without cameras?" he asked.

"If that's the way it's got to be."

"I'll see what I can do. But it would have to be here in Washington. He's not planning to be in New York in the near future."

"Even with his daughter missing?"

"No comment." He laughed. A nice laugh. The kind of laugh that made me want to know more about the voice on the other end of the line. "Can I ask you a question?"

"Sure," I said.

"What was all that about a quick hundred bucks when you answered the phone?"

I told him about the WTBK contest for increasing our ratings.

"That's hard to believe," he said.

"You're right," I agreed. "We're going to be the joke of the TV business."

"No, I mean it's hard to believe you're doing so badly. I like the show. I watch you whenever I'm in New York."

"A fan, huh? You're in a real select minority. Sort of an endangered species."

He chuckled.

"What do you like best?" I asked. "Conroy Jackson's probing questions and analysis? Cassie White's dazzling wit?"

"Actually I like you," Paxton said.

"Aha, a real politician."

"No, I mean it. I think you're really great. You've got a nice, friendly quality on the air. Something that just—I don't know—makes you seem likable. I mean that, honest."

"Hey, it's too bad someone doesn't interview you when they make up the Personality Quotient."

"Personality what?"

"Nothing. Just a small problem of mine. One more thing: What do you think of my hair?"

"It's terrific."

"No kidding?"

"No kidding."

"You don't think it looks a little . . . well, disheveled? I mean, do the words *rat's nest* ever cross your mind when you look at it?"

"Of course not."

"Have you ever thought of owning a TV station?" I asked.

He laughed again. "I'll get back to you on the appointment with Senator Wincott, okay?"

"I'll be on pins and needles."

After I hung up with Paxton, I thought about what to do next. I decided I was hungry. I was always hungry these days. I got up and walked next door to the diner for lunch.

Gergen was sitting by himself at one of the booths. I slipped into the seat across from him. When the waitress came over I ordered a plain salad, no dressing, and a Diet Coke.

"Very impressive," he said.

"I'm going to pretend it's a cheeseburger and French fries," I told him.

"You on a diet?"

I nodded.

"How long?"

"Two days, twelve hours and fifty-six minutes. But who's counting?"

He looked down at his plate. There was a half-eaten tuna fish sandwich there. He started to reach for it, then pushed it away.

"How'd it go with Carstairs before?"

"I don't think he was impressed by my diet."

"What do you mean?"

"He made some constructive suggestions concerning my on-air appearance."

"Such as?"

"Well, basically he said I looked a lot like Phyllis Diller."

Gergen smiled. "Hey, you're not that bad."

"Thanks for your support."

The waitress brought my salad and put it in front of me. I wrinkled my nose. It looked like a plate of grass.

"You got anything for your 'Confidential' segment tonight?" Gergen asked.

"Wait'll you hear this one. Countess Pialo is holding the party of the summer social season this weekend in the

Hamptons. One hundred of the most important and most blue-blooded citizens in our town. And I've interviewed the chef who's been hired to cook for them all.''

''Really?''

''Yeah. Do you know how many hors d'oeuvres you need to prepare for something like this?''

''I haven't the slightest idea.''

''Six hundred hors d'oeuvres,'' I said proudly.

Gergen let out a low whistle. ''Isn't that something?''

''It's the little details that define great reporting,'' I said.

''Speaking of parties, you're invited to one on Saturday.''

''That's my day off.''

''It doesn't matter. It's a Fourth of July party being thrown by Andrew Cafferty, the owner's son. Apparently he's the man now.'' I nodded, remembering what Carstairs had told me. ''Anyway, he wants to meet all his new staff.''

''What's Junior like anyway?'' I asked.

''I don't know. I guess we'll find out Saturday.''

''Is this formal or what?''

''No, it's some kind of a barbeque on the terrace of his penthouse apartment. They said to dress casual.''

''Casual's good,'' I said.

Gergen looked out at the East River lapping along the wooden piers of the wharf outside. He seemed lost in thought. Finally he shook his head.

''It's not like the old days, is it, Jenny?''

''No,'' I said, ''it's not.''

I wasn't sure what he was talking about.

''Do you remember the night Son of Sam was caught?''

''Sure. We were at the *Trib*, and you sent me up to interview one of Sam's neighbors. Only when I got there the guy was scared stiff and sitting behind a locked door holding a loaded shotgun. I heard the click through the door and turned to Bill Armanda, the photographer with me, and asked: 'Is that what I think it is?' Armanda was white as a ghost but said: 'I'm going to ring the bell. If he shoots, you jump to the left and I'll jump to the right.' We got the interview. Only the guy kept the shotgun on us the whole time.''

''And how about Grenada?'' Gergen asked.

"Please, not while I'm eating."

During the invasion of Grenada, when the press was barred from going to the island to cover the fighting, Gergen told me to get there any way I could. So I finally found this old boat captain in the Bahamas and charted his little rig for ten thousand dollars. Only I forgot that I get seasick on the Staten Island Ferry. It took us two nights and three days to get to Grenada and I was hanging over the side of the boat all the way.

"I was green for a month," I told Gergen.

"Yeah, but you were the only correspondent to make it onto the island and provide a first-hand account of the fighting." He shook his head. "You were really something."

"Was is the correct word."

"Oh, you've still got it," he said. "You just tend to rise to an occasion. You need a big story, and you'll do all right. What's going on with that Kathy Kerrigan thing anyway?"

I told him about my conversation with Paxton.

"It's a tough one to figure, isn't it?" he said.

"Yep. If I get an appointment, you think it's worth my time to go down to Washington for a day to talk to Senator Wincott?"

"I'm not sure," he said.

"Me either."

Gergen looked down at his tuna fish. He took one more pass at it, then pushed it away for good.

"Are you feeling okay, Joe?" I asked.

"Yes. Well, no."

"That's a definitive answer."

He looked back out at the water.

"You know," he said finally, "it's the damnest thing the way doctors talk to you. I mean it's like an automobile mechanic talking to you about your car. 'I'm awfully sorry, but that transmission of yours is just about ready to give out. You know, you've got sixty thousand miles on it. I don't think you'll be able to drive it another five thousand miles or so.' It's all so matter-of-fact. So impersonal."

I cleared my throat nervously. "You been to a doctor, Joe?"

He nodded.

"What did he say?"

"My heart didn't pass the sixty thousand mile inspection."

"Christ, Joe, I'm sorry . . ."

"Don't be. These things happen. People get old. People get sick. People die. It's one of the infallible rules of nature. I just never thought the rules applied to me."

"Isn't there anything they can do?" I asked.

"Maybe surgery. Definitely a change in life-style. The doctor thinks I should retire. He says I can buy some more time that way."

"Is that what you're going to do?"

"I don't know. I don't want to. That's what I'm sitting here thinking about."

I reached over and grabbed his hand and squeezed it. I've known him for nearly twenty years and I don't ever remember touching him before. He squeezed back.

"Look," I said, "if there's any way I can help . . ."

"I know. Thanks."

"I mean it."

"Okay, then do me a favor. Listen to some advice from someone who knows."

"Sure."

He looked across the table at me and held on to my hand. "Don't ever get old, Jenny."

I tried to smile. "I'm workin' on it," I said.

Gergen wanted to stay there for a while longer, so I left and walked back to the studio. It was only a half block walk, but I could already feel sweat trickling down the back of my neck. It was going to be another day in the nineties. I was thinking about everything Gergen had said and not paying much attention to anything around me. Finally though, as I approached the front door of the WTBK building, I noticed a black Cadillac parked in front, with one guy behind the wheel and another wearing a three-piece suit standing next to it. I had to walk past them to get to the door.

"Excuse me, are you Jenny McKay?" the guy in the suit said, walking over toward me.

"That's right."

"FBI," he said, flashing a credential from his pocket. "Could we have a few words with you?"

"What about?"

"We're investigating the Kathy Kerrigan disappearance and we understand you might have some information that could be of use to us."

He smiled, reached over and opened the back door of the car.

"I'm sure if you just come down to headquarters we can get this all over with in a very short time."

I looked at the guy in the suit for a few seconds, checked out his partner again waiting behind the wheel of the car.

"Miss McKay," he said, "are you coming?"

"Do you mind showing me those credentials one more time?" I asked. "You ran them by me awfully fast."

He nodded and stuck his hand inside his suit jacket again. But when he took it out this time, there were no credentials in it. Just a gun.

"Get in the car, honey."

I looked around. Cars were going by, but no one was paying attention to us. That's New York for you. I didn't figure it was likely that he'd shoot me down right there in the middle of the sidewalk, but then I didn't want to bet my life on it either.

I got in the car. He sat down next to me in the backseat and pulled the door shut. He was still holding the gun. The guy behind the wheel pulled away from the curb and began heading down South Street.

"Let me guess," I said, "you guys aren't really with the FBI after all."

"R-i-i-i-ght," the one with the gun said.

We drove to the Brooklyn Bridge, got on the entrance ramp, and began heading across the water.

"So how did you make us so quick?" the guy next to me asked.

"Your law enforcement techniques leave a little to be desired. Maybe you should watch a few more Efrem Zimbalist reruns. Learn how to say 'FBI! Freeze!' and neat stuff like that. Besides, you're a little too stylish."

"Is that so?"

"Yeah. The suit you're wearing is pure silk and probably

costs at least eight hundred bucks. And this Caddy is a real luxury job. Feds are on a tighter budget. They shop at sales.''

We were almost across the bridge into Brooklyn now.

"You know, you could drop me off here and I'll walk back to the office,'' I said. "I don't mind the heat.''

The guy with the gun snickered. "Funny lady,'' he said. "Isn't she a funny lady, Mickey?''

"Yeah, Al, she's a regular riot.''

Mickey and Al. I made a note of the names. Maybe I'd put them on my Christmas card list.

When we got off the bridge the driver made a turn to the south and took us along the water for a half mile or so. Finally he pulled into a warehouse area across the water from the Fulton Fish Market. We were far enough away from the main road that it was nearly deserted. The guy with the gun got out of the car and motioned me to walk with him toward the river. We went to the edge of the pier.

"I'm awfully sorry about all this, Miss McKay,'' he said. "But I wanted a chance to talk with you in private. Somewhere where we could be alone for a few minutes away from the hustle and bustle of the city.''

I didn't say anything.

"The thing is I have an editorial suggestion for you. Something that I think will help your career as a newscaster. You don't mind me making a suggestion like that, do you?''

"No problem,'' I said, looking down at the water below.

"Good. Because the thing is . . . well, I think you should forget about Kathy Kerrigan.''

"Uh-huh.''

"I mean there's really no story there at all.''

"You know,'' I told him, "I was just thinking the same thing this morning. That story's run its course, I said to myself.''

"I'm glad to see you're being so cooperative.''

"Hey, cooperative is my middle name.''

"That's good. Because you see, Miss McKay, there's two ways we can do this. There's the easy way—which is a pleasant little chat like we're having here now. Or,'' he continued, looking down at the river, "there's the hard way.

The choice is up to you. It makes no difference to me how you want to play it.''

We walked back toward the car, got in, and began heading back toward Manhattan. We rode in silence this time. About 10 minutes later, they let me out just where they picked me up—right in front of the station. The guy with the gun even held the door for me.

"Have a nice day." He smiled.

A few minutes later they were gone, driving down South Street toward the bridge again. It wasn't until they were out of sight that I remembered I'd forgotten to get the license number of their car.

Terrific reporter, huh?

8

Ms. McKay Goes to Washington

At 8 A.M. the next morning I was aboard an air shuttle, winging my way to Washington.

Washington is a terrific city, probably the only place besides New York where I could live happily ever after. It's beautiful, steeped in tradition, and the people are for the most part pretty sophisticated. Of course, the number of eligible women outnumbers the men by three to one, but you can't have everything.

We touched down at National Airport and I took a cab into the city. The heat had broken and it was a beautiful day in the seventies. It's about a fifteen-minute cab ride from the airport into D.C., and I spent the time trying to pick out landmarks as we got closer. I'd only gotten the Washington Monument, the Capitol, and the White House by the time the cab driver let me off.

I stopped at a coffee shop for breakfast, became nauseous at the thought of looking at more cottage cheese and said the hell with it. I had eggs and sausage and buttered toast and three cups of coffee. I eased my conscience, though, by putting Equal in my coffee instead of sugar. Every little bit helps.

While I ate, I read the *Washington Post*. There was an article on the Op Ed page speculating on the chances of various presidential candidates for the next election. Jonathan Wincott's name was mentioned in the story. It described him as an "intriguing longshot possibility." It did not say anything about his missing daughter. It did not say anything about two mobsters picking me up off the street. It did not say anything about whether or not his administrative assistant, Dave Paxton, was cute. I folded up the paper, pushed myself away from the table, and headed for the Russell Senate Office Building to see Wincott.

Senator Wincott was located on the third floor. A secretary greeted me and led the way down a plushly carpeted hall to an office at the end. Jonathan Wincott was sitting behind a handsomely carved oak desk in front of a window overlooking the Capitol. He was good-looking in a distinguished sort of way, with graying hair and craggy features, and wearing a navy blue pin-striped suit. For some reason he reminded me of George Romney, the guy who ran for president years ago. He stood up when I came in.

"Miss McKay," he said, stretching his hand out to greet me, "how are you?"

I shook his hand and said, "Not pleased, if you want to know the truth, Senator."

"Really?" he said with an upraised eyebrow. He gestured toward a chair in front of his desk. "Have a seat and tell me about it."

"Your people wouldn't let me bring a camera crew with me. Why is that?"

"I'm afraid it wouldn't be appropriate for me to be discussing this matter on TV right now. In fact, I must insist that this whole conversation be off the record."

"Off the record? Why? We're talking about a missing woman here, not Watergate. The missing woman is your stepdaughter, Kathy. All I'm doing is trying to help Kathy."

Wincott smiled slightly. "No, you're not," he said. "You don't give a damn about Kathy."

I shrugged.

"I know a little bit about the press and media, Miss McKay.

Let's be honest with one another—the Wincott family is good copy. You see Kathy's actions as a good news story that will make people watch your station. Isn't that what you're really after?''

"Maybe. But don't you want to try to get your stepdaughter back?"

"Miss McKay," Wincott said, "the story you carried on the air about Kathy disappearing. It was . . . well, rather unfortunate, I'm afraid."

"Unfortunate?"

"Not true."

"Kathy's not missing? Well I did get the story from your *wife*, Senator."

Senator Wincott leaned back in his chair and rubbed his temples wearily with his fingers, as if he'd been forced to deal with this kind of situation many times before.

"My wife, I'm afraid, has some emotional problems. Sometimes when she's—ah, very emotionally upset—she talks a bit too much. Blows things out of proportion."

I remembered the ever-present glass in her hand during our interview.

"She drinks too much," I said.

Wincott sighed. "That's putting it rather bluntly, but yes, I'm afraid it's true. My wife has had this problem for a number of years. Generally, we're able to keep it to ourselves. But on occasion, like the other day when she spoke to you . . ."

I nodded.

"But what about Kathy?" I asked. "Her whereabouts are unknown, right? Your wife didn't make that up."

"Miss McKay, Kathy has some emotional problems of her own."

"Emotional problems?"

"She's been under professional care. I don't want to go into all the details; it's a personal matter. I'm sure you don't want to hear them."

"Try me."

"All right, if you insist. Kathy has a drinking problem just like her mother. Maybe because of her mother. In any case, we've put her through three drying-out clinics in the past five years. She's also been dependent at various times on cocaine and sleeping pills.''

''I see.''

''Not to mention extensive psychiatric care. Believe me, Kathy is a very troubled girl.''

''But doesn't that make you more concerned about what might have happened to her?''

''Kathy's all right. You don't have to worry about her.''

''How can you be sure of that?''

''You'll just have to trust me. I've been through this before. She has these . . . well, these episodes. Then she comes back. We just have to wait her out.''

I didn't say anything.

''And now that you know the facts,'' Wincott said, ''I'm going to ask you to do something for me. As you can see, this is a very private family matter. Not the kind of thing that belongs on TV. I want you drop the story now. Just let it go, Miss McKay.''

I thought about it for a second.

''I'm not sure I can do that,'' I told him slowly.

''Why not?''

''Well, for one thing two guys with mob written all over them picked me up in New York yesterday and told me the same thing. They wanted me off the story too.''

Wincott stared at me with surprise. It seemed to be genuine surprise, but who knows?

''Do you have any idea at all why the mob would care about any of this?'' I asked.

''None at all. I'm astonished.''

''Me too.''

Wincott stood up and walked over to the window. He stared out at the Capitol for a few minutes, seemingly lost in thought. It was almost as if he'd forgotten I was there.

''Look,'' I said, starting to get up, ''if there's nothing else, maybe I should be—''

''Miss McKay,'' Wincott said, ''how long have you been at WTBK?''

''I guess about two years,'' I told him. ''Why?''

''Do you like it?''

"It's all right," I said. "To be perfectly honest with you, I prefer writing for newspapers or magazines to TV work. But it's a living."

He turned around and looked at me.

"Dave Paxton, my assistant, tells me you're very good."

"Well, that's flattering."

"Anyway, that got me to thinking," he said. "You may be just what we need around here."

"Just what you need?"

"Yes. How would you like to come to work for me?"

I sat back down again. "Work for you?"

"That's right. For a long time, I've felt the need to improve my relations with the press. Hire somebody with the credentials who could make that their prime responsibility. Someone who could serve as a sort of a . . . oh, as a sort of a press liaison for me."

"Press liaison?" I said.

I was starting to sound like an echo.

"That's right. Now I don't exactly know what your salary is at WTBK. But I'm certain we could better it here. You could work for both my Senate office and the Wincott family industries. It could turn out to be a very profitable venture for you, Miss McKay, I'd really like you to join the Wincott team."

The Wincott team? Jesus Christ, I didn't know people really talked like that. I stood up again.

"Well," I said hesitantly, "that certainly is a very generous offer, Senator. Very generous indeed. But . . ."

"It's something that's actually been on my mind for some time."

"But you didn't know me until today."

"No, but I've heard good things about you. And after meeting you now, well, I'm even more certain that you'd be a valuable addition to our team."

"Thanks very much," I said. "I really mean that. But the truth of the matter is . . . I don't think I'd be interested. The truth is I think I'll just stick with WTBK for the time being."

"Will you at least think about it?" he asked.

"Sure. Of course, I'll think about it. But I don't think . . ."

"Think about it, Miss McKay," Wincott said. "Give it some serious thought after you leave here."

I nodded. "All right, I'll do that."

"I'll be in touch with you," he said.

On my way out, someone called to me as I walked past the receptionist's desk. I looked back. There was a man standing there. He walked over to me.

"Jenny McKay? I'm Dave Paxton."

"Right," I said. "The president of my fan club."

I looked him over. He looked to be in his mid-forties. Wearing a three-piece Ivy League suit. Stylish long curly brown hair that hung down a bit over his ears. Not great, but not bad either. As long as I had fans like this, the hell with my Personality Quotient.

"How'd it go back there?" he asked.

"Okay," I said. I paused for a second and then added: "He offered me a job."

Paxton looked startled. "Did he?" he asked, trying to sound nonchalant about it. But I could tell he was startled.

"Yeah, I guess I dazzled him so much he just couldn't restrain himself," I said.

"Are you going to take the job?" he asked.

I shrugged. "We sort of left it open."

"I see. Listen, maybe we should talk about this a bit more."

"Sure."

"Are you going back to New York now?"

"This afternoon."

"Well, I'll be there sometime in the next few days. You interested in going out to dinner?"

"You mean to talk about my job offer?"

"Well, that plus anything else that might come up," he said.

"So we're not necessarily talking strictly business here, huh?"

Paxton grinned. "Not necessarily."

"Good," I said. "I hate business over dinner. Okay, give me a call when you get to town."

After I left the Senate Office Building, I went over to the *Washington Post* offices.

There's a guy I know who works there named Bill Rohr.

Rohr and I were together at the *Trib* a few years ago. When it folded, he landed a job writing politics for the *Post*. I figured I could pick his brain a little about Jonathan Wincott.

"So what do you know about him?" I asked after we had exchanged a few reminiscences.

"He's okay," Rohr said.

"Boy, that's a ringing endorsement."

"Listen, I'm not in love with the guy, but he seems to be not corrupt, not stupid, not a complete jerk off. He's okay. In Washington in the 1990s, that's a ringing endorsement."

I smiled. "Ever hear anything about him being involved with the mob?"

Rohr shook his head. "Nope, not a thing. Why?"

I told him about my ride to Brooklyn yesterday.

"Did you tell Wincott that?" he asked.

"Yep."

"What did he say?"

"Well, I think he tried to buy me off with a job."

"No kidding?" Rohr thought for a second. "That really doesn't sound like him. Now his father-in-law, that could be another story."

"King Kerrigan?"

"Yeah, there was a lot of talk in the old days about him having underworld connections. Apparently he started out as a gun runner or bootlegger or something back in the 20s, sort of like Joe Kennedy. So the mob thing was always bubbling under the surface with him."

"How about the son? Michael Kerrigan. Do you remember him?"

"Sure, he was elected to Congress about twenty years ago. Supposed to have a big political future. But he died. Why do you bring him up?"

"Just a wild hunch. Can you see what you can find out about him?"

"The kid who died twenty years ago?"

"That's right."

"I guess so. I'll let you know. Anything else?"

"Yeah, you got a job for me?"

"Are you serious?" Rohr asked.

"Sort of."

"Well, there's going to be something opening up in 'Style.'"

"'Style'?"

"'Style' here really isn't women's fashions. It's mostly long life-style features."

"Long life-style features I could handle."

"And down the road, I think they're going to be looking for someone to join our special investigative team."

"That's even better."

"I'll mention your name," Rohr said.

"It's too bad Ben Bradlee retired as editor. That would have been neat working with him."

"Did you ever meet him?"

"I've seen him at a few parties. He never looks like Ben Bradlee to me though. Jason Robards—now he looks like Ben Bradlee."

"*All the President's Men*, huh? The power of the broadcast media again."

"Right. For that matter, Bob Woodward should look like Robert Redford and Carl Bernstein like Dustin Hoffman."

"How about like Jack Nicholson in *Heartburn*?"

"No, that doesn't work. Dustin Hoffman works."

Rohr chuckled. "You've got to get back to newspapers, Jenny. You're living in a fantasy world."

"Tell me about it," I said.

I caught a five o'clock shuttle back to New York. It was packed with commuters, and in general it felt like being on the Lexington Avenue IRT during rush hour. I curled up in my seat and managed to fall asleep right after takeoff.

I was in the middle of a dream about breaking Watergate and living in a Georgetown townhouse with Dave Paxton when we touched down at LaGuardia.

9

"Life-styles of the Rich and Famous"

WHITE: Tired of those city traffic jams? Want to zip around Manhattan without hassling with red lights, taxi cabs and jay walkers? Why not do what the super-rich do—take a boat?

Of course, we're not talking about the Circle Line. The boat we're referring to is the lavish yacht—once known as the *Trump Princess*—that's been owned by the likes of megabuilder Donald Trump and Saudi arms dealer Adnan Khashoggi. It's the most expensive luxury yacht in the world, worth an estimated twenty-nine million. The boat's in New York Harbor tonight, and our Jenny McKay is aboard for this "South Street Confidential" report. Let's go to her now. Jenny?

They cut to a shot of me standing on the boat.

McKAY: This boat is two hundred and eighty-two feet long. It has eleven individually crafted suites, each one named after a precious stone and complete with television, video recorder, and an array of buttons to summon your own steward or stewardess while afloat; a disco-theque featuring strobe lights and lasers for nighttime fun; even a three-room hospital, which includes a fully-equipped operating room. But this only begins to describe the opulence and sheer wealth aboard this vessel. Standing next to me here is John Lafayette, the head steward. John, can you show us some of the things that make life so grand aboard it?

LAFAYETTE: What we're standing on here is the sun deck. It is accessible by a private elevator from the living room suite and contains such features as a swimming pool and an electronically controlled sun bed.

McKAY: Tell us about the sun bed.

He walked over to a control panel.

LAFAYETTE: This operates it. The bed goes up and down on this hydraulic pedestal. [He demonstrated the up and down movement.] Or I can use this button to rotate the bed so the person in it is always following the sun. [He pushed the button and the bed turned.]

McKAY: Okay, say I've got some sun, but now I want to go to my cabin. What will I find there?

LAFAYETTE: Let's go take a look.

We made our way below to the stateroom, with the camera following us. There Lafayette displayed a huge master control panel filled with buttons.

LAFAYETTE: This allows the occupant control over everything in the room and aboard the boat—from contacting the captain to opening a drawer for a pencil.

McKAY: Okay, say I want a pencil. What do I do?

He pointed to one of the buttons on the console. I pushed it. A motor whirred. Then a drawer filled with pencils, pens, and paper clips opened automatically.

McKAY: I'm thirsty. I want something to drink.

Another button. More whirring. This time a section of the wall opens up and a fully stocked bar emerges.

McKAY: Now how about some TV?

One more button. The motor whirring again. A huge sculpture rotates out of the wall and a TV console appears.

McKAY: One more question. There's a story that when Donald Trump owned this boat he actually had a button that projected an image of Ivana, his wife at the time, onto the ceiling over the master bed? Is that true?

LAFAYETTE (laughing): I never saw that. Maybe by the time I came aboard, Marla Maples had ripped it out.

McKAY: John, a lot of people here in New York made fun of Trump and the boat. They said it was just all too much, too garish. Do you think it's garish for a Donald Trump or anyone else to live like this?

LAFAYETTE: No, I think it's what America is all about.

The picture cut back to the studio.

WHITE: Thank you, Jenny. Well, garish or not, I think I'd like one of those for Christmas. Conroy, how much did she say that cost?

JACKSON: Twenty-nine million. But you know what they say about boat prices, Cassie.

WHITE: What's that?

JACKSON: If you have to ask the price, you can't afford it.

They both laughed.

WHITE: And now, visiting our town yesterday was one

of the country's top stunt actors, Hugh Marlowe. He's done stunts for action stars like Steven Seagal, Arnold Schwarzenegger, and Chuck Norris in a host of hit movies. One of the things he's paid to do frequently is fall off a tall building, landing in a safety net below. I asked him how scary that really was. Well, rather than just tell me about it, he let me find out for myself.

The picture went to a videotape of Cassie on top of a roof. Hugh Marlowe was standing next to her.

WHITE: We're here on top of the WTBK studios where I'm going to fall six stories and be caught in a safety net. I am going to be caught in a safety net, right, Hugh?

MARLOWE: I haven't missed yet.

Cassie moved toward the edge of the roof and looked down. Then she looked up at the camera.

WHITE: If this doesn't work, I'm going to be plenty mad.

As she got ready to make the jump, I reached over and switched off the TV in the stateroom where we were watching the rest of the show.

"Don't you want to see how this comes out?" Sanders asked me.

"It's on videotape remember."

"So I guess she didn't splatter herself all over the sidewalk."

"No such luck."

We said good-bye to Lafayette and the people on the boat and headed for our van parked on the pier by the East River.

"How come she does stuff like that?" Sanders asked.

"I don't know. Maybe she's trying to prove something. Or else maybe trying to make up for some kind of void in her life."

"Like what?"

"Who knows. Maybe she's sexually unfulfilled."

"I'm surprised Gergen lets her do it," Jacobson observed.

"Could be it wasn't his idea," I said.

"You think Carstairs . . . ?"

"It's pretty obvious he's running the show now, isn't it?"

"Yeah," Sanders agreed, "and he'd show open heart surgery on the air if he thought it would get good ratings."

"He has," I told him. "And it did. In Sacramento last year. It pulled a forty-two share."

We talked in the van about the slew of rumors sweeping the newsroom since Carstairs arrived. Sanders drove. Jacobson sat in the backseat and worked on a crossword puzzle, showing little interest in any of it.

"Rumor is," Sanders was saying, "Carstairs is going to clean out the on-air staff. Bring in all new blood."

"Who's supposed to go?" I asked.

"You. Hanrahan. Travers. Maybe even Conroy."

"How about Cassie?"

"Carstairs *loves* Cassie, I hear."

"That figures."

"Travers is pretty scared," Sanders said. "He's got a wife, four kids, and another on the way. He's been sending tryout tapes to stations all over the country for the last few days."

Behind us Jacobson grunted. "Anyone know a five-letter word for arrogant?"

"Yeah," I said, "Cassie."

He looked at me strangely. "That's six letters."

"Not if you spell it right," I told him. "Try *b-i-t-c-h*."

Sanders said there was also talk that the format of the news show would undergo drastic changes.

"Carstairs supposedly wants to take it out of the studio and broadcast direct from places all over the city."

"Like where?"

"Like if there's a big hostage standoff or something. We do a remote with the anchors in front of the scene. Stuff like that."

"What if there's no big story?"

"Then I guess we do it out of a bus station or someplace. Christ, I don't know."

I shook my head. "I got a bad feeling about all this."

"Maybe so," Sanders said, "but they did some quickie overnight surveys, and our ratings are already way up for the past few days compared with the stuff we've done before."

"I guess you can fool all the people all the time," I said.

We were heading through the East Village on the way back to the studio. I told Sanders to stop off in front of a building on E. 5th Street. The Ninth Police Precinct. There's a detective there named Jellinek I wanted to talk to.

Lieutenant Norm Jellinek sat behind his desk, shifted his weight uncomfortably in the chair, and snorted when I told him what I wanted. He was a big man, maybe 6 foot 4 and weighing 280 pounds. I figured him to be in his early fifties or so, with nearly thirty years on the force. We'd worked together on a couple of stories. As cops go, he was okay, I guess. Not a great cop maybe, but solid enough.

"Yeah, I've seen your stories about Kathy Kerrigan," he said. "The girl just took a powder on the eve of her wedding, huh?"

"Maybe. Maybe it's something more than that. You guys looking into it at all?"

"Nope."

"Why not?"

"No reason to. Nobody's filed a missing person report. Hell, the dame's twenty-five years old. She doesn't have to report in to her mother and father every night."

"We prefer not to be called dames," I said.

"Sorry. You one of those women lib broads?"

"*Broads* is not looked upon with great favor either."

"Listen, McKay, whaddya want?"

I laid out for him what I knew. Kathy's visit to the lawyer to talk about her long-dead father just before she disappeared. Senator Wincott's strange conversation with me. The two guys in the Caddy.

"And you think something might have happened to her?" he asked when I was finished.

"It's possible."

"What's the motive?"

"She's the only real blood heir to the Kerrigan fortune," I said. "Six hundred million bucks."

"So?"

"So maybe the mother or the stepfather or the lawyer decide one day it's a lot better for them if she's out of the way and . . ."

"Chrissakes, McKay, you're just fishing," Jellinek said disgustedly.

"Well, you could at least check into it."

"How?"

"I don't know, you're the cop. Go talk to Senator Wincott. You could do that."

"Sure. I could be directing sixth graders at a school guard crossing in the Bronx next week, too. Hey, Jenny, these are important people we're talking about here. He's a U.S. senator. They own one of the largest corporations in America. . . ."

He didn't say anymore, but I knew what he was thinking. Jellinek was a couple of years away from retirement, maybe five at most. He didn't want to do anything to rock the boat. He just wanted to serve out his time, get his pension, and go off and live a nice peaceful life somewhere. He didn't need any complications. He certainly didn't need to take on a U.S. senator and corporate America. I couldn't blame him, I guess. But I didn't feel that way right then.

I stood up. "Sorry," I said. "I thought you might want to act like a real policeman for a change. I guess I was wrong."

I regretted it as soon as the words came out of my mouth

"What in the hell kind of bug got up your ass?" he asked.

"Sorry, I'm just frustrated. I really think there's something going on here. I just don't know what it is."

Jellinek shrugged. "Look, I'll make a few discreet calls, okay?"

"Terrific."

"But don't expect anything to come out of it."

"I understand." I started toward the door, then turned around. "Thanks, Lieutenant. I don't think you'll regret it."

"Are you kidding? I regret it already."

It was nearly ten by the time I got home.

The first thing I did was tell Hobo a joke. This is not as crazy as it sounds. It's a technique I learned from a dog care book.

You tell your dog a joke every night when you come home. It doesn't matter what it is, only how you tell it. If you laugh and seem happy as you do it the animal picks up on that emotion, too, and it makes him happy. It always worked like a charm. Sometimes I read comic strips. Stuff like ''Garfield'' or ''Marmaduke.'' But tonight I tried a dog joke:

> A guy walks into a doctor's office. He's got a dog stuck on top of his head.
> ''Boy, I can see what your problem is,'' the doctor says.
> (Pause for punch line.)
> ''Yeah,'' the dog tells him, ''I can't get this asshole out from underneath me.''

I laughed uproariously. Hobo's mouth turned up at the sides and his tail made a *thump-thump* sound on the floor as he licked my face happily.

''You think that's good,'' I told him. ''Just wait until tomorrow. I'm doing a Rodney Dangerfield routine.''

I took Hobo out for his walk. (Fortunately, I have a dog walker who comes in twice a day, which takes some of the pressure off me.) Then I got undressed, figured out what I was going to wear to the Fourth of July party at Andrew Cafferty's place tomorrow and went into the kitchen to fix dinner.

I cut up some lettuce, a tomato, an onion, and some cucumber. Then I put it all into a big wooden dish and poured some low-cal salad dressing over the top.

When it was ready I took a can of Mighty Dog out of the cupboard, opened it up, and poured the contents into Hobo's dish next to mine on the counter.

I looked at the two of them there side by side. I wasn't sure which one looked more appetizing. Actually I was. Hobo's. I thought about asking to share it with him, but I figured he'd never go for it.

So I put his dish down on the floor and carried mine into the living room.

They were showing *Broadcast News* on one of the movie channels. It was about midway through, right at the part where

William Hurt is picked during the party at his boss's house to do the special news broadcast that turns him into a star.

Maybe that would happen to me tomorrow at Cafferty's.

I chewed listlessly on the salad, watched the screen, and thought about Kathy Kerrigan. I knew the movie by heart already. I'd seen it maybe fifteen times. I watched it all the way through again, though, hoping that this time Holly Hunter might actually go off with William Hurt at the end. I was also hoping something might click in my mind to make sense of the Kerrigan story.

Neither did, and I fell asleep around midnight.

10
Social Studies

Andrew Cafferty lived in a duplex at Fifth Avenue and 63rd Street. It was a big old handsome building that had been designated a New York City landmark about ten years ago. Cafferty's neighbors included the likes of Jackie Onassis, Henry Kissinger, and Laurence Rockefeller. Everything about the place oozed money.

A doorman was sitting at a desk in the corner of the lobby. The doorman didn't ooze money. He sat there watching a Yankee game on a small black-and-white TV and eating a hero sandwich. The image of Don Mattingly at bat flickered on the snow-filled screen. The guy looked up as I came in. There was sauce from the sandwich dribbling down his chin.

"Can I help you?" he asked.

"I'm here for the Cafferty party."

"Really?" He seemed surprised as he looked me over. I was wearing a denim skirt, a blue shirt worn loose over the skirt, a rattan belt, a red-and-blue scarf, and my most expensive pair of Italian sandals. If I had to describe myself, I'd say I was casual chic.

"Yeah. Where's it at?"

He told me.

"Let me ask you a question," I said to him. "Is this going to be real bad?"

"No comment," he chuckled.

"Christ, I hate the idea of spending the day dealing with a bunch of snooty, tight-asses with their noses so far up in the air I'm surprised they don't get nosebleeds," I complained. "That's not my idea of fun."

"Tell me about it." He sighed.

The first person I saw that I knew inside Cafferty's place was Cassie White.

She was wearing a black silk blouse, designer pants that flared at the hips, a silver metal belt, high heels, and an expensive-looking pair of antique silver earrings. I looked around and saw a lot of other people dressed similarly. I was starting to feel underdressed. Maybe I should have tucked my shirt in.

"Boy," Cassie said, "you didn't exactly dress up for this, did you?"

"I thought it was supposed to be casual."

"That's not casual."

"It isn't?"

"No, that's let's dress up like the 60s and go to Woodstock and smoke some dope and listen to Buffalo Springfield records."

"I like your outfit too," I told her.

There were about thirty-five people scattered around the living room and a terrace overlooking Fifth Avenue. A long table by the window was covered with trays of seafood appetizers, cold cuts, and barbecue dishes. A bartender stood next to it filling drink orders. Another man walked around the room with a tray offering appetizers to the guests. On the terrace a man in a chef's hat stood in front of a huge barbecue. Next to him were a collection of uncooked porterhouse steaks, chicken parts, and ribs.

Gergen came over and said hi.

"This isn't the kind of cookout where they're just going to roast weenies, is it?" I asked.

"I hate these things too," he said, "but it's important to be here. Think of it as a career move."

I nodded. "You think I'm underdressed?"

"Don't worry about it. Just remember this is Andrew Cafferty's party—don't insult anybody."

"Who me?"

"Yes, you. And no jokes either."

"No jokes?"

"Some of these people wouldn't understand your sense of humor," he said.

"Is it okay if I chortle to myself once in a while?" I asked. He shook his head and walked off.

I wandered over to find some beer. No luck. The bartender informed me they only had hard liquor or wine. Which would I prefer? While I was considering it, a man came over, introduced himself as Roger Bracken and said I looked familiar. I told him who I was and ordered a vodka tonic. Then I sipped it and listened to Bracken rattle on about himself.

"Yeah, I'm into real estate," he was saying. "Condos. We're building a big new one right now over by Gracie Mansion. Two hundred twenty units, luxury housing, $200,000 to $1 million a pop. And only twenty-two months from digging the first shovelful for the foundation until the first tenant moves in. Pretty impressive, right?"

"Uh-huh," I said and sipped my drink.

"Terrific party," he said. "Andy always throws terrific parties. Were you at his bash on Memorial Day out in the Hamptons?"

"I don't think so," I said. "I was probably busy having dinner with Mick Jagger that day." That one passed him by.

"McKay, huh?" he said. "What is that—Irish?"

"No. Jewish."

"Jewish?"

"It's really McKaystein. I changed it."

"No kidding," he said.

"Yeah, I'm kidding."

I hoped he didn't tell Gergen.

A woman came over to us. She was middle-aged, maybe thirty pounds overweight and wearing too much makeup.

There was a drink in her hand, and she seemed slightly tipsy. She looked at me, then at the man I'd been talking to.

"Who's your little friend?" she asked him.

Little friend. Adorable.

"This is Jenny McKay. She's on the TV news." He introduced her to me as his wife.

"I don't like TV news anymore," she announced. "Want to know why?"

No, but I'm sure you're going to tell me, I thought.

"Why?"

"Too many of them on the air."

"Who's 'them'?"

She leaned forward and whispered to me in a conspiratorial tone. There was a noticeable smell of alcohol on her breath.

"The niggers, spics, and chinks."

"I take it you're referring to the minority hiring ratio in the broadcast news industry," I said.

"Damned right I am," she said. "Give me a good white man to deliver the news any day."

I didn't say anything.

"You know who I hate the worst?" She belched softly. "That slant-eyed woman."

"Connie Chung?"

"Yeah, that's her." She belched again, only louder this time. "A slant-eyed chink woman like that shouldn't be giving me my news, she should be doing my laundry."

She took a big gulp of the drink in her hand.

"Yep," she repeated, "a slant-eyed chink woman like that should be doing my goddamned laundry."

She seemed pleased with herself for saying it.

I saw Gergen walking in from the terrace outside and moved over to him.

"Hey, Joe," I asked, "how far up from the street are we?"

"Ten floors. Why?"

"Because I'm thinking of jumping soon."

He gestured to me to walk with him.

"I want you to meet Andrew Cafferty," he said. "He's over there talking with a Doctor Wolfe."

"Doctor?"

"He's some sort of a big Park Avenue psychiatrist. Cafferty apparently swears by him. Doesn't make a move without his advice."

"A psychiatrist, huh? Sort of like Frasier on 'Cheers.'"

"Life isn't like a TV show, Jenny. There they are now."

He pointed to two men on the terrace. One was a somewhat nerdy looking guy in his thirties, wearing a green blazer, white pants, and open-collared polo shirt. That was Cafferty Junior. Dr. Wolfe was a huge, corpulent guy wearing a three-piece suit with a vest that seemed ready to pop. He was eating a handful of chicken wings from a paper plate he was holding.

"Actually he looks more like Norm than Frasier," I observed.

We went over and Gergen introduced me.

"Well, well," Cafferty said. "Jenny McKay. Bob Carstairs has told me a lot about you."

"None of it is true," I said.

"Huh?"

"Sorry. Just kidding."

"Oh yes, Bob told me that you like to think of yourself as something of a wit. I'm afraid I don't have much of a sense of humor. For a long time I perceived that as a character flaw of mine, not anymore. Doctor Wolfe has changed my thinking."

"That's right," the doctor said. He'd finished the chicken wings, and was now grabbing for ribs and potato salad from the banquet table next to him. I was starting to worry the tablecloth might go next. "I find in many of my patients that a sense of humor is an attempt to avoid dealing with the real problems in one's life."

"Are you trying to psychoanalyze me?" I asked.

"No, I'm just trying to help you put your actions in better perspective. You see your sense of humor as a strength. But maybe it's really a fault. A lot of people do that with their faults to avoid dealing with them." He smiled at me.

I smiled back. "You mean like overeating?" I asked.

Gergen cut in quickly.

"You know Jenny has been doing some very interesting stuff," he said.

"Yes, the 'South Street Confidential' segment," Cafferty said. "That was Carstairs's idea, and I like it very much."

"Well, we got really lucky with that first one," Gergen told him. "Stumbling onto the story about the Kerrigan woman disappearing on the eve of her wedding."

"That's a real good society scoop," Cafferty said.

"Well, I think it might be more than that," I said.

I told him about my encounter with the two underworld hoods.

"Why would they care about a story concerning a society girl's wedding?" he asked.

"That's just the point. I think there's something else going on. This could be more than just a story about a girl missing her wedding. It could be really explosive."

"But it doesn't make any sense," he said.

"A lot of stories don't at first. Until you get the answers to a lot of questions."

"But how do you get those answers?"

"That's what reporters do for a living," I reminded him.

Dr. Wolfe was shaking his head.

"You seem rather obsessed with this, Miss McKay," he said.

"Obsessed?"

"Well, you don't really enjoy doing celebrity and society news that much, do you? You'd probably prefer to be doing hard news stories."

"So?"

"So now you're trying to convince yourself—and your bosses—that this simple society story is really a major news story." Wolfe smiled and ate a mouthful of potato salad. "One might conjecture that you're letting your imagination run wild."

"The two mob guys who picked me up weren't my imagination," I said.

"How do you know they were from the mob?"

"What do you mean?"

"Well, did they identify themselves as members of the underworld?"

"Well, no, but . . ."

"Do you feel you always know what members of the underworld would look like?"

"No."

"Well, maybe this didn't happen the way you now perceive it. Maybe it was just your imagination and your desire for a bigger story working together to create a larger-than-life scenario. You need to get in touch with your true feelings about all this, Miss McKay. Try and do that."

I stared at him. "You want me to get in touch with my true feelings, Dr. Wolfe?"

"That's right."

"My true feeling," I said slowly, "is that you're starting to get on my nerves."

"Well, I'm sorry, I only . . ."

"Look, I said I got picked up by two mob guys, and I mean it. It is true that I didn't get anything in writing to that effect, but I was a little bit concerned about my well-being at the time. Now—if you'd like—I'll go find them again and get them to give me signed affidavits that they are bona fide members of the Mafia. Then we can go find a notary public, get the affidavits notarized and you'll have the proof you need." I paused. "That is if you can tear yourself away from the feeding trough long enough."

There was silence.

"I need another drink," I announced. Turning to Cafferty, I said: "Nice meeting you." Then I headed for the bartender at the table inside.

I'd just gotten there when I felt a hand grab me from behind. I turned around. It was Roger Bracken, the real estate whiz. Minus his wife this time. And a lot drunker than the first time we'd talked.

"Hi, remember me?" He smiled.

"Mr. Bracken."

"Rog, Jenny. Call me Rog."

"Okay, Rog."

"That's better."

"Rog, can I ask you a favor?"

"Sure, anything you want, Jenny. What is it?"

"Take your hand off my ass," I said.

He threw back his head and laughed.

"Boy, you are a spunky little filly."

His hand was still there.

I looked down at the banquet table next to us. There was an expansive array of hors d'oeuvres, dips, potato salad, and other goodies.

"Rog," I said slowly, "I've had a tough day. For that matter, I've had a tough week. None of this is your fault. But if you don't move your hand in the next five seconds, you're going right into the onion dip."

He stuck his face close to mine and smiled. "Try and make me," he said.

I'm not sure what happened next. I didn't mean to do what I did. Or maybe I did. All I know is that when I pushed him away from me, he went flying right into the banquet table.

It was like something out of a Marx Brothers comedy, only in agonizing slow motion. Maybe it was the booze that made him lose his balance. Or maybe I just don't know my strength when I get mad. Anyway, he hovered precariously over the food for a second, then went toppling smack into the center of the table. There was a huge cracking sound, and the table broke in half. Food flew everywhere, people screamed. I wanted to crawl into a hole and die.

Gergen somehow appeared out of the confusion and hauled me off into the kitchen.

"What in the hell are you doing?" he screamed at me.

"Joe, I'm sorry. I just—"

"I'm trying to save your job, and you're doing your best to lose it."

"Maybe if I went back out and apologized to everyone . . ." I suggested.

"Forget it. They'd probably lynch you. Just get out of here. I'll try and smooth things over as best I can."

"Are you sure?"

"Jenny—out!"

I had to walk through the living room again to get to the front door. Everyone stared at me. No one said good-bye. No one wished me a happy Fourth of July. No one said we had to do it again next year.

I took the elevator down to the lobby. The same doorman was still on duty. The Yankee game was over and an Abbott and Costello rerun was playing on the little TV.

"How'd it go?" he asked.

"Not well," I said.

"What happened?"

"I may have committed a social faux pas," I told him.

He looked at me. I was dripping barbecue sauce from my hair and a big gob of cream cheese was stuck to my shirt. There was also a yellow mustard stain down the front of my denim skirt.

"I'll bet you did," he said softly.

11
Aftershocks

Once a long time ago, when I was a little girl, I got this brand-new watercolor set for my birthday. Before she would give it to me, my mother made me promise I would only use it when she was there. She was afraid I'd make a mess. Of course, I promised her—I wanted the damned watercolor set. But I didn't really mean it. What the hell did she know?

The first time she left the house, I took out the watercolors and began to paint. I painted trees. I painted animals. I painted blue skies with billowy white clouds floating through them. I was having so much fun it took me nearly an hour to realize I had also painted much of my room. There was paint all over the walls, the bed spread—even the ceiling.

I knew I was in big trouble, so I reacted the way I always do in that kind of situation. I ran away from it. There was a tree house my friends and I had built down the street, so I ran there and sat in it and thought about how I'd live in it for the rest of my life. Eventually though it got dark and I knew I had to go home. That walk back to my house seemed like an eternity, my mind speculating each step of the way on what kind of horrible punishment awaited me.

That's how I felt now as I went to work on Monday morning after Cafferty's party. Like a little girl going to face the music.

I took a deep breath, sighed, and steeled myself as I stood outside the newsroom.

Maybe I was making too much of it. Maybe everyone was too busy to worry about what I did at a damned party. Maybe no one had even heard about it.

I walked in.

"Hey, there she is," Hanrahan yelled the minute he saw me. "It's the party girl."

They gave me a standing ovation.

"I'd pay a lot of money for a videotape of the whole scene," he told me. "It would be the cult film of the New York media world."

"What happened?" asked Travers, the weatherman, who'd just come in after me.

"You haven't heard?" Hanrahan said. "Jenny here pretended like she was doing a javelin throw with one of the guests at Andrew Cafferty's party Saturday. Threw him head-first right into the banquet table."

"Did you really drop a plate of potato salad over Andrew Cafferty's head?" someone asked.

"I think this story is getting a little exaggerated," I said.

A production assistant came over to me. "Mr. Gergen wants to see you."

"Right now?"

"His exact words were 'Tell her to get her ass in here the second she shows up, if not sooner.'"

I started toward his office with a small wave at the crowd that had gathered around me.

We who are about to die salute you.

On the way there, I met Cassie White.

"Boy, I'm surprised you've got the guts to show your face around here today," she said.

"I say that about you every day," I told her.

"No, I'm talking about your performance at the party. By the way, Gergen is looking for you."

"I know that," I snapped.

"Hey, I'm just telling you. Don't shoot the messenger."

"Why not?"

Gergen was standing next to his desk. When he saw me, he grunted, motioned me toward a chair in front of him, then walked over and slammed the door shut.

Gulp.

"I just spent the last thirty minutes talking with Andrew Cafferty about you, and your little performance at his party," Gergen said. "Do you know what he said?"

"We'll have to do it at my place next time?"

"Don't be flip now, Jenny."

"Sorry."

Gergen shuffled through some papers on his desk.

"This is no time for fooling around," he said. "This is your career we're talking about here. The thing is, Jenny, well, he and Carstairs want me to put someone else on 'South Street Confidential.' "

"Who?"

"Cassie."

"That figures."

"They think she can do it along with her anchor duties for a while anyway."

"And what do they want me to do?"

"Well, that's just it."

"Meaning?"

"In a word—nothing."

I sat there stunned. "I'm out?"

"That's what Cafferty suggested."

"All because of one party?"

Gergen sighed and picked up the papers in front of him.

"Do you know what all this is?" he said.

I shook my head.

"It's a quickie research study about the changes we've made since Carstairs took over. One of the things the researchers found out is that 'South Street Confidential' has the potential to be what they call a turnaround factor. Along with our new contest and an upcoming ad campaign, it could turn the station's entire image around. They want to make a major splash with it—promos all day, ads in newspapers, radio spots, the works. They say this could make all the difference in the world in terms of ratings. That is—with the right personality doing it.''

"And I'm not that personality?''

Gergen looked at me sadly. "That's what they think. Carstairs was going to give you a little time, but now after what happened at the party. . . .''

"What do you think, Joe?'' I asked.

"I think you can do it,'' he said. He paused. "And that's exactly what I told them.''

"Huh?''

"I told them you've been busting your ass on 'South Street Confidential.' That you had broken the Kathy Kerrigan thing and done a lot of other good stuff too. That I thought you could do as good a job on it as Cassie or anyone else. That I thought Carstairs could take his ratings charts and his demographic studies and stick them up his . . . Well, I didn't really say that, but I think he got the message.''

I smiled. "Thanks, Joe. I really appreciate it.''

"Anyway, you're still on 'South Street Confidential.' Cafferty and Carstairs said they didn't agree with me, but I said I was the news director and they'd go along with my judgment. For now.''

"Meaning it's only a temporary reprieve, right?''

"Well, at least you can work out the last month or whatever of your contract.''

"And then?''

"There's this twenty-four-year-old ex–Miss North Carolina down in Roanoke,'' Gergen said slowly, "who's made a big splash in the ratings as a reporter on the station down there over the past six months. She sent Carstairs some tapes of her and he wants to go over them with me soon. She's got this Southern accent and cute little-girl look that he just eats up with a spoon. I think he wants to bring her to New York.''

I let my breath out slowly.

"Look, Jenny, I wish I knew what to tell you. If it was just a matter of getting a new hairdo and taking voice lessons to turn yourself into a Cassie White clone, I'd tell you to do that. Christ, I don't know. Sometimes I don't understand this business any more than you do. You're a good reporter. A damned good reporter. But that's not enough here. Hell, in newspapers we never had to worry about any of this crap. You either came through with the story or you didn't. No one cared how you looked or sounded or what kind of a fool you made of yourself at a party.''

"Once again, I'm sorry about that," I said. "You don't deserve to have to deal with all these hassles. Especially after what we talked about in the diner. How're you feeling, Joe?"

Gergen shrugged. "I've been better." He looked at me. "Did you really mean what you were telling Cafferty about the Kathy Kerrigan story?"

"Yeah," I said. "I think there's something going on. Something pretty big. I just don't know what it is."

"But you're going to keep looking into it?"

"I'd like to. I made an appointment today to talk to the Kerrigan woman's fiancé—this guy Brad Jeffries. As long as I'm still on the job, that is."

"Go for it," Gergen said.

When I went back to the newsroom, Cassie was waiting for me. She had a big smile on her face. Like a piranha moving in for the kill.

"Boy, you don't wait for the body to get cold, do you?" I snapped.

"Well, I just—"

"I didn't get fired if that's what you're wondering. Sorry."

"But I heard . . ."

"You heard wrong."

She glared at me, her nostrils flaring slightly for a second, then turned and walked away.

"Better luck next time," I called after her.

Hanrahan walked over with an amused look on his face.

"What was that all about?"

"Just woman talk," I told him. "We were exchanging recipes."

"Speaking of food, you know your whole party performance sounds real kinky."

"Kinky?"

"Yeah. You can do a lot of kinky things with food. Maybe

you only scratched the surface. How about we get together,
send for some Chinese takeout, and see what happens?''

"How about you don't worry about my personal life?"

"Okay," he said, holding up a phone note, "but then I can't
give you this message."

"Who's it from?"

"Someone named Paxton."

Dave Paxton, Senator Wincott's administrative assistant.

"Sounded real classy," Hanrahan said.

"Something you wouldn't know anything about."

"C'mon, be nice now. I didn't have to do this. I'm not your
answering service, you know."

"What'd he say?"

"He says he's flying into New York today and he wants to
have dinner with you." Hanrahan handed me the message slip.
"You're supposed to call him right away at that number."

"Thanks a lot."

"No problem. Hey, if this thing doesn't work out tonight,
the Chinese takeout order is still open. Why not give me a call
afterward? Come over to my place for a nightcap."

"I think I'll pass on that."

"You'd love my place. I've got it all. Fully stocked bar.
Ten-thousand-dollar stereo system. Strobe lighting. Mirrored
ceiling in the bedroom." He leaned over closer to me and
winked. "Everything you need."

"How about a barf bag?" I asked. "I might need that."

He shook his head. "You're a challenge, Jenny. A real
challenge. But I'll get through to you somehow."

He left and I dialed the number on the message slip. It was
Senator Wincott's Washington office.

"Hi," Paxton said when he came on the line. "I'm a man
who keeps my promise. Dinner tonight?"

"Sounds yummy. Where?"

"You know the Palm?"

"You mean the place on 45th and Second with the terrific
steaks, giant lobsters, sawdust on the floor, and drawings of
celebrities all over the walls?"

"Yeah, that's it."

"Never heard of it," I said.

Paxton chuckled at the other end. "You're a funny lady, Jenny McKay."

"Some people see it as a character flaw—a psychological ploy to cover up my other inadequacies."

"Huh?"

"Just someone I met at a party. I'll tell you about it later."

"Okay. I'll meet you at the bar in the Palm at 7:30."

"Sounds good."

"One thing," he said. "Is this going to be about you and me tonight or are you going to pump me for information about Kathy Kerrigan?"

"Probably both," I admitted.

"Well," he sighed, "I guess I'll have to take you any way I can get you."

"Most people do," I said.

12
Burger King
vs. Lutèce

The Kerrigan Corporation occupied the top floors of a sky-scraper at Park Avenue and 53rd Street.

Brad Jeffries was listed in the directory in the lobby as an executive vice-president. Sanders, Jacobson, and I rode the elevator up to the fifty-second floor and met him in his office, which had an eye-boggling view of half of Manhattan. Jeffries was about thirty, wore a three-piece pin-striped suit, and had close-cropped short hair. He motioned for us to sit down, then kept us waiting for another few minutes while he talked on the phone.

"I don't want to hear any more excuses," he was saying. "You've got to get that deal together this week. It's costing me fifty thousand dollars for every day we can't drill. Tell acquisitions to put a forty-eight hour time limit on our offer, or we withdraw the money. Do whatever you have to, but let's fish or cut bait. I have to get those oil fields operating."

He slammed down the phone and turned to us.

"Sorry about that, but we negotiated this deal with the Mexican government for a new oil field last month, and now we're running into trouble from all the local landowners and municipalities. In the meantime, I'm sitting on this oil that's probably worth millions if I could get it out of the goddamned ground. Can you believe it?''

I didn't say anything.

''Now, Miss McKay, I guess you're here to interview me about Kathy, right?''

''That's right, Mr. Jeffries. Now she's been gone several days and—''

The telephone rang again.

''Jack, how are you?'' Jeffries said to the person on the other end. ''Lunch today? Sure, that sounds fine. What do you say—maybe about one o'clock?''

I was getting bored. I dug around in my purse, found a package of sugarless Life Savers and opened it. Sanders looked over at me and rolled his eyes up toward the ceiling. Jacobson sat slouched in a corner working on another crossword puzzle.

''Lutèce?'' Jeffries was saying. ''Gee, Jack, I don't think so. Not again. Because I just like La Côte Basque better, that's why.''

I stuck one of the Life Savers in my mouth and sucked on it.

''Jack, I don't give a damn what *New York* magazine says about Lutèce,'' Jeffries said. ''You know how I feel about it. So just let me call Henri right now at La Côte Basque and make reservations for us.''

He looked over at me and winked.

''Hey, Jack, I've got to go. Got some TV people here. I'll see you at lunch.''

Jeffries hung up, turned toward me, and shook his head.

''Some people just love Lutèce,'' he said. ''Me, I always thought it was overrated.''

I nodded.

''Now don't get me wrong,'' he said. ''Lutèce is good, but it's just not great. You know what I mean.''

''Sure,'' I told him. ''Actually I have a very similar problem.''

''Is that so?''

''Yeah. A lot of my friends just love the Big Macs at McDonald's. Say the sesame seeds and the special sauce are sensational. Me, I think they're good, but not great. You know what I mean? Now, I prefer Burger King . . .''

Sanders snickered loudly behind me.

"All right, Miss McKay," Jeffries said, holding up his hand. "I get your point."

"If you could spare a few minutes away from the phone," I said, "I'd like to talk with you about Kathy."

"Certainly."

"Now I want to do an on-camera interview in a few minutes. But I'd like to ask you a few preliminary questions about your fiancée. Tell me about her. About your wedding plans."

Jeffries sighed. "Ah yes, the wedding. That's been very much on my mind these past few days. You know, her parents had to cancel an order with the caterer for three hundred dinners. You can imagine what fun that was. Damned embarrassing too. When I think of Kathy disappearing at a time like this . . ."

"Yeah, awfully inconvenient of her, wasn't it?" I said.

"It sure was," he said, apparently not noticing my sarcasm.

"If I might say so, you don't seem too worried about what might have happened to her."

"Oh, Kathy's all right. She's just playing one of her little games. She'll be back soon."

"You know, everybody keeps telling me that," I told him.

"That's because it's true."

"I may be the only one who's not so sure."

"That's because you don't know her."

"Tell me about her," I said.

The phone rang again. Jeffries looked at it longingly, then over at me and sighed. Finally he switched the phone off and started talking.

"Kathy's always been a little—well—confused. She's a terrific girl, I love her dearly. But sometimes she acts just like an immature little kid. I suppose her family has something to do with it. The senator's in Washington so much of the time. And her mother has a—uh, well—this problem. . . ."

"You mean her drinking?" I asked.

"I see you've met Audrey." Jeffries smiled. "Yes, that's right. Anyway, it's made her somewhat less than the ideal parent. Then there's growing up with all that money, too, like Kathy did. I think that it has an effect on a person. It certainly did on Kathy. Most people don't have that kind of life as an impressionable young kid. So it's hard for me or most people to understand.''

"Your family wasn't rich?''

"Oh no,'' Jeffries laughed. "Not at all. I'm a working stiff just like you. Graduated from City College, as a matter of fact. Then went ahead and got my M.B.A. at Harvard after I came here and the company put me through.''

"A self-made man, huh?'' I said.

He laughed again. "I guess you might say that.''

Who just happened to latch onto a gold mine named Kathy Kerrigan, I thought to myself. I really didn't like Brad Jeffries.

"You said something about Kathy being confused. Are you talking about her being under psychiatric care?''

"Yeah, she's had a lot of troubles. She's been seeing doctors—off and on—ever since she was a little girl. You see she had this really traumatic thing happen to her about her father—losing him when she was young really screwed her up.''

"What else?''

"Well, there were the drugs and the booze. . . . Like mother, like daughter, I guess. People tell me that's pretty common. Anyway I thought she had it licked, but when she gets real depressed or upset she sometimes turns to the stuff. I guess it goes back to the whole father thing.''

"Is that what you think now? She's on some kind of booze or drug binge?''

He shrugged. "Sure. What else?''

"Tell me about Kathy's father.''

"Mike Kerrigan? King Kerrigan's son?''

"Yeah. What was he like?''

"Jeez, I only know what I've heard. I mean I was ten years old when it happened. But I guess he was really something. Brilliant, charismatic, almost the perfect politician. Sort of like another JFK from the way they describe him. That's what the old man—King Kerrigan—wanted. Thought he could put his son in the White House just like old Joe Kennedy did. Probably could have too.''

''Seriously?''

''Sure. The kid was the real goods. Did you know he was a Vietnam hero—saved a bunch of guys' lives?''

''He was in Vietnam?''

''Infantry. He volunteered for it. He didn't have to either, I mean King Kerrigan's son could have pulled enough strings to stay out of the fighting. Lots of important people did back then. But Mike Kerrigan wanted to be in the middle of it.''

''So what did he do to become a hero?''

''His platoon got ambushed by the Viet Cong down in the Mekong Delta. A lot of them were killed, the rest taken prisoner. Mike somehow managed to get away and spent the next three days crawling through the jungle and rice paddies to get to a U.S. base camp. He made it, and he was able to organize a rescue force to free the survivors. They gave him the Bronze Star for it.''

''Sort of like *PT 109* all over again,'' I said.

''That's right. I thought of it in the same way. So he went on and got elected to Congress, where he did all sorts of good stuff. Passed a bill to help Vietnam veterans, proposed legislation to rebuild the cities, got on this committee investigating mob influence in American—''

''The mob?'' An alarm went off in my head. I thought about the two guys in the black Caddy.

''Yeah. He said he felt the Mafia was a cancer to our country—draining millions of dollars from the economy, using threats and violence to infiltrate legitimate businesses in our society. He said it was time we stood up to it.''

''Sort of like Robert F. Kennedy with Jimmy Hoffa,'' I pointed out.

''Eerie, isn't it?''

''And then Mike Kerrigan died,'' I said.

Jeffries nodded. ''When he had everything going for him. What a bitch.''

''John F. Kennedy said it: 'Life's unfair,' '' I told him. ''So anyway Kathy's got this terrific father who dies when she's still a little girl. She can't get over it. Hates her stepfather, resents her mother, gets all screwed up on drugs and booze, then cuts out on the eve of her wedding to you. Is that about it?''

''I guess so. Of course, it sounds pretty grim when you say it like that, but I guess it's as good a description as any.''

''What about Senator Wincott, her stepfather. How well do you know him?''

''Oh, he's okay. Nice guy, smart, competent. Got himself elected senator, might even make it to the White House. Only . . .''

''Only what?''

Jeffries smiled. ''Well, he's just no Mike Kerrigan.''

''I guess Kathy felt that way too,'' I said.

He looked up at me and grinned.

''So are you going to put me on TV or what?'' he asked.

I interviewed him for about twenty minutes with the camera running. Afterward, I called Gergen from the phone in the van.

''How'd it go?'' he asked.

''Well, I got the interview. The guy's a bit of a jerk. He seems to care more about some Mexican oil field than he does about his missing fiancée. If I was Kathy, I'd have run away too.''

''Who cares what you think of him? Is it usable stuff?''

''Oh sure. By the time we finish editing it down to a minute or so, he'll come across as a sympathetic, loving boyfriend. Isn't TV wonderful?''

''We'll do some 'South Street Confidential' spots for it. Promos for it during the afternoon. Are you on the way back now?''

''Sanders and Jacobson are coming back with the tape. They're going to drop me off in Midtown. There's something else I want to do.''

''What?''

''I'm going to the library.''

''The library? Why?''

''I want to do some research on Mike Kerrigan.''

''The one who died twenty years ago?''

''Yeah. His name keeps popping up everywhere I turn.''

''So?''

''I'm curious,'' I said.

13
Younger than Yesterday

It used to be when you wanted to go through old newspapers, you went to the main branch of the New York Public Library on Fifth Avenue and 42nd Street. That's the one with the lions out front—a marvelous building with high ceilings and marble halls that looks like a library is supposed to look. Back in those days, you went to a room where they'd hand you a stack of old yellowed newspapers to page through. Now all newspaper records are kept on microfilm in a newer building a few blocks away. Progress, they say. The older I get the more I hate progress.

The librarian behind the counter listened to my request, directed me to a viewing machine, and a few minutes later brought over microfilm copies of the New York papers from the summer months of 1973. After struggling with the projector for a while, I managed to get the microfilm threaded through the right slots and turned on the device. I sat back and began slowly going through the pages of the newspapers.

The summer of 1973. Christ, the memories it brought back. Watergate. *Mary Tyler Moore* and *All in the Family* on TV every Saturday night. Tug McGraw's "You Gotta Believe" cry leading the Mets to the pennant. I was twenty years old then and working as a college intern for a big magazine that summer, and I remember feeling that I had everything in the world going for me. There wasn't anything I didn't think I could do.

Now, two decades later, it's not the same anymore. I'm forty years old, worried about my future, hate my job, and sometimes wonder if I can do anything right. It seemed so easy back then.

It took about twenty-five minutes to find what I was looking for. The date was August 15, 1973, and it got pretty good play in most of the papers. Page one headlines in the *News* and *Post*, the lead obit in the *Times*. I read the *Post* article first:

CONGRESSMAN DIES IN BOAT ACCIDENT

NANTUCKET, Mass.—Michael Kerrigan, Congressman from New York and heir to the Kerrigan oil millions, drowned in a boating accident here over the weekend, authorities said today.

The thirty-one-year-old Kerrigan's boat capsized on Saturday afternoon about two miles off the eastern coast of this island resort, according to Commander Charles Schumbacher of the U.S. Coast Guard station here.

A nearby fisherman saw Kerrigan's thirty-foot sloop roll over shortly after 2 P.M. and spotted the victim struggling briefly in the water several feet away from the wreckage, Schumbacher said.

But the fisherman, Thomas Meehan of Glouster, Mass., said that Kerrigan had disappeared under the waves by the time he was able to maneuver his own boat into the area.

A thirty-six-hour search of the waters proved fruitless, and rescue operations were halted last night.

A family spokesman said Kerrigan had sailed alone out into the ocean earlier in the afternoon from his summer house on the island's exclusive Siasconset community. He'd been spending the weekend there along with his wife, Audrey, and young daughter, Kathy.

The house adjoins the land owned by his father, Thomas Kerrigan, the legendary oil baron and financier who is believed to be one of the richest men in the world.

Thomas Kerrigan was reported in seclusion in the compound after learning of the death of his only son.

The elder Kerrigan—or King Kerrigan as he's often called—has long been known as a major power broker in both political and financial circles. He's personally responsible for the election of a number of congressmen, senators, governors and even possibly a president or two over the past thirty years, many observers say.

His latest triumph was the election of his son to Congress.

The younger Kerrigan was elected last year as Representative from the Silk Stocking congressional district on Manhattan's East Side.

There had been speculation in political circles that Kerrigan would run for the Senate next year and . . .

The rest of the papers were all pretty much the same. Accounts of the accident. Details of the younger Kerrigan's political future. Lots of background on King Kerrigan's financial empire and career.

After the first-day stories, most of the papers kept it going with follow-ups for another week or so. I skimmed through most of them, stopping to make notes on some. One I found particularly interesting was a biography of Michael Kerrigan that appeared in the *Sunday Daily News* that week.

Michael Kerrigan, who died in a sailing accident several days ago, seemed to have everything going for him.

Family wealth. A promising political career. A loving family. He seemed to lead a charmed life until the tragedy off the coast of Nantucket ended it all.

"He had a certain something," one friend said, "a kind of spark that sets some people apart from the crowd so that you never forget them. The kind of thing John F.

Kennedy had. Maybe a few others, but not many. Well, Michael Kerrigan had it.

"Christ, if he'd lived and gone on in politics, he might have been another JFK. I honestly believe that. He had those kinds of qualities."

There was some biographical background on him. He was the only child of King Kerrigan, and his mother had died during childbirth, so he became the apple of his father's eye. The sole heir to the Kerrigan name and fortune. He grew up in the family's townhouse in Manhattan and went to the exclusive Brooke Preparatory School on East 78th Street. Then on to Harvard, where he made the dean's list and starred on the swimming and lacrosse teams. There was an old newspaper picture of him placing first in a relay swim meet with Yale. After graduation came a stint as an executive vice-president with the Kerrigan Corporation, his marriage, and then the run for Congress.

No question about it, Michael Kerrigan seemed to have everything going for him.

I went through the rest of the papers, taking notes as I went along. If I was looking for anything suspicious or sinister, it wasn't here. Frankly, this Kerrigan sounded like a helluva guy. Almost made me wish I'd known him. I began to understand why his daughter didn't seem to want to let go of his memory.

Just before I called it a day, I found one last item dated September 22, about a month after the boating accident. The name Kerrigan in it caught my eye. As it turns out, it wasn't really about Michael Kerrigan, it was about his father. But I found it interesting just the same.

CONGRESSIONAL COMMITTEE:
NO SMOKING GUN
IN MOB PROBE

WASHINGTON—A special Congressional subcommittee set up to investigate the influence of mob activity in the U.S. political process adjourned yesterday after four months of taking testimony.

John Warham, the committee's co-counsel, conceded the panel had been unable to make any significant headway in documenting organized corruption by any of the targets it was eyeing during its probe.

Among the most notable public figures who appeared before the committee was Thomas (King) Kerrigan, the legendary industrialist and political boss who has ruled much of New York and Massachusetts politics for the past quarter century.

Several top reputed underworld figures also appeared, but invoked the Fifth Amendment to avoid testifying. . . .

After leaving the library, I found a pay phone that worked on Fifth Avenue.

My first call was to Tom Sewell, the Wincott family attorney. Something had crossed my mind while going through all those clips. Something I didn't have the answer to. I figured Sewell would.

"What?" he asked when I put it to him. He sounded surprised.

"Where is Michael Kerrigan buried?" I repeated.

"What kind of question is that?"

"Well, I was thinking about Kathy's fierce devotion to her father's memory while I went through all the stories about him. And it suddenly occurred to me, what better place for her to go if she was upset than her father's grave site? I mean it's a long-shot, but it's still a shot. So where's the body?"

Sewell chuckled. "I'm afraid you're really off-base this time, Miss McKay."

"You mean you already checked and she hasn't been there?"

"There's nothing to check."

"What do you mean?"

"There is no grave site. That's because there never was any body."

"No body?" I wasn't ready for that answer.

"That's right. Mike was lost at sea, remember?"

"I know. I mean, well, I just assumed the body had turned up somewhere later."

"It never did."

"Don't drowning victims usually wash up somewhere?"

"Not always. Especially not that far out at sea."

"But . . ."

"Miss McKay," Sewell said softly, as if he were talking to a child, "you seem to be continually looking for something that's not there. There's no mystery of any kind going on here. As I explained to you before, Kathy's just gone off to be by herself for a while. That's all. It's as simple and innocent as that."

After I hung up, I thought about it for a while. Maybe Sewell was right. Nobody seemed to be taking it that seriously. Not him. Not the cops. Not Kathy's stepfather. Not her fiancé.

Nobody was really worried about Kathy but me.

And her mother.

Audrey Wincott was worried about her. I knew that because she'd asked for my help in finding her that first day at the penthouse.

I tracked down her number and dialed it.

"Mrs. Wincott, I'd like to come up and see you again today," I told her when she came on the line.

"I—I—I don't think that's a good idea," she said. It was only a little after noon, but her speech was already slurred. Probably started on the bottle at the crack of dawn. The early bird gets the worm.

"I need to talk to you," I said.

"Why?"

"You asked me to help find your daughter. Remember?"

There was a silence on the other end.

"I was wrong to do that," she said finally.

"Why?"

"Because I overreacted. Kathy's all right. It's just that sometimes . . . well, I've been taking this medication and it occasionally makes me a little lightheaded. Anyway, I was wrong to talk to you."

"Is that what your husband says or what you say, Mrs. Wincott?" I asked.

She didn't answer.

"You were worried about Kathy? Aren't you still worried?"

"She's fine."

"How can you be sure?"

"I . . ."

"She could be dead," I said. "Or at least need help. You're her mother, for God's sake."

"Miss McKay, please . . ."

"I want to help her," I said. "I think you do, too."

"I'm sorry, I can't talk about this anymore."

"But if you'd just—"

"I'm sorry. I really am sorry."

There was a loud click and the phone went dead.

I stared at the receiver for a second, then dialed the number for my friend Bill Rohr at the *Washington Post*. The operator asked for my long distance calling card number. I gave it to her, then held my breath because I hadn't paid my phone bill for the past two months. I was afraid the computer might spit that back at me. But it didn't. She put the call through for me, thanked me for using AT&T, and wished me a happy day. Service with a smile.

"Did you come up with anything yet on Mike Kerrigan?" I asked Rohr.

"Not yet. It's been a little tougher than I expected. Give me another day or so."

"No problem. Check on one more thing while you're at it, okay?"

"Sure."

"Twenty years ago a congressional subcommittee held a whole batch of hearings on the mob. One of the counsels was someone named John Warham. I think Mike Kerrigan helped head up the committee too before he died. There've got to be some people still around who were involved in that."

"Probably. What do you need from them?" Rohr asked.

"I want to find out why they talked to Mike Kerrigan's father," I said.

14
Romantic Interlude

Dave Paxton was standing at the bar of the Palm with his back to the door when I got there a little after eight.

"Buy me a drink, big fella," I whispered, slipping silently into the space next to him.

He whirled around in surprise, then smiled when he saw me.

"Sure," he grinned. "What'll it be?"

"Vodka and tonic."

He ordered it along with a bourbon and water for himself. The bartender brought both drinks and put them down in front of us along with a big bowl of peanuts.

"Oh great," I said, reaching over and scooping up a handful of the peanuts. "We don't even have to wait for a table. We can just pig out right here."

"You look hungry," he observed as I began popping peanuts into my mouth.

"I'm on a diet," I said.

Paxton looked at me quizzically. "Peanuts? Peanuts are part of your diet?"

"Yeah, well, I'm not fanatical about it."

I finished off the peanuts in my hand and reached for some more.

"Gee," Paxton said, "I wouldn't think you needed to worry about dieting. You look great to me."

"You know, I like you, big fella," I said, winking at him. "I think this is gonna work out real fine."

He took a sip of his drink and smiled.

"No, I'm serious. You don't seem overweight."

"It's just that I'm approaching a crisis point. Five more pounds and I'll have to buy all new jeans."

"You fit your jeans okay, I'd say," he observed.

"Yeah, well it can't be too bad yet. I walked past a construction site today, and still got some wolf whistles from the workers."

"Doesn't that bother you?"

"Hey, when they stop doing it, that's when I'm going to know it's really time to start dieting."

The guy who runs the Palm came over and told us a table was ready. He took us to a table along the wall, where a drawing of Elizabeth Taylor looked down at us.

"So how was your day?" Paxton asked after we were seated.

"Okay," I said. "I talked to Brad Jeffries, Kathy Kerrigan's fiancé."

"What'd you think?"

"He told me Kathy was crazy, an alcoholic, a drug addict, and that she'd screwed up all the catering plans for the wedding."

"You didn't like him."

"Well, I don't think he's going to win any merit badges for standing by his woman in a time of crisis."

Paxton smiled.

"Do you know him?" I asked.

"We've met at a few social gatherings."

"And?"

"No comment."

"What a politician," I said.

The waiter came over to our table. There are no menus at the Palm, you just give the waiter your order. This is sometimes a problem for newcomers who aren't sure what's available or what they want. I knew what I wanted.

"I'll take the filet mignon, cook it medium and butterfly it," I said. "Plus a salad with Russian dressing and a big plate of half onion rings and half cottage fries."

They've got great onion rings and cottage fries at the Palm.

"I'll have the lobster." Paxton smiled.

"Boy, that takes guts," I told him after the waiter left.

"What?"

"Ordering lobster on a first date. It's real big and messy, and they put a bib on you and everything."

"Is this a first date?" he asked with a twinkle in his eye.

"I'll call it a first date if you will," I said.

The waiter brought our salads.

"Tell me about you," I said. "How'd a nice guy like you get mixed up in politics?"

"Just the way things work out, I guess. I don't think anyone ever plans to be a political aide. Actually I started out as a writer."

"No kidding? What'd you write?"

"A lot of stuff for magazines and newspapers. Free-lance, mostly. Did some fiction too. Even wrote a novel once. Of course, it sold only about thirteen copies. But it's nice to have on a bookshelf."

"I'm impressed."

"Later, I moved out to Hollywood and got plugged into a part of the film community. Did a few screenplays. Mostly B-movie stuff. Quickie horror movies, action films—the kind of thing that used to play on the bottom bill at drive-ins."

"Name one. Maybe I saw it. I go to a lot of movies."

"How about *Terror Tower*? It's about a maniac who's killing people in a skyscraper."

"Jeez, I think I missed that one."

"Yeah, well a lot of people did." He laughed. "Anyway, I did a bunch of them that never saw the light of day. Hollywood does that, you know. Buys up a lot of options, then never puts out the movies. And when they do, it generally looks very little like the thing you originally wrote. It's really a frustrating business."

"Is that why you left?"

"Partly. That and also because I needed a steadier job—with health insurance and all—because of a lot of medical bills."

"Were you sick?"

"Not me. My wife."

"Wife?" A warning bell went off in my head.

"She died a year and a half ago," he said.

"Oh, I'm sorry."

Paxton shrugged. "I'm sort of getting used to it now. Anyway, after she was gone, I just stayed on with Wincott for a while. It seemed as good a place as any. Until I figured out what I really wanted to do, that is."

"Which is?"

"I haven't figured that out yet."

"Me either," I said.

The waiter brought our food. I sliced into the steak with my knife and devoured a piece hungrily.

"Speaking of Senator Wincott," I said, "tell me a little about him."

Paxton smiled and shook his head.

"Notice the clever way I segued into that topic," I said.

"Is this turning into an interview?" he asked.

"Not really. I was just curious. Is Wincott okay?"

He dug out a piece of lobster and dipped it into a dish of butter next to his plate.

"How about we talk about you for a while instead? Tell me something about Jenny McKay."

"There's not a lot to tell. I'm forty years old, used to work in newspapers and now I'm on TV, I live alone . . ."

"You always lived alone?"

"No, not until recently."

"How recently?"

"What time is it?"

He looked at his watch. "10:05."

"One week, one day, and four hours," I told him.

I related the sad story of Tony heading for greener pastures in Hollywood and my search for new living quarters.

"What about before Tony?" he asked.

"I was married once," I said.

"And?"

"He left me, too."

"Boy, you're really popular, aren't you? What do you have—the plague?"

I smiled. "Technically I left my husband."

"Were there a lot of problems?"

"Just one. Her name was Vickie."

"What happened?"

"He was a reporter at the same paper I was. Covered City Hall. For about a month, he was coming home late every night because there was a big budget crisis he said he had to write about. One night I decided to surprise him at City Hall and go out to dinner after he finished. I found him on a couch in the Budget Director's office with one of the secretaries. They were in the middle of a very delicate maneuver."

"They were making love?"

"Well, I don't think they were discussing the budget deficit."

I picked up a cottage fry and nibbled on it. "So anyway, tell me about Senator Wincott."

"Boy, you're relentless," he said.

"I have been described as a tenacious interviewer," I admitted.

"Wincott's like a lot of politicians, I guess, no better or worse," Paxton said. "He's not dishonest or anything, if that's what you mean."

"Maybe not," I told him, "but I think he tried to buy me off with a job the other day in his office so I wouldn't pry anymore into the disappearance of his stepdaughter. What do you make of that?"

Paxton sighed. "Listen, if he did do that—and I'm not saying that was his intent—then it was just concern about a lot of unfavorable publicity and what it might do to him and his family. He's got big political plans. He doesn't want anything to happen that might upset them."

"Where's he come from?" I asked. "What's his background?"

"Oh, he was an up-and-coming young executive in the Kerrigan Corporation at the time of Mike's death. Afterward, he and Audrey went out a few times, liked each other, and eventually got married.''

"I'll bet he was a lot more up-and-coming after that."

"Huh?"

"You know, like Brad Jeffries. Sounds like a fortune hunter."

"No, not really. Listen, the Senator's okay. Honest."

"How'd he wind up getting into politics?" I asked.

"That was mostly the old man's doing."

"King Kerrigan?"

Paxton nodded. "Yeah, he was really bit by the Kennedy syndrome, I guess. You know, push your son to be what you never were—in this case, president of the United States. Hell, King Kerrigan owned just about everything else. Why not the White House? Anyway, the way I hear it he figured his kid—Mike Kerrigan—was going to be his JFK."

"But the son died."

"Yeah. And it was his only kid, too. There was no Bobby or Teddy waiting in the family wings. So there was no choice. His son-in-law had to become the stand-in. Not even really a son-in-law. He was just married to his son's widow. But there was nobody else."

"So he persuaded Wincott to use the Kerrigan fortune and influence to run for office?"

"I don't think it took all that much persuading. But anyway, yeah, he was elected to the East Side Congressional seat that Kerrigan's son had at the time of his death. Wincott spent some time in Congress, then ran for the Senate four years ago and won. So here we are."

"You think the old man's going to push him for the presidency?"

"King Kerrigan doesn't really do much pushing anymore. He's in retirement—a virtual recluse—up in Nantucket these days. Has been for years. Plays almost no role in the company anymore or even in Wincott's political organization. But he makes all his money and contacts available to him, which is what counts. If Wincott wants something, the old man gives it to him. And yes, I think he's going to run for president."

"I'll bet it isn't the same for Kerrigan though. Having his son-in-law rise to power like this, instead of his son."

"Maybe that's why he keeps his distance. In the old days, I'm told he was everywhere—had his fingers into everything. Fundraising, political platforms, campaign organization—the whole thing. Now we never hear from him."

"Interesting," I said.

"Well, he's also pushing eighty now," Paxton said. "Maybe he's just too sick and old to care anymore."

We had both finished our meals. He'd made it through half of his lobster. I'd cleaned my plate and finished off most of the cottage fries and onion rings.

"So what's for dessert?" I asked.

The waiter came over and went through the dessert menu. I stopped him when he got to the chocolate cheesecake. We also both ordered coffee. We sat and talked over it for a long time. Until I looked at my watch.

"Hey, I've got to get home," I said. "The opposition news comes on at eleven. I have to see what they've got. Plus I want to watch a tape I made of myself on the Six doing the Brad Jeffries interview."

We paid the bill and walked out onto Second Avenue. It was hot, like it usually is in New York in July, but the worst of the humidity was gone for the time being. Above us the sky was almost crystal clear, and you could see stars twinkling. I took a deep breath of air. I felt good. Better than I had at any time I could remember since Tony left for Hollywood.

"You want to come back to my place with me and watch the news?" I blurted out.

Paxton looked at me. "Sure. I'd love to."

We hailed a cab and headed downtown toward the Village.

"Did you ever meet Kathy Kerrigan?" I asked.

"Once or twice," he said. "At a few social affairs."

"What did you think?"

"Like I say, I only talked to her briefly. But . . . well, I thought she seemed confused. Mixed up. Looking for something she didn't have. Even though she seemed to have everything. Definitely not a happy girl."

"That's my impression, too," I said.

"You? I thought you never met her."

"I didn't. . . ."

"But . . ."

"I just feel as if I know her."

The cab pulled up in front of my apartment house and we got out.

"Listen, you're not allergic to dogs or anything, are you?" I asked as we headed for the door.

"No. Why, you got one?"

I nodded.

"What kind?"

"A dachshund."

"No kidding. I used to have one when I was a kid. Always wanted to get another. They're great dogs."

"I know, but he can be a little weird sometimes. Don't get too upset if he barks or bares his teeth at you or something."

"A good watchdog, huh?"

"I hope so."

I turned the key in my lock, opened the door, and we walked in.

Hobo came bounding out of the bedroom, took a look at Paxton, and stopped dead. He let out one short yip of a bark. Then he walked over to him, his tail wagging furiously and rolled over on his back at Paxton's feet.

"Yeah, he looks like a real killer," Paxton laughed as he reached down and petted Hobo's stomach.

Hobo reached up and licked his face.

We walked Hobo together, then I made some coffee and brought it into the living room where the eleven o'clock news was playing on the TV. They didn't have anything I didn't know about. Afterward, I popped in the tape of our six o'clock show and we sat on the couch, watching it and drinking coffee. Hobo maneuvered himself into a spot between us—his head resting on Paxton's lap and his tail on mine. While we watched, Paxton scratched him behind his ear.

As I'd told Gergen earlier, the tape with Brad Jeffries had been edited well enough to make him seem relatively sensitive and normal. When he talked about his missing fiancée, he looked directly into the camera. He was certain nothing was wrong, he said, but his biggest hope in the entire world right now was to hear from her. It was a nice performance. Sincere. Loving. Caring. The perfect fiancé.

When my segment was over, the camera switched back to Cassie and Conroy at the anchor desk.

"I don't know, Conroy," Cassie was saying. "He looks like quite a catch to me. If I were Kathy Kerrigan, I wouldn't throw him back. I'd reel him in and marry him while I had the chance."

"Well, from what I hear about your social life, Cassie," Conroy replied, "you don't throw any men back."

"Oh, wicked!" Cassie cackled. "Actually I know one I'd throw back. And he's sitting right next to me."

I let out a loud groan. "My God, they're terrible!" I screamed at the TV.

Hobo turned around and looked at me quizzically for a second, then rolled over and went back to sleep again. He looked very content. Paxton glanced over at me and smiled as he continued to scratch his ear.

"Some watchdog, huh?" I said.

15

Madison Avenue Comes to South Street

We were taping a series of ad promotions for the six o'clock news show.

The promos were Carstairs's idea. He said it was important that we let the viewer know who we are. That way when they were watching "F-Troop" or "The Munsters" or some of the other daytime rerun fare, they'd be prodded to tune in later to the news. I wasn't sure exactly what kind of demographic group we were going after. I mean the people who advertised on these shows were mostly party phone lines and schools, where you could learn how to get into well-paying, fast-paced careers like truck driving and air-conditioning repair. But then beggars can't be choosers.

There was a series of ads—some featuring us individually, another with us all together in the newsroom.

"We want to let the viewer know we're a family," Carstairs explained. "A happy family that laughs and kids around with each other."

"How about we forget the ads and go on 'Family Feud'?" I suggested.

Carstairs ignored me.

"The important thing is to foster this atmosphere of camaraderie," he continued. "An aura of good feeling, of higher expectations, of exuberance. . . ."

"Sort of like Mary Tyler Moore throwing her hat up in the air and catching it at the beginning of the old show," I said.

"Exactly," Carstairs agreed.

Someone laughed.

"I know it may sound funny," Carstairs said, "but that's exactly what I'm looking for. That simple act—tossing the hat in the air, spinning around on a Minneapolis street, then catching it—summed up the message of her show in a nutshell: A feeling that things were going to get better. Like the last line in the theme song when it said 'You're gonna make it after all.' That's the same thing I want to do here."

The ad contract had been awarded to Oglyvy and Rothman, a medium-size Madison Avenue firm. The deal had been worth about one hundred thousand dollars, according to the whispers around the office. A woman who was producing the ads stood up after Carstairs and explained the procedure to us. The ads would take about two hours to shoot, she said. Then they would be edited, approved by the station, and be on the air within a matter of days. Most of them would be shot right here in the newsroom, a few on location around town, she told us.

"Now let's get to work," she said. I expected her to say "Lights! Camera! Action!" but she didn't.

The first ad shot was about Cassie White. It went like this:

Cassie White has jumped off a building (cut to shot of her doing stunt leap); jumped out of an airplane (shot of parachute jump); and jumped into a tense hostage drama (picture of her walking out of the bank with the gunman). She'll do anything to get the story for you.

So when it's six o'clock, it's time for *you* to jump to the "News on Six."

The switch is on!

With Conroy Jackson, the idea was to portray him as a distinguished veteran journalist. A man who could give you insight into everything from the Board of Estimate to detente.

Which was pretty funny because Jackson couldn't even pro-
nounce detente, much less give anyone insight on it.

> Conroy Jackson. Journalist. For twenty years he's been
> giving you the news as he sees it.

There was a shot of him supposedly asking a question at a
mayoral press conference (he hasn't left the office in years);
one of him working at his typewriter on deadline (he doesn't
write his own stuff); and one of him conferring with a reporter
in the newsroom on a story (he barely talks).

> When you've tried all the other news shows, it's nice to
> come back to the voice of authority—Conroy Jackson and
> the "News on Six."
> The switch is on.

For me, we did a series of on site location shots in front of
some of the city's most famous restaurants. Four Seasons, 21,
Lutèce, the Russian Tea Room.

> Wherever the rich and powerful dine and play, Jenny
> McKay is there. Her "South Street Confidential" gives
> you a ringside seat at the tables where the city's power
> brokers and celebrities wheel and deal.
> It's a look at the beautiful people for those of us who
> don't always (cut to a shot of me eating a hot dog from a
> vendor on the street outside 21) live so beautiful.
> "South Street Confidential." Try it. Only on the
> "News on Six."
> The switch is on.

I sort of liked mine. Especially the self-deprecating humor of
the hot dog shot. Travers and Hanrahan weren't so lucky.
Hanrahan had to dress up wearing a different piece of
athletic gear on each part of his body—a football helmet,
catcher's chest pad, ice skates, basketball short pants.
Travers's was the worst—it showed him saying there was a
big shower on the horizon—and then a bucketful of water was

dumped on his head. Sort of like the old "sock-it-to-me" bit Judy Carne used to do on "Laugh-In" during the 60s. I felt sorry for him.

Then there was one with all of us together in the newsroom. Scrambling around after a big-breaking story. Putting it on the air. Then sending out for sandwiches, which we all ate together sitting around the news desk. Yep, we were just one big, happy family. Just like "The Brady Bunch" or the Andersons on "Father Knows Best."

Afterward, I talked to Travers in the dressing room as he dried off from his drenching.

"I'm a black man," he said.

"Yeah, I've noticed."

"My ancestors withstood slave ships, bus protests, cross burnings, segregated bathrooms—all so we could get to the point where we are today. They didn't go through all this so I could get a bucket of water dropped on my head."

"That's pretty heavy," I said.

"Okay, how about this: I felt like a damn fool out there."

"That I can understand."

"I'm outta here," he said as he put the towel down. "This is the last straw. I've got my tapes out all over the country. The minute I get a nibble, I'm taking it."

"Are you sure?" I asked. "You'll have to leave New York."

"I'm not sure it's even my decision to make anymore."

"What do you mean?"

"I hear Carstairs has been conducting a talent search around the country for people who'll fit into what he's trying to build here."

I remembered Gergen talking about the anchorwoman in Roanoke.

"For all of us?"

He shrugged. "I know he's talked to a weatherman in Austin. This guy's a real sweetheart. He dresses up in a rain slicker on camera when it's going to be showers and a bathing suit for sunny days. Then he sings the forecast."

"Damn!"

"I don't know if Hanrahan knows it, but they're also

looking at a sports guy in Louisville. He's sort of a cross between Warner Wolf and Sam Kinison, the late loudmouth comedian. He screams all the scores.''

"It sounds like they're planning on breaking up that old gang of ours," I said.

"Sure seems that way."

"Kind of makes it hard to maintain that family feeling Carstairs was talking about for the ads," I told him.

"The only hope we've got is Gergen. If he can stand up to Carstairs. He's the only guy who could be strong enough to stop this insanity."

I thought about what he'd told me in the diner.

"I wouldn't count on that," I said slowly.

"Well, he's done it before. You told me he once defied the publisher of the *Trib* in the middle of the city room. Threatened to quit if the publisher pulled a story about some big advertiser being caught for drunk driving. You said the publisher backed down."

"That was a long time ago, Larry," I said.

He looked at me strangely. "Is Joe all right, by the way? He's looking a little tired."

"Probably just tense," I told him.

Later that afternoon, I shot my "South Street Confidential" segment.

It was an astrologer who did horoscopes for the stars. She told me why the Prince Charles–Princess Diana marriage could never work. "He's a Scorpio, you know," she confided. "That explains it all."

I nodded solemnly, as if I really knew what she was talking about.

That night, as I was leaving the building after the show was over, a thought struck me. It was Carstairs talking about the beginning of the old "Mary Tyler Moore Show"—when she throws her hat in the air and catches it. And how that seemed to signify all the hope in her life. I was wearing a hat—a man's wide-brimmed job, sort of like Diane Keaton in *Annie Hall* or Robbie Robertson in *The Last Waltz*. I stood in front of the WTBK sign on the building and—with the security guard at the front door, a few passersby, and some surprised motorists looking on—I flung it straight up in air.

Would I catch it like Mary? Or fumble it like Rhoda did at the beginning of her show? Somehow it seemed to matter.

"You're gonna make it after all," I sang.

The hat came down, landed in my hand, and . . . bounced off.

From behind me I heard someone laugh. It was the security guard.

" 'Mary Tyler Moore,' right?" he said. "The opening credits?"

"Yeah."

I reached down to the sidewalk, picked up the hat, and put in on my head.

"You're not Mary Tyler Moore," he observed.

"Tell me about it," I said.

Then I hailed a cab and got in.

16
Lost Lives
and Loves

"Name?"

"Jenny McKay."

"Age?"

I thought about it for a second before answering. Honesty is the best policy. Truth wins out. Liar, liar, pants on fire.

"Thirty-six," I answered.

The realtor taking the information at the apartment-rental agency didn't blink. She just wrote it down on the application form in front of her. More important, lightning didn't strike me from above. So far, so good.

"Address?"

I smiled. "That's why I'm here. To find a new one. You do find apartments, don't you?"

The woman didn't smile back. Maybe she'd heard that one before.

Her name was Lois Childs. She was middle-aged, with her hair pulled back in a severe bun and a grim expression on her face. She didn't look enthusiastic about finding me an apartment. She didn't look like she was ever enthusiastic about anything.

"No," she said, "I mean, what is your address at the moment?"

"Eighty Washington Place."

"Occupation?"

"Broadcast news."

"Pardon me?"

"I'm a TV newswoman. I work for Channel Six."

Lois Childs looked up at me now with interest. Her icy, businesslike manner began to melt away. Before, I was nobody for her to worry about. Now, I was somebody. Now she wanted to be my friend. I didn't want to be her friend. I simply wanted an apartment. But if I had to be her friend to find an apartment—well, it was a small price to pay.

"I thought you looked familiar," she was saying. "I have seen you on the news. You look a little different in person. But I guess people always tell you that, huh?"

"Sometimes," I admitted.

"My, my, a real TV star here in my office. You must live a really exciting life."

"Yeah, it's sort of like being in Disneyland every day."

"And you're here looking for an apartment."

"Right. I'm in the middle of a delicate domestic dilemma that forces me to seek new accommodations."

"Well, let's fix you up then."

I looked at her with surprise. "You do have apartments?"

"Of course."

"It's just that I've been looking for days. And there doesn't seem to be anything out there. Anything livable that is."

She smiled. "That's why we're here."

"But none of the ads seem to . . ."

"We have apartments aimed at people like you," she said soothingly. "People who are able to afford an ultrasophisticated style of living. People who want to live in a manner fitting their position."

"I'm not looking for the Taj Mahal," I told her. "Just a simple one-bedroom apartment."

"No problem."

The rental agency was located at 63rd Street and Lex. We took a cab over to a new high-rise that had just been built, in the 60s along the East River Drive. The apartment was on the fourteenth floor. Everything in it smelled of newness. The paint on the walls, the shiny parquet floors, the fully electronic kitchen. There was a wall-length glass picture window with a breathtaking view of the East River. It was getting dark now, and outside I could see the lights from boats on the river and buildings on Roosevelt Island and Queens in the distance.

"How much?" I asked.

"Oh, it's very reasonable," she said.

"How reasonable?"

She paged through a notebook she was carrying. "Let's see—Apartment Fourteen B. Oh, here it is . . . Twenty-four hundred and fifty is the rent."

"Twenty-four fifty a month?"

"Yes. Now with that you also get a three-hundred-dollar-a-month rebate for the first three months."

"Terrific."

"If you're looking for something a little bigger, we can take a peek at a two-bedroom on the twenty-third floor. That goes for"—she checked the notebook again—"thirty-nine hundred dollars."

"Thirty-nine hundred dollars," I said.

"Right. Or if you don't like the idea of spending money on rent, we do some co-op and condominium sales, too. For instance, there's a new building down on Union Square where the prices start as low as four hundred thousand dollars . . ."

I thanked her for her time and said I'd be in touch. She gave me her card. When I got outside, I ripped up the card and threw it into a metal canister that said KEEP NEW YORK CLEAN. Then I caught a subway home to the Village.

When I got there, I found my landlord on the front steps with the super. They were discussing what days the garbage was picked up. The timing seemed perfect. I had a new plan for dealing with the apartment issue. Actually I had two plans. Call them Plans A and B. Plan A involved attempting to deal rationally with the super over the problem.

"My name is Jenny McKay," I said.

The landlord stopped midsentence and turned to look at me.

"I live in Apartment Six D."

"Not for long you don't."

It wasn't a good beginning, but I plunged on ahead anyway.

"Look," I told him, "I've lived in this apartment for four years with a man named Tony Richards. Now the aforementioned Tony Richards has moved out. But I want to continue living here as I always did. Can't we work something out?"

"Why?"

"Pardon me?"

"Why should I let you stay here? You're name's not on the lease, you have no legal right to it. If I turn the apartment over to someone new, I raise the rent by thirty percent. So what's in it for me to keep you?"

"Well, it just seems to me like it's the right thing to do."

He snorted. "You're wasting my time."

Plan A didn't seem to be working too well. I decided to try Plan B.

"As you may know," I said, "I work for a TV news show."

"So?"

"So I meet a lot of important people. One of them is a lawyer named Tom Sewell, who represents the Kerrigan Corporation. I've told Mr. Sewell about my problem with you, and he's agreed to seek legal recourse. He feels your eviction notice is a clear-cut violation of my rights as a tenant, a woman, and a human being."

I was bluffing, of course, but there was no way for the landlord to know that. I figured I'd throw a scare into him.

"And you're gonna throw this high-priced legal talent at me?" There was an amused expression on his face.

"That's right."

"I'm shaking."

He turned back to the super and continued with his conversation about whether the garbagemen picked up on Mondays, Wednesdays, and Fridays or Tuesdays, Thursdays, and Saturdays.

Somehow I had the feeling I hadn't scared him too much.

I went upstairs to my apartment, said hello to Hobo and took him out for a walk. When we got back, I told him his daily joke.

When we'd finished laughing over it, I pulled out my

financial records and tried to figure out how much money I had. Now that was really funny. I counted up everything. Money markets, mutual funds, savings bonds, passbook accounts. It came to $12,132. Christ, where did it all go?

It certainly wasn't enough to buy a co-op on Union Square. Was it enough to rent a twenty-four-hundred-dollar-a-month apartment in an antiseptic building like the one I'd just seen?

Well, yes, if I devoted most of my paycheck to it and didn't spend any money on anything else. Only I didn't know how much longer that paycheck would be coming in. So what then? I'd have an expensive new apartment that I hated and no way to pay for it.

The telephone rang. I picked it up.

"Will you accept a collect call from a Tony Richards?" the operator's voice said.

My mouth suddenly went dry. I licked my lips.

"Ma'am, will you accept this collect call?"

"Yes," I heard myself say.

A few seconds later Tony came on the line.

"Hi," he said.

"Hi."

"Look, I know you're probably furious with me, but . . ."

"Furious doesn't come close to describing how I feel."

"I'd like to talk to you about it sometime."

"So talk."

"Not like this. Not over the phone. It's too impersonal."

"Impersonal?"

"Yeah. Maybe when I get settled here, you could fly out. We could spend a week together."

"I work weekends."

"You know what I'm saying."

"No, what are you saying, Tony?"

"Look, Jenny, things happen. I realized that I had to do this with my life now. It won't be forever. I don't want to be without you forever."

"Give me a break, Tony."

"I mean it. In fact, when I get settled here, I'd like you to move out and join me. There's plenty of TV stations and newspapers in Southern California. You should get a job easy.

And you'd love it here. It's sunny all the time, the beaches are great . . ."

When you live with someone for a long time, you get to know them well. I mean really well. You know what they're up to, what they're going to do next. Tony wanted something from me. That's why he was calling.

"What do you need, Tony?"

"Need?"

"You didn't call just to give me a travelogue on California living."

He cleared his throat. "Well, there is one little thing . . ."

I rest my case.

"See when I left, I was in a hurry—I mean I was so busy—I forgot one of my portfolio scrapbooks. It's got a lot of studio stills and stuff of me in it. It's in one of the drawers of the dresser I used in the bedroom. You remember which one?"

I said I remembered.

"It would really be a big help if you'd send it out here to me."

"Just where would I send it?"

He gave me an address. It was for a post office box in Venice.

"You're a real sweetheart for doing this," he said.

"Yeah."

"Listen, I've got to run. But we'll talk again soon. Promise?"

"Sure. You got a number I can call?"

"I'll call you," he said.

"When?"

"Next week sometime. And honey, don't forget the scrapbook."

"I won't."

"Take care, Jenny."

The phone went dead.

I stood up and walked over to the dresser. When I opened it, there was a smell of men's cologne. The kind of smell a man leaves behind long after he's gone. It brought back memories of other times. Better times. Times when the house was full of love.

Sure enough, the scrapbook was there. I paged through it slowly, looking at Tony's face smiling back at me from picture after picture.

Then I took out a pair of scissors and began cutting up all the pictures. First in half, then in quarters and finally into little pieces. When everything was in shreds, I dumped the whole mess down the incinerator in the hall. Then I went back and sprayed so much Lysol in the dresser drawers that they didn't smell like Tony anymore.

Hobo watched me the whole time. "Just a long overdue good-bye," I explained. "You want supper?"

He gave a yip.

I went into the kitchen and fixed some dog food for him and tuna without mayonnaise, a salad with low-cal dressing, and a Diet Pepsi for myself. I was very proud of my willpower. Of course, I also felt a little bit guilty because I had eaten three hot dogs that afternoon during the promo with the street vendor outside 21. But then nobody's perfect.

I was carrying supper into the living room when the phone rang.

Tony again?

"Hi, Jenny," a voice said.

It took me a second to place it. Then I realized who it was. Bill Rohr, my friend from the *Washington Post*.

"Sorry to call you at home this late," he said, "but I wanted to give you an update on that Michael Kerrigan stuff you asked about."

"No problem. Tell me what you've got."

"Well, it's kind of funny actually."

"What, do you mean?"

"I really couldn't find out much."

"Hell, it's only been twenty years. It shouldn't be that hard to track down information on the guy."

"I know."

"So?"

"That's what's so funny. There isn't any."

I was confused. "Are you telling me Michael Kerrigan didn't exist?"

"Oh, he existed all right. He just doesn't seem to have existed the way those clips you read described him."

"Huh?"

"Nothing checked out. There should be records in Congress of his speeches about the mob, with the Department of Defense about his military awards for Vietnam—all that stuff. But everything's missing. Almost as if someone has been wiping out all traces of Michael Kerrigan's existence."

"Jesus," I said.

"And one more thing. The people I found who do remember him from back then? They gave me a very different picture of him from the one you heard."

"How different?"

"A lot. They say he was no JFK. That he was lazy, not bright, barely showed up for congressional sessions. Some of them remember some problem in the military they heard rumors about, but nothing about any heroism. And this stuff about him being a one-man mob buster—well, the word I hear is he was in the mob's pocket. But I don't have anything hard."

"Can you keep checking on this, Bill?"

Rohr said he would.

"Jenny?"

"Yeah."

"What the hell is going on anyway?"

"I don't know," I said. "But I'm going to find out."

17

More Questions

Brooke Preparatory School, where Michael Kerrigan went as a boy, is on East 78th Street in Manhattan.

I paid a visit there the next morning. The headmaster was a man named David Kellerman. He was very pleased when I told him I was interested in doing a feature on the school. For twenty minutes, he regaled me with tales of the rich and famous offspring who'd passed through the institution's portals.

"Over the years many of our students have been the children of diplomats, corporate leaders—even a president of the United States," he said proudly. Then he quickly added, "But we have people from all walks of life. And all of them get the best education in New York City."

I nodded and acted as if I were interested.

"How about the Kerrigan family?" I asked casually. "Didn't I hear somewhere about them being involved with this school in some way?"

Kellerman nodded. "The Kerrigans have been very generous. In fact, this whole wing of the building was built with funds they provided."

"How long ago was that?" I asked.

"Oh, sometime back in the 70s, I guess."

"The Kerrigan kid went here, right?"

"Uh-huh. After he died, his father bequeathed a large amount of money to the school in his name for the construction."

"Did you know him?"

"Who?"

"Michael Kerrigan. The son who died."

"No, that was before my time."

"Would anyone here still remember him?" I was still trying to act casual. If he asked me why I was so interested in Michael Kerrigan, I wasn't sure what I was going to say. But he didn't.

"The only one who might is Arthur Faust. He was headmaster here for years. Finally retired in 1982."

"Where is he now?"

"Moved down to Florida."

"Boy, he sounds as if he could be a gold mine of information about the old days," I said. "Any idea how I could get in contact with him?"

"Sure," Kellerman said. "He lives in Boca Raton. Here, I'll get you the number from our files."

He stood up.

"While you're at it," I asked him, "do you think I could just look at your records on Michael Kerrigan?"

He looked puzzled. "Why?"

That was the question I didn't want to hear.

"Oh, I just thought it might be interesting to look at one student from the past—someone with some name recognition— and see some of the highlights of their academic career here," I smiled.

It wasn't a great answer, but it was good enough.

"Hey, that's good," he said. "I'll bring it all back for you. Wait here a minute."

While he was gone, I looked around the office. There were trophies, scholarship awards, and pictures of graduates. I checked to see if any of them belonged to Michael Kerrigan. None did, but there was a plaque attached to the wall near the door.

THIS WING OF THE BROOKE PREPARATORY SCHOOL
DEDICATED IN MEMORY OF MICHAEL KERRIGAN, 1942–1973

Interesting.

Kellerman came back and sat down behind his desk. He didn't look happy.

"Here's the number for Faust," he said, handing me a slip of paper.

"Problem?" I asked.

"I can't find Michael Kerrigan's records."

Surprise, surprise.

"Maybe they're misfiled," I said.

"I suppose so, only . . ."

"Only what?"

"Well, I really looked very thoroughly. And our files are always up to date."

"No one's perfect," I said.

"I guess so. I just find it extremely frustrating when I can't find something I want."

"I know the feeling," I told him.

I went back to the WTBK office and called the number he'd given me for Arthur Faust. Faust was as happy to talk to me about his old school as Kellerman had been. He told me more about the good old days. The Brooke School seemed to be one big happy family, according to these guys. Sort of like the WTBK News team.

Then I asked him about Michael Kerrigan.

"Uh-well, yes, he was a student at Brooke."

I thought I detected a change in his tone of voice.

"And?"

"And what?"

"What happened?"

"Oh, he died a number of years back, you know. It was a terrible tragedy."

"I know about that. I mean what happened to him while he was at Brooke?"

He coughed nervously. "Michael was an excellent student, as I remember. A real leader. The boy had tremendous potential . . ."

"His records are missing," I said.

"Pardon me?"

"I asked to see his file when I was at the school. They said it's missing. Why do you think it would be missing?"

"I have no idea."

"Then you're my only source of information. Tell me absolutely everything you remember about him."

Another nervous cough. "I'm going to have to get off now," Faust said.

"It would just take a few more minutes. . . ."

"I don't have any more time for this."

"What are you trying to hide, Mr. Faust?"

There was a click and the phone went dead.

Next I called Harvard, where the newspaper clip in the library said Kerrigan graduated with honors. No records there either. He'd attended some classes, it appeared, but no one could tell me any more than that. Nothing about the dean's list or the swimming team or the lacrosse team.

More troubles when I checked with the Army on his military record. Everything was missing. No one knew why. A Vietnam hero, Jeffries had said. A Bronze Star winner who saved a lot of lives. Okay, but where was that information coming from?

I got up and walked to Gergen's office. I wasn't sure what to do next. Maybe he'd have an idea. Only he wasn't there.

"Where's the boss?" I asked his receptionist.

"Haven't seen him yet today," she replied.

"Gergen? Late for work? That's sacrilegious," I muttered. "Sort of like Mother Teresa taking money out of the poor box."

I went back to my desk and reached for my phone again. Only it wasn't there. Someone had removed the receiver part, and I was holding a cucumber in my hand. A large cucumber that they had scotch-taped to the telephone wire.

"All right, who's the wise guy?" I screamed.

There was loud laughter. I recognized the laughter. Hanrahan.

"What's the idea?" I asked him.

"I wanted to remind you of me," he chuckled.

I looked down at the cucumber in my hand.

"And this is supposed to do it?"

"Sure, babe. You know what I mean."

"No, what do you mean?"

"Doesn't that make you think of a certain body part?"

"Oh yeah," I said. "It does look a lot like your head."

He smiled. "You can kid around all you want, babe, but you're just trying to hide your real feelings."

I took the cucumber and dropped it into the trash on top of some empty coffee cups and bagel wrappers.

"Those are my real feelings," I told him.

"C'mon, you want it from me. You know you do."

"No, no, no."

"Sure you do."

I sighed. "All right, Bill, you're right. I do like you. I'm crazy about you."

"I knew it . . ."

"But I'm not going to do anything about it. It's too dangerous."

"What are you talking about?"

I motioned him to come closer to me.

"You know that Cassie White and I don't get along very well, right?" I whispered.

He nodded.

"Well, the thing is I have to work with her and I don't want to make our relationship any worse. If I started seeing you, she'd hear about it and get jealous. She's already trying to get me fired. I don't want to take any chances."

"You mean . . . ?"

"Sure, Cassie's hot for you," I told him. "Has been for a long time. You don't know that?"

Hanrahan made a face. "You're bullshitting me."

"Nope. Do you remember that office party a few months ago? Well, Cassie had a bit too much to drink. I ran into her in the ladies' room and she was talking about how she'd really like to get to know you better. Told me and that receptionist from down on the third floor that you were a real hunk. Said you reminded her of Don Johnson."

"I don't know . . . Cassie White said that?"

"Yep. You were wearing that 'Miami Vice'–style suit and

had the two-day growth of stubble on your face. It really turned her on.''

''Cassie?''

''Don't believe me, if you want,'' I shrugged. ''It's your loss. But that's what she said. Listen, I've got to get back to work, okay?''

''Yeah, yeah, sure,'' he said as he began walking back toward his own desk. He turned around and looked at me. ''Don Johnson, huh?''

''Don Johnson,'' I said.

Hanrahan went back to his desk. I could see him thinking about what I'd said. He wanted to believe it. And, in the end, he didn't disappoint me. He got up and began heading over to Cassie White.

I smiled broadly.

Now there, I thought to myself, is a match made in heaven.

I reattached my phone to the cord and dialed the number for Jellinek, the cop I'd talked to at the Ninth Precinct.

''Boy, you're the last person I want to hear from this morning,'' he said when he came on the line.

''What's wrong?''

''I just got reamed out royally upstairs on the Kerrigan thing. Apparently the senator or someone in his office complained. The chief called me in to find out why I've been bothering people with questions about the daughter. He pointed out that there's been no missing persons complaint and therefore no open police investigation.''

''The brass didn't like it?''

''I don't think I'm exactly up for a medal of commendation, if that's what you mean.''

''So you think they got some pressure from Wincott to lay off this?''

''Yeah. I know this may come as a surprise to you, but a U.S. senator does have a bit of clout around here.''

''What about doing your duty and all that? Don't you guys have some sort of motto? Like 'neither rain nor snow or pressure from Washington big shots . . .'?''

Jellinek snorted.

''So what now?'' I asked.

"Are you kidding? I'm out of it."

"What do you mean? You're giving up? What about the girl?"

"I don't give a damn about what she's doing. If she wants to come back, fine. If she wants to stay out there doing God-knows-what, well, that's fine too."

"But, Lieutenant—"

"See you around, McKay. Thanks for everything."

Another click.

I sat there staring at the phone again. A lot of people were hanging up on me these days. Maybe it was me. Maybe I needed to work on my phone manner. Maybe I should take one of those courses on phone salesmanship. My stomach growled. Maybe I should go down to the diner and order a big piece of chocolate cream pie with whipped cream on top.

I walked over to Gergen's office again. Still not in. Where the hell was he? Why did he have to pick this day, of all days, to be late? I needed to talk to him about all this Kerrigan stuff.

"Jenny?"

I turned around. It was Gergen's receptionist again. She was coming back from the ladies' room.

"Yeah? You heard from him?"

"Mrs. Gergen just called before," she said. "Joe's wife." Her eyes were red and she looked as if she'd been crying.

"What's wrong?"

"Joe collapsed this morning while he was getting ready for work."

"My God!"

"He's all right, but they want to keep him in the hospital for observation."

"What hospital?"

"Cabrini. On East Twentieth Street. Listen, Jenny, Joe . . . well, Joe's really embarrassed by this."

"Embarrassed?"

"I know it sounds silly, but he doesn't want people here to know yet. He thinks he'll be out of the hospital and back to work soon and he doesn't want a lot of sympathy. So no one else knows. I only told you because I know the two of you go back a long way together."

"I understand. And thanks."

I started to walk away.

"Where are you going?" she asked.

"To Cabrini. Where else?"

"Joe can't see anyone yet. They're not allowing any visitors."

"I'm going anyway," I said.

18
Hospital
Zone

I've spent a lot of time in hospitals over the years.

Cop shootings. Stakeouts for interviews with crime victims. Deaths of important people. I was at Roosevelt Hospital the night John Lennon got shot. At New York Hospital when Andy Warhol died. At Kings County Hospital in Brooklyn the night they brought in two of Son of Sam's victims. If you added up all those hours and hours of waiting, I've probably spent more time in hospitals than Ben Casey.

But I've never really gotten used to it.

I've never been in a hospital overnight myself. Never been admitted. Never even been treated in one for anything worse than poison ivy since I was a kid. For that matter, I haven't been to a doctor of any kind in years. Not that I'm particularly healthy, I just don't want to know about it. I operate on the theory "if it ain't broke, don't fix it." Hey, I saw *The Hospital* with George C. Scott. I watched "St. Elsewhere." I know what goes on in a hospital, and I don't want any part of it."

Maybe it all goes back to when I was growing up. I was ten years old when my father died. He had cancer and spent the last five years of his life in and out of hospitals. My memories of that period are of my mother, her face grim and eyes red from constant crying, leading me through doctors' offices and into countless hospital rooms in the losing battle against the disease that was ravaging his body. The one incident that sticks out above all the others occurred near the end. We were sitting by his bed while a doctor was explaining why they were going to try another operation—his fourth in five years. There was a look of horror on my father's face. When the doctor left, my mother began to tell him how it was an excellent hospital and he would be getting the best possible medical care, etc. My father looked at us both and said: "If I could do it all over again, I would have never set foot in a doctor's office or hospital at all. If I'm going to die, so be it. But let me die with dignity." I've never forgotten that.

Now I stood on East 20th Street in front of the hospital.

CABRINI MEDICAL CENTER
EMERGENCY ROOM ENTRANCE

Cabrini was a few blocks away from Gergen's home near Gramercy Park, so the ambulance had brought him here. I took a deep breath and walked inside. There was a hatched-faced, middle-aged woman in a nurse's uniform sitting at a desk near the entrance. I told her who I was looking for.

"Gergen? With a J?"

"G."

"And you say he's a patient here?"

"He was brought to the emergency room this morning."

She thumbed through some cards in a metal filing cabinet in front of her.

"Mr. Gergen was treated in our emergency facility this morning," she said finally. "He was admitted as an in-patient to Room-nine-two-three-seven for further testing."

"How is he?" I asked.

Hatchet Face looked down at the card again. "Critical condition," she said.

"Critical?"

"Heart patients are always routinely listed as critical when they're admitted." She looked behind me. There was a man holding a cloth to a wound on his head. Off to the side sat a young boy with a broken arm and a woman who looked zonked out on drugs. "Next?"

"Can I see him?" I asked.

"He's in Intensive Care," she said. "There are no visitors allowed in Intensive Care."

"Do you think you could make an exception in my case because . . ."

"No exceptions," she snapped.

I walked back outside onto 20th Street. Rebuffed, but not defeated. I've been a reporter too long to take no for an answer that easily. For a good reporter, sneaking into a hospital is as much second nature as covering a fire or a City Council meeting.

The classic way of doing it is to pay off someone or get ahold of a doctor's smock and pass yourself off as a member of the medical staff. Or maybe do both. As it turned out though, I didn't have to do either. There was a service entrance around back. When I went in, I found an employee's elevator. I pushed the button for nine, rode up, and found Room 9237 within a matter of minutes. No one stopped me. No one asked what I was doing. No one seemed to care whether I was there or not. I'll bet Hatchet Face downstairs would be horrified if she knew.

Gergen was lying in bed, hooked up to a lot of tubes and a heart-monitoring machine. He was awake, but seemed kind of doped up. When he heard me, he turned his head slowly in my direction. Then he smiled.

"Jenny!"

"How are you, Joe?"

"I've been better."

I pulled up a chair next to the bed and sat down.

"What are you doing here?" he asked.

"I'm working up a lunch order for the Pastrami King. You want something?"

He smiled. "Yeah. A pastrami sandwich. Nice and thick, with extra fat."

"Is that on rye bread?"

He reached over and took my hand. There was an IV

connected to the back of it with some sort of clear fluid trickling into his vein. A white hospital identification bracelet was around his wrist. That made me think of my father again.

"I'm scared, Jenny," he said.

"Me, too."

I squeezed his hand. He squeezed back.

"We've got to stop meeting like this," I said hoarsely.

He seemed agitated. "Don't tell them at work what happened to me, Jenny."

"Jesus, Joe, I can't keep something like this . . ."

"Just tell them I have the flu or something. That I'll be back in a few days."

"Why?"

"They'll get rid of me."

"No, they won't."

"Carstairs wants to run the station. Make it his kind of place. I have to fight him. I can't let him do it. I have to stand up to him. . . ."

"Joe, don't worry about that now. Forget about it."

"I can't. That's all I've been thinking about."

A doctor appeared at the door. He was young. Everybody keeps looking younger to me these days. Policemen. School teachers. Now doctors. Doctors are supposed to look like Marcus Welby. Or at least Trapper John. The doctor walked over to Gergen with a needle in his hand.

"What's that for?" Gergen asked.

"Just something to help you rest." He pricked Gergen's arm. "You need rest."

Sure enough, within a minute or so, Joe's eyes closed and he was asleep.

"He's been like this ever since they brought him in," the doctor sighed.

"He's very upset," I told him.

"I know. But there are some things he's just going to have to accept. He appears to have a serious heart condition. It may or may not require surgery. Those are the facts, whether or not he wants to face them."

I looked at Joe sleeping peacefully on the bed.

"Can I stay with him for a while?" I asked.

"It's against the rules."

"Please."

He stared at me.

"Are you a relative?"

I shook my head.

"Well, then . . ."

"I'm a friend."

The doctor shrugged. "Sure. If you get caught though, don't give me up as an accomplice."

He started toward the door, then turned around and looked at me.

"Do I know you from somewhere?" he asked.

"I'm on TV. Channel Six News."

"That's it. You look . . . well, you look different in person."

"Everybody says that. Better or worse?"

He smiled. "Just different."

After he left, I sat there next to Joe for a half hour or so. He was totally out and unaware that I was there, but that was okay. I've always gone to Joe whenever I have a problem on a story. Talked it out with him. Now I wanted to do it again. Even if he couldn't hear me. He was still better than anyone else I could talk to.

I recounted out loud everything that I'd found out over the past twenty-four hours. The stuff from Rohr. My visit to the Brooke School. The calls to the ex-headmaster and to Harvard and to the Army. The pressure from Senator Wincott's office to keep the police out of it.

So what do you think's going on, Jenny? I could almost hear Gergen saying it.

"Well, I have a theory. But that's all it is. Just a theory."

Let's hear it.

"Okay, I think Kathy Kerrigan stumbled onto something."

What?

"I'm not sure. Maybe it was about her father and how he died twenty years ago. Maybe it had something to do with a congressional investigation into ties between the underworld and the Kerrigan family. Or maybe it's something else altogether. But whatever it is, Kathy found out something about it.

I think it upset her enough that she went searching for some answers.''

Anything else?

''Yeah. I think Kathy has shaken something up, and a lot of things have come falling out. Things that she doesn't even know about. Things that have been hidden for many years. Things somebody wants to stay hidden.''

And you think it's all connected to her father's death?

''I do. I don't know how, but I really do.''

So what now?

''Simple answer. I have to find Kathy Kerrigan.''

Gergen lay there snoring silently on the hospital bed, his chest rising and falling with each breath. I leaned over and squeezed his hand again. Then I hugged him through all the tubes and monitoring devices.

''Thanks, Joe,'' I said. ''Our talk helped.''

When I got outside again on East 20th Street, I found a pay phone and called the office.

''Where the hell are you?'' Sanders asked when he came on the line.

''I had something I needed to take care of.''

''Well, you better take care of 'South Street Confidential' for tonight pretty soon. Carstairs was looking all over for you.''

''Hey, McKay's the name. Celebrity gossip's my game.''

''I'm serious.''

''I'll come up with something. I'm on my way in now.''

''Damn, it's a really weird day,'' Sanders said. ''You're not here. Carstairs left a little while ago for some assignment upstate with Cassie. Gergen isn't around either. The place is empty.''

I didn't say anything.

''Hey, what's with Joe anyway?'' Sanders asked. ''Is he just out for the day?''

''I don't know. Listen, what the hell is Carstairs doing upstate with Cassie?''

''Oh, some big assignment on the death penalty.''

''The death penalty?''

''Yeah. You're gonna love this. They're interviewing the guy up at this prison who's in charge of the electric chair and

carried out the last execution in New York State. Then—hold
on to your hat now—Cassie's going to sit in the electric chair
herself and demonstrate what it feels like to be a condemned
person."

"You're kidding?"

"Nope. They're going to strap her in and everything. Even
put that metal cap on her head like they do in the movies."

"Are they going to turn on the switch?"

Sanders chuckled. "No such luck."

"I'll bet you dinner she uses the line 'I really got a charge
out of this' somewhere in her report," I said.

"You're on."

"Anything else?"

"Some woman called for you a couple of times this
morning. Said she had to talk to you."

"What's her name?"

"She wouldn't say."

I thought for a second. Maybe it was Lois Childs at the rental
agency.

"Did she mention anything about an apartment?" I asked.

"Nope. Just wanted to know when you'd be in."

"Well, I'm on my way now."

I caught a cab on Third Avenue and asked the driver to take
me down to South Street. He said he didn't know where South
Street was. I told him it was near Chinatown. He didn't know
where Chinatown was. So I told him to just get on the East
River Drive and take it to the South Street exit. He didn't know
where the East River Drive was.

We finally made it about thirty minutes later, with me
directing him every block along the way. The fare was $4.90.
I gave him a five dollar bill, told him to keep the change and
use it for the first down payment on a Hagstrom's city road
map.

Then I went upstairs to work.

19
Love—
Italian Style

"So what's the answer?" I asked.

Dave Paxton looked over at me and grinned. It was later that evening, and we were walking on Park Avenue near the Kerrigan Corporation offices. Most of the rush-hour crowds were gone by now, and the street was peaceful. Paxton was eating an ice cream cone that he'd bought at a Baskin-Robbins. I was munching on a carrot.

Determined. Resolute. Brimming with power. That's the name of my game.

"Boy, you don't quit, do you?" he said.

"Never."

Paxton had called me that afternoon to say he was in town again, so I made plans to meet him after the show. Strictly business, of course. I needed to ask him a lot of questions about the Kerrigan business. On the other hand, if something else should develop. . . .

I was working hard on both fronts as we stopped at a light on Park and 49th.

"You're asking me if I know whether the Senator put any

pressure on the police to stop asking about his missing stepdaughter?''

''That's the question.''

''The answer is no.''

''No, he hasn't?''

''No, I don't know.''

''Honest?''

''Honest.''

''But he could have.''

He took a lick of his ice cream cone and sighed. ''Look, Jenny, the Senator has an image to protect. You know that. What's more, he's got the power of his position. Okay, say he uses that power once in a while to pull some strings here and there with the authorities? A lot of people do. I'm not condoning it, just telling you what could have happened.''

The light changed and we started walking again.

''Is he going to run for president?'' I asked.

''Are we off the record here?''

''Sure.''

''Yeah, he probably is.''

''Then his stepdaughter could be an embarrassment again in the future. To say nothing of the drunken wife. What's the plan—ship them both off to some rest-cure spa somewhere until he makes it to the White House?''

''Everyone has family problems. Even the Kennedys. It's not that unusual.''

''Does he love her?'' I asked.

''Who?''

''The senator and his wife.''

I took another bite of my carrot and nodded. Somehow his ice cream looked a lot better.

''Yeah, I guess he loves her,'' Paxton muttered.

''Why do I think this isn't one of the great romances since Romeo and Juliet?''

''We do what we have to do sometimes,'' he said.

''Meaning he doesn't want to be cut off from the Kerrigan money and power. So he stays in the marriage. My, my—how convenient.''

Paxton shook his head and chuckled. ''It's always easy to

criticize other people's relationships. Are you an expert on relationships?''

I thought about Tony. Maybe he was right. Maybe people who live in glass houses shouldn't throw stones.

''Not really,'' I said. I took another bite of the carrot, made a face, and threw the rest into a trash can. ''Just screwed-up relationships.''

We were in front of a fountain on Park Avenue. Paxton finished off his ice cream cone, sat down on the concrete edge of the fountain, and patted the spot next to him. I plopped down.

''How about we change the subject?'' he suggested.

''Okay. Let's talk about Michael Kerrigan.''

He looked at me strangely. ''Why?''

''I've been studying up on him.''

''Why does Michael Kerrigan matter?'' he asked.

''I'm not sure, but I think he does. Did you know him?''

''Me? No, that was long before my time. I've heard about him, of course. Everyone who has any contact with the Kerrigan family has. I think probably the senator is sick of hearing about him, of always being compared to him. The heroic young leader cut down at such an early age.''

''Was he?''

''Was he what?''

''A heroic young leader?''

''What are you talking about?''

''I don't know, a lot of things about him don't make sense.''

I told him what I'd found out about Michael Kerrigan over the past few days. Or to be more exact, what I hadn't found out about him.

''Why would someone lie about something that happened twenty years ago?'' he asked when I was finished.

''I don't know the answer to that either.''

He smiled. ''So what do you know?''

I looked down in my purse and saw two more carrots.

''I know I'm acquiring a deep and abiding loathing of carrots,'' I told him.

''You want to have dinner someplace?''

"How about we go back to my apartment and I'll whip something up," I suggested.

"Even better."

An hour later, we were sitting in my living room wolfing down manicotti, stuffed shells, linguini and garlic bread from Emilio's, an Italian restaurant on Sixth Avenue that does take-out. Hobo was at our feet snatching up any bits we dropped and waiting to lick the plates.

"When you said you'd whip something up," Paxton said as he nibbled on some linguini, "I thought you were talking about cooking it yourself."

"I'm not that domestic."

He looked at the spread of food and half-empty dishes around us. "Isn't this a bit of a diet buster?"

"I ate a carrot before," I pointed out.

"I don't think it works that way."

"Hey, fat is in. Look at Oprah Winfrey. Delta Burke."

I reached over and pressed a button on my VCR remote control. A second later a tape I'd made of that night's news show came on. "Shhh. I want to hear this."

My picture appeared on the screen.

McKAY: I'm here at a bagel shop in Great Neck. This is not just any bagel shop. It's the place where Rob Camilletti, Cher's on and off young boyfriend, once worked as a bagel maker before she took him away from all that. Now that Cher's been seen around town with her favorite boytoy again, we went back to find out what Rob was really like when they first met.

I turned to one of the workers.

McKAY: Tell us about Rob Camilletti. Did you know him?

WORKER: Uh . . . yes.

McKAY: Good guy?

WORKER: Oh sure, he was fine.

McKAY: Did he make good bagels?

WORKER: Sure. He worked right here with the rest of us. All our bagels are good.

The camera panned to a tray of freshly cooked bagels coming out of the oven.

McKAY: What was his favorite kind of bagel?

WORKER: [after long pause] Garlic. Garlic and cinnamon. I think he liked garlic and cinnamon.

I turned to Paxton. "Who says there's no place for investigative journalism on TV?"
He smiled. "This is really hard-hitting, all right."
After my spot, Cassie White came on with her segment on the electric chair. Sure enough, it showed her strapped into the thing. She even acted out what would happen when the juice was turned on. When the taped clip from the upstate prison was over, she turned to Conroy Jackson in the studio and said: "Well, Conroy, I can honestly say that's one story I got a real charge out of."
I ran over to the TV and kissed the screen. "Thank you, Cassie, baby. I knew you wouldn't let me down. That's worth a free dinner to me."
Paxton looked around my place.
"Nice apartment," he said. "A little short on furniture. But still I like it."
I told him about Tony and the furniture and the lease.
"Jeez, what a jerk," he said.
"Very perceptive comment."
"How did you ever get mixed up with someone like him?"
"A weakness of the flesh."
"What?"
"I was swayed by a pretty face."
"He was good-looking, I take it."
"The best. That was his strong point. I saw him for the first

time in this Off-Broadway show and couldn't take my eyes off him. I went back eight nights in a row. Finally, I waited for him outside the stage door and just walked up and introduced myself. I used to do stuff like that.'' I paused and looked at him. ''Pretty pathetic, huh?''

''What do you think he saw in you?''

''I was never sure. Something he needed at the time, I guess.''

''So what happened?''

''I guess he stopped seeing it.''

I took a big bite of my manicotti. A glob of tomato sauce dribbled down my chin.

''Well, you've told me about your husband and you've told me about Tony,'' Paxton said. He picked up a napkin and moved closer to me. ''Any more like that?''

''Oh, tons.'' I thought about it for a second. ''I don't have very good luck with men.''

He used the napkin to wipe away the tomato sauce from my mouth.

''Doesn't Ellen Barkin say that to Dennis Quaid in *The Big Easy*?'' he asked.

''Yeah. That's where I got it.''

Our faces were very close now.

''And then,'' he said, ''Dennis Quaid tells her, 'Darlin', I think your luck's about to change.' ''

''Uh-huh.''

He kissed me on the lips. Soft. Tenderly. Like a swimmer testing out the water in a pool for the first time.

''If I spill more tomato sauce on my face, will you do that again?'' I asked.

''Why bother?''

He kissed me a second time. This one was longer and deeper. The third one was even better. After that, I lost count. I was too busy maneuvering our way into the bedroom and getting my clothes off.

Later we lay there in each other's arms for a long time. Neither of us said anything. It seemed too good to be true.

''You know, a disturbing thought just crossed my mind,'' I said finally.

"What's that?"

"Well, maybe Wincott sent you here to woo me and make love to me so you could find out how much I know about his family affairs. Maybe your job is to take my mind off the story."

He leaned down and kissed me on the cheek. "Did it work?"

"Temporarily," I admitted.

"You know I could say the same thing," he told me.

"What do you mean?"

"Well, maybe you just bedded me down to find out what I knew about it. Maybe this is the way you work a source. Maybe you're just using me for some cheap thrills while you—"

I held up my hand. "Good point," I said.

"Truce?"

"Truce."

I rolled over and reached for a joint from the drawer next to my bed. I lit it and offered him some. He shook his head. I inhaled some of the marijuana smoke.

"Isn't that illegal?" he said.

"So's coitus without the benefit of marriage. I won't turn you in if you don't turn me in."

"It's a deal."

"You know, you're pretty pretty good at that," I said.

"Illegal coitus?"

"Yeah. You must get a lot of practice down in Washington."

"Not really."

"You're kidding. I'll bet a hotshot like you has a harem down there."

"Actually you're the first."

I looked over at him. He wasn't smiling.

"The first?"

"Well, the first since my wife died. That was two years ago."

"You've been celibate all that time?"

He nodded. "Disgusting, isn't it?"

"Startling is more like it."

"But it was okay for you, right?"

"It was great," I smiled. "The earth moved. I saw the rocket's red glare and everything."

"I'm glad. I was worried that . . . well . . ."

"I guess it's like riding a bike. Once you know how, you never forget."

I lay back on the pillow.

"Tell me about your wife," I said.

"What's there to say? We knew each other forever. We got married right out of college. High school sweethearts and all that. I even took her to the high school prom in Schenectady, New York, where we came from. Ever been to Schenectady?"

"Not that I know of."

"Well, you're not missing much. Grim place. Anyway, we moved to New York, then to Hollywood; I was writing movie scripts and things were going pretty good."

"It sounds terrific."

"Yeah, except for one thing—we wanted to have a family. But it never worked out. The doctors said she couldn't have kids. So we accepted that and went on with our lives. And we were happy, too, really happy."

I nodded. He was talking about a kind of world I'd never known.

"Then, about two and a half years ago, a miracle happened. She got pregnant. God, I don't know how, but it just happened. They even told us that it was going to be a girl. They can do that now, you know." He shook his head sadly. "Only, one day when she was about seven months into it, we were in New York and she left this building at Fifth Avenue and Fifty-fourth Street and started to cross the street. A cabbie was barreling down Fifth Avenue, didn't see her, and went through the red light—" His voice broke off.

"She died?" I asked.

"No, not right away. But our baby did. Right there in the middle of goddamned Fifth Avenue and Fifty-fourth Street inside my wife—without ever even seeing this world. Why? It's a question I must have asked myself a million times. But there's no answer."

"And your wife?"

"She hung on for six months. Then she . . . well, the doctors said they thought she just lost the will to live."

I looked over at him.

"Why me?" I asked.

"Huh?"

"Why me? After all that time, why did you decide to make love to me tonight?"

"I didn't decide. It just happened. And it seemed . . . well, it seemed right."

I lay my head down on his chest.

"I'm forty years old," I said.

"So?"

"You don't think I'm damaged goods? A little past my prime? A few too many miles on the old odometer?"

He laughed. "Of course not. You know, forty's not that old. A lot of women these days have babies after forty."

I felt my body stiffen.

"I don't do babies," I said.

"What?"

"I don't do babies. I don't even really do marriage. So if that's what you're shopping for, you better move on."

I took my head off his chest and sat up. The mood in the room seemed to have changed. And not for the better.

"Hey, I'm sorry."

"No problem."

"It's just that I think you really need . . ." He didn't finish the sentence.

"What? What do I really need?"

"Never mind."

"No, tell me. I want to know."

He took a deep breath. "Okay, I think maybe you really need to take a long look at your life, Jenny. You're a terrific woman. But you seem to be on some sort of treadmill, just running frantically all the time from story to story. There's more to life than just the news."

"How do you know about my life? You've only known me for twelve seconds."

"Well, it's pretty obvious how obsessed you are with your

job. Even when we were making love, I'll bet you were thinking about it and—''

I threw my hands up in the air.

''Oh great, now you're going to criticize my bedroom technique. First Tony, now you. What is this? Dump-On-Jenny-McKay Month?''

''Look, now you're mad.''

''You bet I'm mad.''

''I just thought if we're going to have any kind of relationship it was best to . . .''

I got out of bed and clicked on the TV.

''Maybe it's best if I leave. . . .''

I didn't say anything.

He got up and started pulling on his clothes. The eleven o'clock news was just starting. There was a coup in Central America, a fire on Wall Street, a murder-suicide on Staten Island. I stared at the screen.

Paxton was dressed now. He leaned over and kissed me on the cheek.

''Look, I'll call you,'' he said.

I didn't answer him. I just kept watching TV. There was a fire marshal on, talking about inoperative smoke alarms.

''It's not real, Jenny,'' he said.

''What?''

''The fires, the murders, all the juicy gossip on the stars—none of it is real. It's a make-believe world. What happened here between us before in bed, that was real. Think about that.''

I glared at him.

''You want to know something else that's real?'' I said. ''The door. Use it.''

He stood there for a second longer, then shrugged and walked out. I heard the door slam behind him.

I sat watching the TV screen for a while longer, then got up and looked around the living room. It was a mess. Paper plates all over. Half-eaten dishes of Italian food. There was a napkin lying on the floor. The one Dave Paxton had used to wipe his face before our first kiss.

I bent down to pick it up, then suddenly burst into tears.

I lay there on the floor sobbing until I felt something touch my face. It was Hobo. He was licking my cheek. Dogs have instincts, like that. Tell them a joke, and they laugh with you. Cry, and they're unhappy too.

"I really blew it, didn't I kid?" I said to him.

You betcha, Hobo said.

Well, he didn't really say that. He didn't say anything. Never does. But I know that's what he was thinking.

Boy, did I blow it.

Shit!

20

The Morning After

The next morning started out as one of those days when nothing goes right.

First off, I made it to the doughnut shop around the corner too late to get the ones filled with grape jelly. All that was left was raspberry or apricot. I don't like raspberry or apricot jelly. I like grape jelly. This did not seem to be a good omen.

I bought two glazed doughnuts instead, along with a giant container of black coffee, and carried them back to my place.

I switched back and forth between the three morning news shows while I ate. Paula Zahn. Katie Couric. Joan Lunden. None of them had my style. None of them had my pizzazz. On the other hand, none of them had my problems either.

Then I got dressed. Or tried to. Virtually everything in my closet was wrinkled, dirty, torn, or stained. Finally I found a rust-colored blouse and tan slacks that seemed wearable. The slacks were a bit tight around the waist. But I solved that by leaving the top button open, wearing the blouse outside the pants, and using a wide belt to hold the whole outfit together.

After that I tried to catch a cab. Just stick your hand up in the air and wait, right? Wrong. There were packs of people on every corner of Sixth Avenue battling for the few open cars. At first I tried to be nice. Then I became determined. Finally I became ruthless. After about twenty minutes of frantic maneuvering, I outran two guys in suits, a blonde-haired woman, and an old man with a cane to grab one sitting at a red light. I got lucky with the cab driver though. During the entire trip downtown, he did not make any lewd remarks, political pronouncements, or try to rob, rape, or murder me. It seemed too good to be true. I had to pinch myself to make sure I wasn't dreaming.

Yep, all in all it was shaping up as one rotten day.

Work was even worse.

There was a staff meeting starting just as I arrived. It was top-level stuff with Andrew Cafferty himself down from the top floor to help Carstairs run it. The topic was our improved ratings. I found a chair next to Sanders and sat down. Jacobson was sitting on the other side of him working on a crossword puzzle and looking bored.

"I need a seven-letter word for happiness," Jacobson said.

"Good sex," I whispered.

He looked at me strangely. "That's two words."

"You pick your happiness and I'll pick mine."

Cafferty glared over at me.

"Glad you could find the time to drop by, Miss McKay. Is it all right if we proceed now?"

I smiled at him. I had a hunch he was still mad at me from the party. Call it women's intuition.

Then he looked over at Carstairs. Carstairs stood up and began talking.

"In recent days, our ratings have risen dramatically. If this trend continues, it could mean several hundred thousand dollars in additional advertising revenues for us. So obviously we're very pleased."

He looked around at our faces. I tried to look pleased.

"Much of the credit for this dramatic improvement, I believe, is due to the introduction of our very popular 'Dialing-for-Cash' contest, the new friendly atmosphere by our on the air news people, and the more relevant, tabloid-style stories we've been covering. Therefore . . ."

Oh Christ, I thought to myself, here it comes.

''Therefore we're upping the contest calls from six to twelve times a day and increasing the individual prize money from one hundred dollars to two hundred fifty dollars. I also want more relevant stories, things our viewers really care about. Tragedies, miracles, even things that might at first glance seem supernatural.''

''You mean like UFOs?'' I said. ''Devil worship?''

Carstairs ignored me.

''In addition,'' he continued, ''I want to increase our 'friendliness' quotient even more than before. I don't think there's any story that can't be delivered in a more upbeat manner than we used to. Nothing is totally grim. Let's look for the happy side of news. That's what's gotten us this high in the ratings, and it can get us even higher. I want all of you to think about that next time you're in front of the camera.''

''Maybe I should put on a party hat,'' I whispered to Sanders.

''What's that, Miss McKay?'' Cafferty said. ''The rest of us didn't quite hear you.''

''I said 'Can you believe that? A big rise in the ratings, huh?' ''

He scowled. Carstairs went on.

''Now a perfect example for all of you to use as a role model would be Cassie White's performance on the air,'' Carstairs said.

Cassie smiled broadly.

''When you watch her, you're seeing exactly what I'm looking for. Someone who puts life into the news. Someone who's not afraid to relate to the audience. Someone who . . .''

He kept talking for another fifteen or so minutes, but I'd tuned him out. I amused myself the rest of the time daydreaming about taking a Caribbean vacation and also by imagining what Cassie White's face would look like if it were covered with pimples. Both were very pleasant thoughts.

After the meeting, Carstairs called me into his office and shut the door.

''You look like hell,'' he said.

''I had a rough night. Anything else bothering you?''

''Yeah, that was real cute with Cafferty out there.''

I didn't say anything.

"Do you have a death wish or something? Do you want to be fired?"

I shrugged.

You're going to fire me anyway, I thought, so what's the difference?

"By the way," I told him, "all that stuff about how we need contests and relevant stories and friendliness quotients to get big ratings is a bunch of crap, you know."

"Is that so?" There was a bemused expression on his face.

"Yeah. There's other stations in town that do well without doing those stunts. And I'll bet their demographics are a lot better than ours. I mean the kind of people who would go for this aren't exactly rocket scientists."

"I don't need you to tell me about demographics," he snapped. "I just need you to report. What are you reporting on these days?"

"Well," I said slowly, "I'm still working on the Kathy Kerrigan thing."

"Has the girl shown up?"

"No, not yet."

"Then what's the story?"

"She's still missing."

"We've already reported that."

"I know, but—"

"And when she turns up again, we'll report that, too. Is there anything else to say?"

I told him an edited version of what I'd found out about the family. Not all of it. I didn't want him to know all of it. I didn't trust his reaction. As it turned out, I was right.

"It sounds like you're pretty far out in left field," he said.

"I think it's all connected."

"And it doesn't really sound like something for a 'South Street Confidential' segment."

"This is bigger than just a 'South Street Confidential' item," I told him. "It's a story. A big story."

"I don't see it. And I don't see the point in chasing after something that happened twenty years ago."

"That's what you sometimes have to do on a big story," I

explained. "Go after things that don't seem to make sense at first. You just pull on a thread and see where it leads. And you don't know whether or not you're wasting your time until it's all over."

But Carstairs wasn't listening.

"You know how many Elvis Presley fan clubs there are in this country?" he asked.

"Elvis Presley?"

"Elvis Presley. You have heard of him, haven't you?"

"The King? 'Don't be Cruel.' 'Heartbreak Hotel.' But what does that have to do with Kathy Kerrigan?"

"Nothing. But there's a lot of these fans in clubs in the tristate area. Some of these people think Elvis is still alive. Let's go talk to them."

"You want me to do a story on whether Elvis is still alive?"

"You know what I'm saying."

"No, what are you saying?"

"Forget this goddamned Kathy Kerrigan nonsense and give me a story on Elvis Presley fan clubs."

I stood up.

"Elvis Presley," I said. "You got it."

When I got back to my desk, Bill Hanrahan was standing there.

"Hiyah, Jenny," he said. He checked me out from head to toe. "You're looking good."

"Sorry I can't say the same."

I picked up the phone and started to dial the number for Cabrini Hospital. I wanted to check on Gergen.

"So how's the diet going?" Hanrahan asked.

I thought about the glazed donuts for breakfast.

"Okay," I lied.

He leaned down close to me. "You know what I hear is the best way to lose weight."

"No, what?"

"Exercise. Hard, vigorous exercise. Something like . . . well, like sex, for instance. Did you know that during sex you lose up to one thousand calories every time you—"

"Bill," I said, "this is all terribly fascinating, but why don't you go tell it all to Cassie White?"

"Oh her," he grumbled.

"Yeah," I smiled, thinking about the way I'd gotten him interested in her the other day. "Did you two ever get together?"

"Sure. We went out last night."

"No kidding!" I put down the phone. This I wanted to hear. "How'd it go?"

He shrugged. "Nothing special. Cassie's not that great, you know."

I stared at him.

"She's not very attractive at all up close," he said.

"Are you serious?"

"Sure. You know something, Jenny? As far as I'm concerned, you're a lot sexier than her. You've got her beat hands down."

I smiled. I was loving this.

"Did you go to bed with her?"

He shook his head.

"She wouldn't?" I asked.

"I didn't want to."

"C'mon, Bill," I said. "You'll have sex with any warm-blooded mammal."

"Hey, after I was with her for a while, she just didn't turn me on. It was my choice."

"Honest?"

"Honest."

I looked at his face. He seemed like he was being straight with me. Or as straight as Bill Hanrahan can ever be.

"You know, Bill," I told him, "maybe you're not so bad after all."

He leaned over close to me. "So does this mean maybe you and I can get together at my place later?"

"Don't push it," I said and went back to the phone.

The hospital said Gergen was off the critical list and doing better. They offered to put me through to his room. After several seconds, his voice came booming over the line. He seemed in a lot better spirits than yesterday.

"Sorry I nodded off in the middle of our conversation," he said.

"Men do that to me all the time," I told him.

I filled him in on everything that was happening in the office, assured him that no one but me and his secretary knew about what happened to him, and said I'd be by to see him soon.

"You better hurry. I'm not going to be here long."

"We'll see."

"What does that mean?"

"Well, old Hatchet Face may have something to say about that."

"Who's that?"

I thought of the unsmiling woman at the front door.

"She's the warden," I said.

When I hung up, I found a message on my desk to call Bill Rohr at the *Post*.

"I may have something," Rohr said when he came on the line.

"Yeah?"

"Remember you asked me to check up on this congressional probe into the mob back in 1973. The one this guy Kerrigan was supposed to be leading. Well, it turns out one of the big targets of the probe was the dealings of a guy named Vincent Delvecchio. Know him?"

"He's one of New York's top crime bosses, isn't he? Still around, too, I think."

"That's right. But here's the hitch. One of the people Delvecchio is rumored to have done a lot of business with is none other than King Kerrigan."

"Michael Kerrigan's father."

"The same."

"So the kid was investigating his own father?"

"Maybe. Or maybe the old man got him on the committee to make sure the investigation stayed headed on the right track. Away from him and his business dealings with Delvecchio."

"Interesting," I said.

"It gets more interesting. There was a rumor around—albeit an unsubstantiated one—that young Kerrigan was doing more than investigating Vincent Delvecchio's young wife pretty closely."

"Are you telling me Michael Kerrigan was having an affair with a mob kingpin's wife?"

"I'm saying it's possible."

"How come something like that never came out?"

"Why would it? Jack Kennedy was boffing Judith Campbell Exner in the White House, at the same time brother Bobby was going after her mob boyfriend, Sam Giancanna. This was before the end of Watergate, remember. People didn't write about these things then."

"Where's Mrs. Delvecchio now?"

"Dead."

"When did she die?"

"Three weeks before Michael Kerrigan."

My mouth felt dry. "How?"

"She died in a boating accident."

"Jesus Christ!"

I hung up the phone and sat there thinking for a while. Thinking about the Kerrigan family and the deep, dark secrets that seemed to be coming to the surface. About Dave Paxton. About my life. About Elvis Presley fan clubs. And, most of all, about the fact that my stomach was making ominous sounds of hunger. The glazed doughnuts hadn't done the trick. I checked my watch. Still too early for lunch. Maybe I'd just nibble on something to tide me over. I got up and started toward the concession stand in the lobby of the building, with visions of potato chips and ice cream cups dancing in my head. I was halfway across the room when my phone rang again. Sanders reached over and picked it up.

"It's for you," he yelled.

"Who?"

"Some woman. Won't give her name." He paused. "I think it's the same one who tried to get you yesterday."

I walked back and picked up the receiver.

"Jenny McKay," I said.

"Miss McKay, I want to talk to you about the Kerrigan story you've been working on."

"So talk."

"Not like this. I'm at a phone booth next to Washington

Square Park. The north side, near the arch. Do you know where that is?''

"Yeah, sure, that's near my house. But . . .''

"Meet me in twenty minutes.''

"Hey, wait a minute!''

"Twenty minutes. No more.''

"I need some idea of who you are before I go running off to meet you.''

The person on the other end sighed.

"Don't you know?''

"No.''

"I'm Kathy Kerrigan,'' she said softly.

21
Kathy
Kerrigan

I met Kathy Kerrigan on the corner of Fifth Avenue and Washington Square Park, near the arch at the front end of the park.

She was wearing jeans, sandals, and a baggy T-shirt with GUNS N' ROSES TOUR, '92 written across the front. Her hair hung in her eyes and looked darker than it had in the pictures I'd seen. Maybe she'd dyed it. Her face looked tired and drawn. All in all, she didn't look much like the Kerrigan heiress at the moment.

"Hello, Kathy," I said, extending my hand. "I'm Jenny McKay."

She took it. "Thanks for coming."

I looked around. The sidewalk was filled with lunchtime crowds.

"Let's go somewhere and talk," I said.

She nodded.

"You want something to eat?" I asked.

"Yeah, I could eat." Her voice sounded flat. Listless. As if talking was an effort.

"I know a good restaurant on Tenth Street and—"

"Maybe we could just go sit in the park," she said. "I've been there for a while. It's so peaceful."

"Sure." I looked around and saw a vendor with a food cart on the other side of the street from us. "How about I get something over there for us?"

She said that would be fine.

I walked across the street, bought two hot dogs with mustard and sauerkraut and a couple of Cokes, then took them back to where Kathy was waiting. I pointed to an empty bench in the middle of the park.

"Over there," I told her.

We sat down. As I handed Kathy her hot dog and Coke, she looked at me and said, "I really screwed up, didn't I?"

"We all screw up." I took a bite out of my hot dog.

"Not like this. Not in front of the whole world. Not so that you wind up on the six o'clock news every night."

"Okay," I smiled, "so it was a major league screwup. You want to talk about it?"

"Yeah. I need to talk to someone."

"I'm sort of curious—why me?"

"Huh?"

"Why me? Why not someone you know?"

"I have no one else."

"What about your mother? Or your fiancé? Or the senator?"

"I have no one else," she repeated.

She said it almost defiantly.

"Look, I saw you on TV," she went on as if she somehow had to explain it to herself, too. "You were talking about me, and you just . . . well, you just seemed like a nice person. Like you really cared. I felt I could trust you." She shook her head. "I know it doesn't make much sense. None of it really does. But you seemed like the only person in the whole world I could go to for help."

I took a drink of my Coke and looked around the park. A girl with green hair rolled by on a skateboard. On the grass behind us a tall, blond-headed guy in cutoff jeans and a T-shirt was throwing a ball to an Irish Setter, who kept bringing it back to him with his tail wagging. Nearby two lovers leaning on a tree made out. Just a lazy summer day in Washington Square Park. And here I was sitting with Kathy Kerrigan.

"So where've you been, Kathy?"

She took two bites of the hot dog. Big bites. More than half of it disappeared into her mouth. I wondered when she'd last eaten.

"Sobering up," she said, after she'd chewed and swallowed.

"Where?"

"Some fleabag hotel on the Lower East Side. At least that's where I woke up."

"What happened?"

"What do you think happened? I drank myself silly, did a lot of coke, some uppers, some downers—fucked myself up real good."

"Why?"

"Because that's what I do. I don't need a reason to get fucked up. Didn't my lovely family tell you that?"

I shook my head.

"I'm not buying it, Kath," I said. "I think you had a reason this time. Why not tell me about it?"

She hesitated. "I—I—just had to get away. . . ."

"Away where?"

"It's . . . it's sort of personal."

"Is it about your father?"

Her head jerked up in surprise. "How do you know about my father?"

I finished up what was left of my hot dog.

"I've heard a lot about him in the past few days. It seems that people who know say you were showing a lot of interest in him and the circumstances of his death before you disappeared. Almost a bizarre interest. I figured it might be connected somehow, so I did some research."

"He was a wonderful man, wasn't he?" Kathy said. "A great man."

I thought about the Michael Kerrigan I'd heard about. The one who might have been connected with the mob. Who might have slept with a mob boss's wife. Who, when you scratched the surface, seemed less like a hero and more like an enigma. But the look on Kathy Kerrigan's face told me she wasn't

thinking about that man. She was thinking about the man she'd
been told about since she was a little girl.

"Yeah," I said, "he was."

She smiled.

"I'm sorry he had to die so young," I started to say. "It
must have been traumatic—"

"He's still alive."

She said it in the same flat voice, almost without emotion.

"What?"

"My father is still alive," she repeated.

I leaned back on the park bench and sighed deeply. Next to
us the dog was still chasing the stick, bringing it back, then
starting all over again. I felt like the dog. Chasing leads,
bringing them back, then starting from the beginning again. At
least the dog looked as if he was having fun.

"Your father is dead," I told her.

"No, he isn't."

"Sure he is. He's been dead for twenty years."

Kathy shook her head violently from side to side. "I saw
him."

"Where?"

"On TV."

She took a videotape out of her purse.

"I've been carrying this around," she said. "I went to the
station that showed it and got a copy made. I must have
watched it a thousand times—over and over. Slow motion,
freeze frame. It's always the same. It's him."

"Who?"

"My father."

"But . . ."

"You think I don't know how crazy it sounds. That's why I
didn't tell anyone. No one at all. Not until today."

I took another sip of my Coke. What a crazy world, I
thought. She doesn't trust anyone but me. And she trusts me
because she saw me on TV. I seemed nice. Christ, Marshall
McLuhan was right. The medium is the message.

"What's on the tape?" I heard myself asking.

"It's a show about the homeless. They went out onto the
streets of New York and shot pictures and talked with a lot of

them. You know—the people who live in cardboard boxes, panhandle money, and keep warm in the winter by setting fires in trash barrels.''

''I know about the homeless,'' I said somewhat impatiently. ''I see them all the time. So what's the point?''

''My father is one of them.''

''One of the homeless?''

''Yes.''

''Why would your father be living on the street?''

''I don't know.''

''And if he were alive, why wouldn't he contact you and your mother?''

''I don't know that either.''

I looked at her eyes. They seemed clear, but I wondered if she was on something now. Booze. Coke. Or God knows what else.

''Look,'' I said, ''you probably saw someone who looked a little like your father used to and—''

''No, it was my father.''

''But he's long dead.''

''That's what I thought, too. But not anymore.''

''Kathy, how can you be sure what your father would even look like if he were still alive? It's been twenty years. . . .''

''I know that. And, as a matter of fact, he didn't look very much like the pictures I've seen of my father. He was older, of course, and he had this mangy hair and beard.''

''Well, then how . . . ?''

''There was something in his eyes,'' she said. ''His eyes were the same as I remember from when I was a little girl. I'm sure, Miss McKay. It was my father I saw on this tape. And he was very much alive.''

The dog had stopped chasing the stick now. His master lay sprawled on the grass a few yards away from us, trying to get a suntan, and the dog was sleeping peacefully next to him. Rest for the weary. Maybe that's what I should do. Go to sleep. Just head on home, crawl into bed, and pull the covers over my head. It would solve a lot of problems.

I looked at Kathy. ''So you went looking for him, huh?''

''That's right.''

"Where'd you go?"

"The Bowery. Central Park. Penn Station. Everywhere bums and homeless people hang out. Believe me, there's more of them than I ever knew existed."

"What did you find?"

"Nothing."

"No one knew him?"

"No."

"No one at all?"

"Well, there was this one prostitute—an Asian one—who actually said he looked familiar. Her name was China, and I found her on Lexington Avenue. But I could never really pin her down. And I didn't push it. I guess I didn't want to think about my father being with someone like her. She was really spaced out anyway. Probably just made it up to get some money out of me."

"How long did you spend talking to these kinds of people?"

"Oh, a day or so, I guess. Then I decided it seemed hopeless."

"And that's when you went on your binge?"

"Yeah. I got depressed."

"How long did the binge last?"

Kathy looked down at the ground. "I'm not sure."

"A few days?"

She nodded. "Probably. I woke up in the hotel I told you about. I don't know how I got there. My purse was gone, my money . . . anyway then I turned on a TV and saw your account about me missing the wedding and all. I was too embarrassed to go home. So I've been wandering around the city ever since." She began to sob quietly. "Oh hell, I've messed things up so badly."

"You need to talk to your mother," I said. "And your fiancé. Your stepfather, too. Tell them what happened."

"I can't."

"Why not?"

"They'll never forgive me."

"If people love you, they can always forgive you," I said.

She didn't say anything.

"You can't stay on the street forever."

"Can I stay with you?" she asked.

"What?"

"You said you lived near here. Maybe I could sleep there. At least for tonight."

I thought about it for a second and then nodded. "Okay, but I want to do an interview with you on-camera. For the news. Is that okay?"

"Sure, why not? I can't mess up things any more than they already are."

I stood up and pointed to a pay phone across the street. I told Kathy I had to make a call.

"Who are you calling?" There was concern in her voice. "Not my family . . ."

"No. Just my office. I need to tell them where I am."

When I got Sanders on the line, I told him what had happened. But I told him to keep it quiet.

"Make up some excuse to Carstairs about why I'm not there," I said. "Tell him I've got an exclusive interview with Meryl Streep, tell him I'm jogging with Madonna—tell him anything you can think of. Just cover for me."

"I'll do my best. But why not tell him the truth?"

I looked back to where Kathy was sitting.

"I'm not sure."

"You don't trust him."

"Something like that. Anyway you and Jacobson meet us here. I'm going to get the Kerrigan woman on-camera. And then I want to get a picture of that face she saw on the videotape she's carrying."

"Okay, we're on our way. Hey, Jenny?"

"Yeah?"

"You think this Kerrigan guy really is alive?"

"No."

"But then what . . . ?"

"I think Kathy Kerrigan is close to the edge. I also think she was having second thoughts about the wedding. So she sees this TV show and she'd always been hung up on her father anyway and—well, her imagination just ran wild. But something funny's going on in this family. And I want to find out what it is."

I hung up and walked back to where Kathy was sitting.

"Some friends of mine are coming," I said. "You can trust them."

"All right."

"While we're waiting for them, let's talk some more."

"About what?"

"About your father. Tell me everything you can remember about him. Let's start with the last time you saw him—twenty years ago."

She hesitated for a minute, then nodded and began telling me the story.

"We were all in Nantucket, at my grandfather's house . . ."

22

The King and
His Castle

The next morning I was on a plane headed out of LaGuardia for
Nantucket.

The trip takes a little more than an hour. Everyone else on
the plane seemed to be on vacation, headed for some fun in the
sun. The conversation around me was all about wave heights,
sailboats, and the best seafood restaurants. I figured I was the
only person aboard the plane going there on business. I thought
about what I was doing. I had no real plan, just a theory of
sorts. A theory that Thomas (King) Kerrigan somehow was at
the center of all this. And that if I shook him hard enough,
maybe the family secrets would come tumbling out.

I'd brought along a biography of Thomas Kerrigan that I
skimmed through during the flight. It corroborated a lot of
what I already knew about him and added some more details.
He was one of the titans of business and politics during the 40s,
50s, and 60s. A man who got whatever he wanted, whenever he
wanted it.

Kerrigan ran his empire with an iron fist from corporate
headquarters in New York and Washington and from the
compound in Nantucket. There was a multimillion-dollar

townhouse in Manhattan, another one in Georgetown, and a beachfront estate in Palm Beach. A private jet or helicopter was always standing by to whisk him to one of these spots. There was also a sophisticated communication network that kept him in constant contact with his far-flung business enterprises throughout the world.

But even more than money, King Kerrigan's life seemed to be dominated by a need always to be the winner, always to come out on top.

The book told one anecdote about him playing golf. It seems that he would always have an aide standing by just in case he was losing. If that happened, the aide would rush onto the green and interrupt the game. He would announce that some urgent business had come up that had to be attended to immediately. Kerrigan would apologize profusely to his opponent and then quit the course. That way he never lost.

Another time his boat finished second in the annual Nantucket sailing regatta. The next year there was no sailing regatta. Kerrigan simply used his influence to get it canceled. If he couldn't win the race, what was the point in holding it at all?

The author then told a story about the legendary patriarch of the Kennedy family, which he said summed up Thomas Kerrigan perfectly. Someone once asked the elder Kennedy what he really wanted out of life. "Everything," Kennedy replied. According to the book, Kerrigan was the same way.

Looking down at the white Nantucket coastline as we approached it over the Atlantic, I wondered about how a man like that reacted to losing his only son. A son he'd hoped would someday become president. That's not something money can do anything about. Or is it?

We got into Nantucket a little after eleven. At the airport I rented a battered 1984 Chevette with 102,000 miles on the odometer, a huge gash along the passenger side, and a front bumper that was tied on with rope. The guy at the rental counter told me it was the last car they had left. He didn't say "take it or leave it," but the message was clear. I drove into town and found the visitors' bureau off Main Street. A woman gave me a map and helped me with directions on where I wanted to go.

By now it was almost lunchtime, so I looked around to see if there was a health food place that sold wheat germ or carrot sticks. I didn't see any, so I settled for a seafood restaurant where I sat out on the patio and had lobster thermidor, corn on the cob drenched in butter, and a chocolate mousse for dessert. Hey, I tried, didn't I?

An hour later, I was on the road to King Kerrigan's house. I opened the sunroof on the Chevette, let the early July heat beat down on me, and clicked on the radio. They were playing "Surfing U.S.A." by the Beach Boys. Along the road I passed all kinds of bikers carrying towels and radios and picnic lunches to the beach. A car ahead of me was pulling a sailboat. Going to the beach sounded like a good idea. Maybe I should just forget about all this for now and . . . I shook my head and pushed the idea out of my head. I wasn't here on vacation, I was here to work.

Thomas (King) Kerrigan lived on the eastern part of the island, north of a little town called Siasconset. It wasn't nearly as built up as the area around the town of Nantucket itself, and the woman at the visitors' bureau told me there were a number of wealthy estate-type homes here. I figured Kerrigan would have one of the wealthiest, and I wasn't wrong. It stood majestically on a cliff overlooking the Atlantic. A tall fence with a locked gate surrounded it. There was a sign on the gate:

PRIVATE PROPERTY
NO TRESPASSING

and a buzzer beneath it. I rang the buzzer. After a few minutes, a man who looked like a security guard came out to greet me. His job obviously was to keep out unwanted visitors. After taking a quick look at me and my car, it was clear he included me in that category.

"No one is allowed past this point without specific authorization, ma'am," he said. There was a small smile on his face as he told me this. Imperious. Haughty. A man who loved his job.

"My name is Jenny McKay, and I'm a reporter from Channel Six in New York. I'd like to see Thomas Kerrigan."

He smiled again. He liked this. Probably made his day. "I'm sorry, but that's not a good enough answer."

"How about 'I'm the Avon Lady and they're in desperate need of free samples inside,'" I suggested.

"Funny," he said. "You're a funny lady, aren't you? Well, listen, funny lady, just take this"—he looked disdainfully at my Chevette and its battered exterior—"this thing you're driving . . ."

"It's an antique," I told him.

"Well, you and whatever-it-is just turn around and head back to town."

I reached into my purse, took out a letter Kathy Kerrigan had written for me before I left New York, and passed it through the fence to him.

"Give this to Mr. Kerrigan. It's from somebody he cares about very much. I think he'll want to see me. But I'll wait here just to make sure, if you'd like."

The guard looked down at the letter for a moment, frowned, then walked toward the house.

I got back in my car to wait. The sun was getting hotter, probably pushing ninety. I switched on the radio again. Now they were playing "Little Surfer Girl." Must be a summer golden oldies show. I sang along with the Beach Boys for a while. Boy, that took me back. Sitting in a car alongside the water on a hot summer afternoon listening to Beach Boys' music. I had flashbacks to when I was a teenager. Nineteen years old, sitting in a convertible with a gang of guys and girls in bathing suits, drinking cold beer. I closed my eyes. Nineteen! Christ, where did all the years go? How did I get to be forty so fast?

"Miss McKay?"

I looked up. The guard was standing at the fence again. Only this time he had opened up the gate to let me in.

"Mr. Kerrigan will see you," he said. "Just leave your car here."

I shut off the engine, got out, and slammed the door shut. The whole car vibrated when I did that. "Keep an eye on it, willya?" I told the guard. "Make sure it doesn't get any scratches on the paint job."

He ignored me, so I followed him silently up the road to the huge house overlooking the water. We went up the steps and inside through a long hall to what appeared to be Thomas Kerrigan's study. There were pictures of him with famous people all over the walls. John and Robert Kennedy. Lyndon Johnson. Richard Nixon. But I noticed they all seemed to stop in the 70s. Nothing since 1973 when Michael Kerrigan died on his boat.

An aged white-haired man shuffled into the room. Another man, who seemed to be in his 60s, was alongside him.

"Miss McKay," he said. "I'm Thomas Kerrigan." He pointed to the other man. "This is Robert Dalton, my assistant."

Dalton. I remembered reading about him on the plane. He was Kerrigan's legendary right-hand man back in the old days, one of the most powerful people in the world. The man behind the Kerrigan throne.

I shook hands with both of them.

"You know my granddaughter?" Kerrigan asked.

I nodded.

"Is she all right?"

"She's fine."

"Good. I know she had another . . . another problem. Anyway, sit down and tell me everything." He pointed to a chair in front of his desk. "Would you like something to drink? Wine? Beer? Iced tea?"

"A Coke will be fine, if you have it," I said.

He nodded to Dalton, who disappeared for a few seconds and then came back carrying a tray with a can of Coca-Cola and a glass of ice. He sat it down on the table next to me and, after a nod from Kerrigan, left the room. So that was the legendary Robert Dalton. The man behind the throne of King Kerrigan. Well, I guess there wasn't that much to do in the old palace these days.

Kerrigan's appearance was shocking. I'd been expecting to meet a Joseph Kennedy or a Nelson Rockefeller–type figure. Instead, the person sitting across from me looked like the type of old man you might see in a park feeding pigeons. He was stooped over, his skin looked sallow, and he needed a cane to walk. But worst of all was the expression on his face. He looked defeated, as if he'd given up on life a long time ago.

The old man eased himself down into the chair behind his desk. Behind him was a picture window with a breathtaking view of the ocean. He looked down at the letter I'd brought with me and frowned.

"My granddaughter says I should trust you."

"That's right."

"Why? You're a TV reporter, aren't you? You're only interested in a story."

"I'm also a friend, Mr. Kerrigan. I care what happens to your granddaughter."

"A friend, huh?" he said. "How long have you known Kathy?"

"I met her yesterday."

He smiled. "That's not a very long friendship."

He leaned back in his chair and looked at me.

"So why are you here anyway?" he asked.

I took a deep breath and plunged ahead. "It's really about your son, Mr. Kerrigan."

The old man's eyes opened wide. "You mean Michael? What's Michael got to do with this?"

I paused and looked for a second at a picture on the wall near me of the two of them—Thomas Kerrigan and his son— meeting President Eisenhower at the White House. Michael Kerrigan looked like he was maybe twelve years old. His father was beaming with a proud expression on his face.

"Tell me what happened the day he died," I said.

"Why?"

"I think it has something to do with what happened to your granddaughter."

"I still don't understand. . . ."

"Let me help you," I said. "Here's what your granddaughter remembers about that day. She says there was some sort of commotion that morning, an argument or a fight. Maybe between you and Michael. Or you and someone else. Or Michael and some other person. Do you remember that?"

Kerrigan shook his head. "No. I mean that was twenty years ago."

"Anyway, Kathy says she ran outside to see what was happening, but someone stopped her. They took her back and put her into her room. And then they told her a terrible thing had happened—that her father had drowned on his boat. He was dead."

"That's pretty much what happened," Kerrigan said. "We wanted to protect her. Michael and she were so close. . . ."

"There's only one problem," I told him. "She also has a memory of seeing her father for the last time. Standing there by the water near his sailboat."

"So?"

"Kathy says she saw him *after* they told her about the accident."

Kerrigan shrugged. "She was very young. And it was a terribly traumatic thing to happen to a little girl. How does she remember what she saw and heard that day?"

"Yeah, I guess."

I reached into my purse and took out a picture of the homeless man I'd made from Kathy Kerrigan's videotape the previous afternoon. I handed it to him.

"Do you recognize him?" I asked.

Kerrigan looked at the picture. I hoped for a flicker of surprise or recognition in his eyes, but I didn't see any. Finally he turned back to me.

"No," he said. "Should I?"

"Your granddaughter thinks it's her father."

"Michael? How could that be Michael?"

"Kathy thinks he's still alive."

I expected him to be shocked or angry or maybe even jump to his feet and have me thrown out. But he didn't do any of these things. He just looked down at the picture again.

"Who is he?"

"A beggar on the streets of New York. That picture is from a TV show on the homeless. That's where Kathy saw it."

"My granddaughter has emotional problems," Kerrigan said. "Serious emotional problems."

"I know."

"So that's why she's telling you all this crazy nonsense."

"She didn't seem all that crazy to me," I said.

"You mean you believe all this?" He pointed to the picture.

"I don't know," I said. "I suppose it could be just wishful thinking on Kathy's part."

He sighed impatiently. "Why are you here, Miss McKay?"

"Because Michael was your son. And because in checking out this story, I've uncovered a lot of questions of my own about his life."

I told him some of what I'd found out at the Brooke School and Harvard and from Washington.

He listened quietly.

"Do you want to try to explain any of this?" I said.

"I don't have to explain anything to you. I don't even know what the hell you're talking about."

"What really happened to your son, Mr. Kerrigan?"

A pained expression crossed his face. "My son's been dead for twenty years," he said. "Why are you the only person who sees something wrong with that?"

"Because I'm the only one looking. There's no reason for anyone else to. Michael died tragically, so everyone accepts the official version of what happened. It's only that when you start to scratch the surface of your son's life . . . well, nothing really is what it seems to be."

"What do you want me to say, Miss McKay?"

"I want you to tell me the truth."

He looked around the room. At the pictures of him with the leaders of the world. At the trophies and awards on the shelves. At the photograph of him and his son meeting the president of the United States that long-ago day at the White House.

"Life lost any meaning for me twenty years ago," he said.

I nodded, thinking again about how everything in the room seemed to have stopped after 1973.

"I don't do much of anything anymore, just sit here and remember. Jonathan Wincott, Tom Sewell, some other people— they run the business. I don't care, none of it really matters."

The sun shining in glistened off his glasses as he sat there. Behind him, through the big picture window, I could see the waves crashing into the shore below us.

"Now you sit here in front of me," he said, "and tell me some cock-and-bull story of how my son could still be alive.

And living on the streets of New York as some sort of homeless person. My son! Michael Kerrigan. Congressman Michael Kerrigan. My son—who could have had all this. My son—who could have been president . . ."

He stopped in midsentence, collected himself, and stared at me.

"My son is dead," he said evenly.

"But your granddaughter—"

"My son is dead," he repeated. "Let him rest in peace."

He whirled around and looked out the picture window with his back to me.

"Our conversation is over, Miss McKay."

Outside I could hear the waves crashing into the rocky shoreline. The ocean. The mighty ocean. The same ocean where Michael Kerrigan had died twenty years ago. Or had he?

"I'm—I'm sorry, Mr. Kerrigan."

No answer.

"Mr. Kerrigan?"

He was alone now. Alone with his memories.

I stood up, put the picture back into the purse, and walked out of King Kerrigan's house.

23

Jenny McKay, Where Are You?

There was a bomb scare at Grand Central. A coed murder in Brooklyn. A five-alarm fire in the Bronx.

I listened to it on WINS, the all-news radio station, on the cab ride back into the city from LaGuardia.

Jenny McKay, where are you?

That's probably what Carstairs was saying right now. I'd been gone without telling him. My disappearance yesterday afternoon might have been acceptable. Today's probably wasn't. But I didn't care. I had a secret weapon—an interview with Kathy Kerrigan.

It was a little after 5:00 P.M. when I walked into the newsroom and plopped down at my desk.

Everyone was rushing to meet the deadline for the six o'clock show. Hardly anyone even paid attention to me. Finally Hanrahan looked up from the sports copy he was writing, saw me, and came over.

"Boy, is Carstairs looking for you," he said.

"That's what I figured."

"He's real mad."

"I'll bet."

"You seem to be taking this very well. Why so happy?"

"I have a song in my heart and an exclusive in my hand."
I looked at him.

"By the way, what's your problem?" I asked.

"What makes you think I have a problem?"

"Well, something's wrong. We've been talking for a good thirty seconds, and you haven't made one sexual innuendo. Are you sick?"

He shook his head. "No, just depressed."

"What's wrong?"

He reached down and showed me his copy. "This is the latest thing they want me to do. Starting next week I do the sports out of people's living rooms."

"Why?"

"Because some station in Houston did it last month and it got big ratings. You get lists of season ticket holders for Jets and Mets fans and the like. Then you just turn up at the door, drink beer in their den, and report the sports live from there. It's supposed to show how much we relate to the common fan, I guess."

"That sounds terrible. My God, I'm gone two days, and this place really is going nuts."

"Wait, there's more. You know the cash giveaways? Well, people love 'em. In fact they love 'em so much, there's now an even bigger prize. They're giving away"—he made the sound of a drum roll—"a new car."

"You're kidding."

"Nope. Once every month to a lucky viewer. Cassie and Conroy will do a raffle on the air in between the weather and the world update."

"Christ, I can just see it now: 'The lucky winner of the brand new Ford Escort is Mrs. Emily Hunt of Maspeth. Happy driving, Mrs. Hunt. And now to our next story: Five hundred people have died in a tragic earthquake in Albania.'"

Hanrahan sighed and went back to his copy.

"Do me a favor, huh?" I said. "Just to cheer me up. Make some sort of sexual innuendo, just for old times' sake."

He looked at me and smiled. "Like what?"

"I'm sure you can think of something."

"Okay, how about after the show we go to some place quiet, with candlelight and violin music and . . . and . . . I suck on your toes all the way up the kneecap."

"Get lost, pervert," I screamed.

Carstairs came out of his office and saw me.

"McKay! In here! Now!"

Uh-oh. I got up and followed him inside his office. He slammed the door shut behind us. This seemed to be becoming a regular part of our conversations.

"I guess you've been looking for me," I said.

"You're damned right I have. For two days."

"Don't tell me—I'm the winner of the new car."

He glared at me.

"What's next?" I asked. "A Vanna White look-alike spelling out the words for the big stories on the screen. I can see it now: 'The category is *Triple Homicides on Staten Island*. Gee, Pat, can I buy a vowel for that?' "

"Put a lid on the smart answers, McKay. I could fire you right now, you know. And I think I may do just that. Unless you come up with a great explanation of where—"

"I have an exclusive interview with Kathy Kerrigan," I told him.

His jaw dropped. "What?"

"I met Kathy Kerrigan. I talked with her. I have her on videotape."

"Jesus!"

"There's more. She thinks her father—her real father, the one who's supposed to have died twenty years ago—is still alive."

"Shit!"

"Am I still fired?"

"We need to get this on in time for the six. Can you do that?"

I looked at the clock. It was 5:05.

"Yeah, I think so."

"Can you do a crash-and-burn?"

A crash-and-burn is a fast edit on deadline.

"Crash-and-burn is my specialty," I said.

"Get going."

Carstairs picked up the phone and called the control room.

"I want to do a teaser promo on the bottom of the screen every five minutes right up until the news show starts," he said. "Make it say: 'First interview with missing heiress Kathy Kerrigan. Exclusive on "South Street Confidential." Coming up on News at Six.'"

Then he headed for the newsroom.

"Cassie, Conroy, we're changing the opening of the six," he yelled. "'South Street Confidential' goes first. Jenny will do copy for the intro."

"But Bob," Cassie wailed, "we've got the evacuation of Grand Central because of the bomb scare."

"It doesn't matter."

"But I was there when the device was dismantled. I snuck up and got to stand right next to the guy who did it. I watched from two feet away while he cut the wire. We've got film of me doing it. I mean it wasn't a real bomb, but nobody knew that then. . . ."

"Okay," Carstairs said impatiently, "so if it was a real bomb, it would go first. Since it's not, 'South Street Confidential' does."

Cassie glared at me after he left.

"What can I say?" I said. "From the outhouse to the penthouse with just one story. This is some crazy business we're in."

I went to an editing room and sat down with Bobby, one of the production guys, to pull out Kathy Kerrigan's best quotes, do the voice-overs on tape, and get it ready for air time in less than an hour.

"Hey, I'm famous," I told Bobby.

"What are you talking about?"

"They're going to be running a promo for me across all the programs for the next fifty minutes or so," I said. "Everybody'll see it. Pretty neat, huh?"

Bobby just shrugged. "You know what programs are on Channel Six between 5 and 6:00 P.M.?"

"No. What?"

"Reruns of 'Gilligan's Island' and 'My Mother the Car.'"

"Oh," I said.

Sic transit gloria.

At 6:00 P.M. the theme music for the newscast came on and Cassie said to the camera:

WHITE: Here's what's happening tonight. A coed was found murdered on the campus of Pratt Institute in Brooklyn. A five-alarm fire raged out of control for three hours at a row of stores in the Bronx, leaving hundreds homeless. And there was a bomb scare at Grand Central, that yours truly almost got a real—well, blast—out of covering. But first, our top story of the night—the reappearance of missing heiress Kathy Kerrigan. For an exclusive report, here's our Jenny McKay with "South Street Confidential."

The camera shifted to me.

McKAY: Kathy Kerrigan, who disappeared more than a week ago on the eve of her wedding at St. Patrick's Cathedral, contacted me yesterday to tell her story for the first time.

The account answers some of the questions about what happened to her during those missing days.

But it also creates a new mystery.

It concerns Kathy's father, the late Michael Kerrigan, who died twenty years ago in a boating accident.

Or did he?

Here's what Kathy told "South Street Confidential":

The picture went to Kathy Kerrigan, with the backdrop of Washington Square Park. She told the story of her search for her missing father and her belief that he was still alive. The picture of the homeless man was superimposed over the screen as she talked. Finally it came back to me in the studio again.

McKAY: So is the Kerrigan heir really alive? Kathy Kerrigan thinks so, and if he is, what is he doing on the streets of New York begging for handouts? No one, including Kathy Kerrigan, has an answer to that. I should add that Channel Six earlier today showed the picture to Thomas Kerrigan, patriarch of the Kerrigan empire.

The camera went to a picture of the elder Kerrigan.

McKAY: Kerrigan told Channel Six this was definitely *not* his son. "My son is dead," he said. "He's been dead for twenty years."

Then back to me in the studio again.

McKAY: So Kathy Kerrigan is back. Back with more questions than ever before. In the upcoming days, "South Street Confidential" will be trying to find the answers to those questions. Stay tuned for more on this explosive story.

Cassie's face appeared on the screen. Her jaw was hanging open. She was as stunned by all this as everyone. And jealous, too. I knew she was wishing she had the story. I loved it.

WHITE: Thanks, Jenny. And now on to other news. [She said it almost with relief, glad to put me behind her.] At Grand Central Station today, a real-life bomb drama, which delayed thousands of commuters, was played out. And this reporter, who covered the story almost found it to be even more—uh, explosive—than expected. . . .

Kathy was still at my place when I got back there after the show. I'd left some bourbon in one of the cabinets from last Christmas, and I idly wondered on the way home whether she might have gotten into it. Or maybe even done some more drugs. My God, that's all I needed—Kathy Kerrigan doing a drug overdose in my apartment. But nothing like that happened. She seemed fine, sitting on my living-room floor playing with Hobo.

Hobo jumped up when he saw me. He trotted over, put his paws on my lap, and licked my face. Then he raced back to Kathy and rolled over on his back for her.

"Traitor," I told him.

"I fed him," she said sheepishly. "That must account for it."

"Nah," I said. "I think he's just tired of my jokes. Have you eaten anything?"

"No, I'm starved."

I found some ground meat in the refrigerator and put it in a skillet for hamburgers. While they were cooking, I got out some bread, lettuce, tomatoes, mayonnaise, and ketchup. I also had some frozen French Fries, which I stuck in the oven. What the hell, you can't diet all the time. And I did eat a carrot the other day.

"Where'd you find him?" she asked.

"Hobo?"

"Yeah. In a pet store?"

"He was a stray. We just picked him up off the street one day and brought him home."

"Sort of like me, huh?" she said.

I smiled.

"I always wanted a dog," she said.

"Didn't you ever have one?"

She shook her head. "My mother never let me."

"How come?"

"Because she hates me."

"I doubt that."

"I'm serious."

"Now why would a mother hate her own daughter?"

"I'm not sure. But I have a theory." She paused. "I think I remind her of my father. And I don't think she wants to be reminded of him."

The hamburgers were frying now. I flipped them over, sprinkled some salt, pepper, and onion powder on them, and took out several pieces of cheese to put on top.

"You said 'we' before when I asked you about Hobo," she said. " 'We picked him up off the street.' Who's 'we'?"

I told her about Tony and how he ran out on me.

"I'm sorry."

"Don't be. It's probably for the best."

"But you're alone now."

"Hey, being alone isn't the worst thing in the world," I said. "It's better than being with the wrong person."

She nodded. I remembered Brad Jeffries and the wedding that never was. I asked her about him.

"Jenny, I've been trying different things all my life to try and find a little happiness. The drugs. The booze. Even the marriage to Brad, I suppose, falls into that category. I figured if I got out of the house and started my own family, maybe things would be different."

"Have you called him yet?"

"No."

"Well, doesn't it bother you that you missed your own wedding?"

She shrugged. "Did you talk to Brad?"

I said I had.

"What did you think?"

"You want me to be honest?"

"Brutally."

"Okay, I think you could do better."

She nodded. "Yeah, that's what I've been thinking, too."

I turned off the stove, put the hamburgers and the rest of it on paper plates, and carried it all out to a table in the living room. "Help yourself," I said. While she did, I reached over and clicked on my VCR to watch a tape of the show.

"Did you watch it?" I asked.

"No, not yet."

"Why not?"

"I don't know. I guess I just . . . well, I wanted someone here with me when I did."

The face of Cassie White appeared on the screen.

"Why does she talk like that?" Kathy asked as she munched on her hamburger.

"Like what?"

"Like she's got marbles in her mouth."

I laughed.

"That's the way they teach us to talk. All the big TV people do it."

"You don't."

"That's because I never learned how. That's why I'm a failure."

She giggled and finished off the rest of her hamburger, then reached for another. The kid seemed really hungry. Well, I could identify with that. I went for a second myself. A good hostess always makes her guest feel comfortable.

On the screen Cassie was finishing up her introduction, then I came on.

Kathy listened to the whole thing intently, her chin resting in her hand as she stared at the picture of herself on the screen. When the shot of the man she thought was her father came on, she still seemed startled. Even though she'd seen it hundreds of times already. She asked me to run the whole thing again. I rewound the tape and ran it a second time.

Finally, she turned to me and said, "So what happens now?"

I looked down at the remains of the hamburger on my plate. I shouldn't have eaten so much. I felt bloated. And I knew I was going to feel guilty as hell tomorrow when I stepped on the scale.

"I think you should go home."

"When?"

"Soon. First thing tomorrow morning, if you can. They know you're back. You have to talk to them."

"I'm—I'm not sure I'm ready. Maybe if I stayed here for the weekend. . . ."

"No, you've got to go home. I'll go with you if you think you need—"

"I can do it myself," she said slowly. She scratched Hobo's head. "But why the hurry?"

"We've set some stuff in motion here," I told her. "Stuff that's likely to upset some people."

"What do you mean?"

"I mean I think the shit's really gonna start hitting the fan now."

24
Meet
the Press

It hit the fan on Monday morning.

That's when Senator Wincott flew into New York and said he wanted to read a statement to the press.

We gathered at his New York office to hear it. The *Times* was there The *News*. The *Post*. All the TV stations. A month earlier, he had called a press conference to announce a new plan for attacking the federal budget deficit and two reporters showed up. Now it looked like Woody Allen–Mia Farrow.

The senator arrived late, with Paxton and two other aides alongside him. I tried to catch Paxton's eye, but he kept his gaze on a door at the back of the room. Probably wished he could run out of it. Wincott took out a piece of paper and began to read from it:

"Ladies and gentlemen of the press, this past weekend my daughter returned home to my wife and myself.

"We are delighted she is back, and she appears to be safe and sound.

"I had hoped to keep this entire unfortunate matter personal but events outside my control"—he glared in my direction—"have forced it to be aired in public.

"Let me simply say this: My daughter is a troubled young woman with a history of emotional problems. She has been treated by some of the best people in the country and—until the recent incident—had appeared to be making significant progress.

"I only hope that the setback she has suffered here does not do any lasting damage to her fragile psyche."

He paused and looked in my direction again.

"One final thought: I personally believe that the TV reports of this case have been sensationalistic journalism at its worst—a blatant attempt to take advantage of a confused young person in order to score a few cheap ratings points. I don't blame all of you for this—just one desperate station and one desperate reporter.

"I have always been an outspoken supporter of the First Amendment. Freedom of the press is an essential for this country."

Oh God. I rolled my eyes.

"But like any other rights," Wincott was continuing, "freedom of the press cannot be totally without restrictions. You cannot yell 'fire!' in a crowded movie theater and claim it's your First Amendment right to do so. That's been tested in the courts. And—well, I just think that the actions of Jenny McKay of Channel Six have been the equivalent of yelling 'fire.'

"That is all I will have to say on this matter. Thank you, ladies and gentlemen."

There was a stunned reaction in the room.

"Is that it?" I yelled.

"What?" Wincott asked sharply.

"That's all you're going to say? How about Kathy's claim her real father's still alive? We're supposed to just ignore all that?"

"I told you—Kathy's sick—"

"She didn't seem sick to me."

"I think I made myself clear in my statement—"

"What about the allegations of mob connections to the Kerrigan empire?" someone else yelled.

"That's total innuendo—"

"Does this affect your chances of running for president?" someone else asked.

Then everyone began shouting questions. Wincott seemed stunned by the intensity of it. He looked around helplessly at Paxton and his other aides. The reporters in the crowd smelled blood. And when the press smelled blood, it was like feeding time at the zoo. Finally Wincott just shook his head and said: "This press conference is over." He headed for the door.

"C'mon," I yelled to Sanders and Jacobson and ran to cut him off before he got there.

I made it in time. When Wincott saw me standing there in front of him, his face froze.

"What *did* happen to Kathy's real father?" I asked.

Wincott stuck his face close to mine.

"I think you're scum, McKay. I think you're shit. You're the most despicable, disgusting thing I've ever seen in all my years in this business."

His face was flushed with anger. Paxton appeared quickly at his side and tried to get him away from me.

"You didn't answer the question," I said.

"Take your question and stick it up your—"

"Senator!" Paxton shouted, drowning out the rest of it.

Cameras were whirring all around me. Microphones were in my face. Christ, this is incredible, I thought. I'm going to be on every 6 o'clock news show in town.

Paxton began dragging him out of the room.

"Hey, Senator!" I yelled after him.

He whirled around one more time.

"Is this going to hurt my chances of joining the Wincott team?" I asked.

And then he was gone.

"Wow!" Sanders said.

"Yeah. Did the honorable senator from the state of New York really call me a shit?"

"Not very presidential, is it?" Sanders laughed.

"Not even very senatorial."

"Wait'll Carstairs sees this."

"You think he'll like it?"

"Does Donald Trump like money?"

Sanders was right, of course.

"This is great," Carstairs said back at the station after he watched a rough cut of the tape. "He actually called you a shit. And he called you scum. Sensational!"

"People've been calling me things like that all my life. I didn't know it was so good."

"Don't you understand? This thrusts you right into the middle of the story. It makes you a part of it. It makes us a part of it."

"I thought you weren't supposed to do that. Isn't that one of the basic rules of journalism? Just report the story objectively, don't become the story yourself?"

"That's the old rules. There're new rules now."

"Damn," I said. "I was just starting to learn the old ones."

I walked back to my desk and checked for messages. There was one from Lieutenant Jellinek. Interesting. I called his number.

"I thought you weren't speaking to me," I said when he came on the line.

"I'm not."

"So?"

"I've been watching your stuff on Kathy Kerrigan. And thinking about what we talked about the other day. So I made some checks."

"Police checks?"

"I can't do anything official, I told you that. But I've got this friend with the Massachusetts State Police. He's retired now, but he was around when the Kerrigan kid had his boat accident. Anyway, he says something about it always seemed funny to him. It just didn't seem to hang together. No one wanted to hear this, though, even back then."

"Anything specific?"

"Well, there was a witness who saw Kerrigan land in the drink and then go under the waves. A fisherman named Meehan."

"Yeah?" I remembered that from the newspaper clips.

"My friend talked to this Meehan guy. Said Meehan seemed real nervous. My friend didn't like his story at all. In fact, he thought it smelled like week-old mackerel."

"What did he do about it?"

"Nothing. He says the brass took him off the case the minute he filed a report questioning the drowning story. They clamped a real tight lid over the investigation."

"You think the Kerrigans . . . ?"

"Who knows? They've got a lot of money and influence up there though. Hell, they've got a lot of money and influence everywhere."

"Does your friend have any idea what really might have happened?"

"Nope. Just that he doesn't believe the story that came out. Anyway, that's it. Use it as you will. The rest is up to you."

"Thanks."

"And, McKay?"

"Yeah."

"You didn't hear this from me. Got that?"

"I don't even know your name."

"That's the way I like it."

There was a click and the phone went dead.

I sat there staring at it.

Okay, now what? Something was going on, that was for sure. But the Wincotts didn't want to know about it. Neither did the cops, at least on an official level. Old man Kerrigan threw me out, Mrs. Wincott had clammed up, and Kathy's fiancé didn't care about anything but the price of Mexican oil and the wine list at La Côte Basque. So who was left? Nobody seemed to care much about this nasty piece of business from the past that Kathy Kerrigan had dug up. Except me. I cared.

Something crossed my mind. Something Audrey Wincott had said to me during that first conversation in her living room. "Tom Sewell has been a lifelong friend as well as sort of a substitute father for Kathy." And then what Sewell had told me about his relationship with Michael Kerrigan: "He was almost like a brother."

Tom Sewell. He cared about Kathy. He cared about Michael Kerrigan. Not only that, he once bought me lunch. Seemed to like me. Maybe he'd help. At the very least maybe he'd buy me another lunch.

I called him.

"Can I come over and talk to you, Mr. Sewell?"

"About what?"

I started to say Michael Kerrigan, but I thought better of it. Why scare him off?

"I need some legal advice."

"You?"

"Yeah, me. It's a real estate matter."

"You mean you're buying a piece of property?"

"No. I'm getting evicted from my rent-controlled apartment."

I told him about my problems with the landlord and the lease.

Sewell chuckled. "A rent-controlled apartment, huh? Miss McKay, do you really think you can afford my fees?"

"I don't know. What are they?"

"If you have to ask, then you can't."

"Okay, I don't want to talk about real estate."

"I never thought you did."

"It's about Kathy Kerrigan."

"Well, now we're really getting into it, aren't we? By the way, I've already heard about what happened at the senator's press conference."

"It won't wash," I told him.

"What do you mean?"

"The senator can't just keep saying 'my daughter is sick.' There's too many questions for that. The truth's going to come out, the only thing you people can do is determine how that happens."

There was a long pause on the line.

"Mr. Sewell, are you still there?"

"Yes."

"So when can I come over to talk to you about it?"

More silence.

"If I cancel my next appointment, can you do it right now?" he said finally.

"I'm on my way," I told him.

25

JFK, Jimmy Hoffa
and Other Heroes

Tom Sewell sat behind a big oak desk and smiled at me.

"You're the most tenacious reporter I've ever met," he said.

"Tenacious, huh? Well, I've been called a lot worse. Especially today."

Behind him was a breathtaking view of Manhattan looking east. The U.N. The East River. Roosevelt Island beyond that. On the water sailboats floated by, looking like little toys in a bathtub. Then a huge ship came into view with little dots that looked to be people. Probably the Circle Line. I took the Circle Line once. I almost got mugged.

"The senator was pretty rough on you, I guess."

"Let's just say he lost my vote."

"You have to forgive him. These are very tough times."

"Tell me about it."

"No, I'm serious. He really has had a lot on his mind the last few days."

"Like what?"

Sewell sighed. "Where do I begin?"

"How about with Michael Kerrigan?"

"You don't quit, do you?"

"What happened to him?"

"I told you. He drowned in an accident."

"I don't think that's what really happened."

He shrugged. "So prove it."

I stared at him.

"I can do it, you know."

"What?"

"Prove it."

Sewell laughed. "Stop blowing smoke at me, McKay. If you had anything at all, you wouldn't be here. You'd be on TV spilling it to the whole city."

"Not now," I said. "I can't prove it now. But I will—in time."

"What do you mean?" He sounded wary now.

"I've got a retired Massachusetts state cop who thinks the only witness to the whole thing, some fisherman named Meehan, lied through his teeth. I checked it out. Meehan's still alive and living up there. How long do you think it would take to shake his story?"

Sewell didn't say anything.

"And then there's Kerrigan's life. Every time I poke around in it, I turn up something interesting. Vietnam hero? Star student? Respected congressman? Maybe not. Want me to keep digging?"

"No," he said quietly.

"Well, give me some answers."

"What do you want to know?"

"Let's start with the truth?" I said. "That's always a good jumping-off point."

Sewell took a cigar out of a case on his desk, lit it with a match, then puffed on it thoughtfully for a few seconds. I watched the Circle Line fade out of sight as I waited.

"I like you," he said finally. "I'm going to do you a favor."

"Uh-oh."

"What's that mean?"

"I get nervous when someone says that to me. It makes me want to check to see if my purse and wallet are still there."

He shook his head. "You're a good reporter. A damned

good reporter. I mean . . . I guess if someone gets to break this . . .''

More silent thought and cigar smoke. I waited some more. I had plenty of time to kill. I could wait him out all day if I had to.

"Look, I'm going to tell you some things," Sewell said, "but we've got to set some ground rules."

"Okay."

"First, everything I say has to be attributed to a source. Second, my name can't be connected to it in any way. Third, if someone asks me about it I'm going to deny it. Agreed?"

"Agreed."

"Okay, here it is."

He took a deep breath.

"Mike Kerrigan didn't die in a boating accident," he said.

Jesus, he really was telling me! I tried to control myself and act calm.

"That's a start."

"It's just . . . it seemed the easiest thing to do twenty years ago to put out that story. And through the years . . . well, one thing led to another and the story stood. It didn't really seem to bother anyone. I mean no one was hurt or anything and it kept certain people from a lot of painful—"

"Until Kathy Kerrigan thought she saw him on TV and went looking for him."

"Yeah. That's what shook everything loose. And now it's all come tumbling down."

I couldn't believe this. He was spilling the whole fuckin' thing. Visions of Emmys danced in my head.

"Is Michael Kerrigan still alive?" I asked.

Sewell shook his head sadly. "No, he died twenty years ago. That part's true."

"So Kathy really imagined seeing her father on that TV show?"

"Uh-huh."

"Then why all the mystery?"

"What you have to understand, Miss McKay, is that Mikey was a very vital man. Brilliant, tough, a great leader—I have no doubt he would have made it to the White House had he lived. But like all great men he was, uh, flawed.''

''Flawed how?''

''Well, Michael had a weakness of the flesh.''

''He chased skirts?''

''Exactly.''

''Did he catch them?''

Sewell smiled. ''More often than not.''

''What kind of women did he like?''

''He preferred them to be breathing.''

''I mean did he go for redheads, blondes, brunettes . . .''

''Yeah, all of the above.''

''In other words, he liked women.''

''You're getting the message.''

I smiled. ''Nothing wrong with that. Lots of men do. It's what makes the world go round. It's not generally fatal.''

''That depends on which skirt you chase,'' Sewell said.

I thought about the story Rohr told me of Kerrigan having an affair with the wife of a mobster.

''Did you ever hear of Vincent Delvecchio?'' I asked.

Sewell's eyes widened in surprise. ''What do you know about him?''

''I know Mike Kerrigan was supposed to be investigating him twenty years ago. I know there was some suggestion he wasn't investigating all that hard, I also know he may have been investigating Mrs. Delvecchio, so to speak, at the same time. You take it from there.''

It was quiet in the room. Just the whir of an air conditioner. From an outer office somewhere I heard a telephone ring. Sewell rustled through some papers on his desk and then covered his face with his hand. When he took it away again, his eyes were tearing.

''They killed him,'' he said simply.

''Who?''

''Delvecchio's people.''

''Vincent Delvecchio murdered Michael Kerrigan?''

Sewell nodded.

''They lured him down to the beach that day. Had Vincent's wife call up and say she wanted to go boating with him. She was there all right. But so were some of Delvecchio's goons. I'm not sure exactly what happened, but somehow they knocked him out, stabbed him to death, then''—his voice cracked—''they cut up his body and stuffed it into an oil drum. They killed Mrs. Delvecchio, too, and put her in another oil drum. Then they dropped both of them into the ocean.''

Sewell's eyes were glistening now. He reached up and wiped them with his hand.

''Sorry,'' he said. ''It's been twenty years but it still doesn't get any easier. I've lived with it all these years. But no one talks about it, no one brings it up anymore.''

''They *were* having an affair then? Kerrigan and Mrs. Delvecchio?''

Sewell nodded. ''They met while Mike was investigating her husband. And well . . .''

''But why the phony story about the drowning?''

''It seemed . . . well, it just seemed like the thing to do then. Christ, you've got to understand—Mike Kerrigan was supposed to wind up in the White House. He was the shining light in his father's life. To be killed because he was caught in the saddle with a mobster's wife seemed too much for the old man to handle. So we . . . we made up the story of the accident so he could die a more respectable death. A noble death at sea.'' He paused. ''A Kerrigan death.''

Sewell leaned back in his chair and sighed. ''Now when I think about it, I wonder if it was worth all the trouble. I mean I hear these stories about JFK sleeping with all those broads while he was in the White House, even the mobster's girlfriend— what's her name again?''

''Judith Exner.''

''Yeah. Anyway it makes me think maybe we should have just told the truth when it happened. I mean, now what happened to Mikey doesn't seem so bad, does it? I mean, he could be a hero for this. What do you think?''

''Sure.'' I didn't really know. I didn't know anything anymore. ''How about Delvecchio?''

''What do you mean?''

''He goes free because you covered up the murder. Doesn't that bother you?''

"Miss McKay, do you know anything about the mob?"

"I did a five-part series on them a few years ago. 'The Mob's Tentacles Get a Hold on New York.'"

"Then you know he had an airtight alibi. And we could never pin the murder on him in a million years. Even if we know he did it. So what's the point?"

I didn't know the answer to either.

"So what now?" he asked.

"What do you mean?"

"Are you going to go on the air with this?"

"I think I have to."

"Why? It's been twenty years. There's no reason to dredge up these memories now. All you'll do is hurt people—King Kerrigan, Mrs. Wincott, the senator, Kathy."

"There's really no choice," I told him.

"Sure there is. There're a lot of choices. Some of them quite lucrative."

I looked at him. "Are you offering me money?"

"You bet."

"How much?"

"Fifty-thousand dollars. No questions asked."

I let out a low whistle. "And what do I have to do for it?"

"Nothing. You do nothing at all. Just walk away from this story."

I stood up. "Sorry, I can't do that."

"Why not?" he asked.

"Because it's the truth. You can't run away from the truth. It always catches up with you."

I wasn't sure what I meant by that, but it sounded good. I started for the door.

"Hey, McKay," he yelled. I turned around. "How about that apartment problem of yours? You want to talk about it?"

"I'll handle it," I said.

"Okay. But here's some free legal advice for you: Pay the guy."

"Huh?"

"Bribe him. Grease him. Slip him something under the table. It'll take care of your problem."

"That's all?"

"Sure. A thousand, maybe fifteen hundred, tops. That's what he's looking for."

"Money. Of course. Jesus, I never thought of that!"

Sewell smiled. "It's what makes the world go round," he said.

I took the Lexington Avenue IRT back to the office. The trip was pretty much of a blur to me. All I remember is thinking about what I'd stumbled onto. And wondering what to do next.

Not that there was really anything to think about.

What a great story! What a great exclusive! What a great reporter I was! All that was left now was to put it on the air. Just report what Sewell had told me and credit it to a source close to the family. I'd blow the socks off of everyone else in town.

Yep, that was all there was to it.

I walked into the studio and was stunned to find Gergen there.

"What's going on?" I asked.

He whisked me into his office so no one else could hear us.

"The hospital released me."

"What did they say?"

"They said to take it easy for a few days. Then they'd do some more tests."

I looked around the office. There were three TV sets on at the same time. Outside I could hear the clacking of wire machines. People were shouting.

"This is taking it easy?" I asked.

"Hey, you've got enough troubles in your own personal life. Don't tell me how to run mine."

That seemed fair enough.

"What are you working on?" he asked.

I told him about my conversation with Sewell.

"That's dynamite!" he said when I was finished.

"Yeah. Dynamite."

"I can't believe you're not more excited."

"Well, it is good," I agreed.

"So what's the problem?"

"Doesn't it seem almost too good?"

"I don't get you—"

"I don't know. It just seems too simple. The Kerrigan family lawyer drops this whole thing right in my lap. And think about the story—it's like a composite of other famous legends. The stuff about the kid boffing the mobster's wife—well, that's JFK and Judith Exner. Then the whole thing about him being lured to the killing site, murdered, and his body put into an oil drum—doesn't that sound a little familiar?"

"Jimmy Hoffa," Gergen said. "That's what they think happened to Hoffa."

"Exactly."

"Now everything I've checked out about Michael Kerrigan so far has turned out to be a lie. The Brooke School. Harvard. His congressional record. The boating accident. Why should this be any different? Why not assume it's just one more smoke screen?"

"Or it could be true."

"Yeah, except for one thing. Sewell says Delvecchio's wife lured Kerrigan down to the boat that day. Only that's wrong. Delvecchio's wife was already dead. She died three weeks before that."

"So Sewell lied. But why? Why give us a phony story that'll embarrass the family when it comes out?"

"I can think of one explanation."

"Yeah," Gergen said. "Me too. The real story is even worse."

"Right. There's something else, too, Joe. Kathy Kerrigan says her father is still alive. She saw him on TV." I took the picture out of my purse and laid it on the desk. "We've got to find this guy."

"How?"

"I've got an idea. Kathy says she ran into a hooker who recognized him."

"So you're—"

"I'm going looking for the hooker."

26

A Walk on the
Wild Side

The hooker Kathy Kerrigan had talked to—the one she thinks
might have seen her father—called herself China.

I went looking for her on Lexington Avenue. I found out
from some people on the street that she hung out on the corner
of 25th Street. I also found out she usually showed up around
noon. I found out, too, that a woman alone on this street—even
a forty-year-old woman like me—could still attract plenty of
interest from the locals.

Forty years old and you still got it, kid. Of course, the only
people you've still got it for are winos and perverts. But, hey,
beggars can't be choosers.

Forty. I'm forty. I still can't believe it. Suddenly I thought
about one of the birthday cards I'd gotten. The one from the PR
guy at the telephone company.

The telephone company.

I walked over to a phone booth with a clear view of the
corner of 25th. I had an idea. I was full of ideas, just no
answers. I dialed the number for my pal at the phone company.

"Jenny, how are you?" he said.

"Well, I need a favor."

His name was Rick Malone and I'd known him for about five years. Sometimes I thought he had the hots for me. Other times I thought he was gay. In any case, he seemed to like me.

"I want to run a check on someone's phone calls for the past few days," I told him. "I'm trying to track something down, and I'm hoping it will give me a lead. Can you do that?"

"There was a long pause."

"Rick?"

Malone cleared his throat. "Listen, Jenny, that's illegal."

"So's taking drugs. But that didn't stop you from laying out those lines of Peruvian powder at your New Year's Eve party last year."

"What's your point?"

"My point is that we all break the law at times. This is one of those times."

Another pause.

"Okay," he sighed, "what's the number?"

I read him Tom Sewell's phone number. I didn't know what I was looking for. But I was pretty sure Sewell had lied to me. Twice. Once when he told me the original story about the boating accident. And again at his office with the revised version. So maybe he'd talked to someone interesting about the changes.

"Local calls are a bit tricky," Malone said. "That could take a while. But the toll stuff—I can get back to you right away with that."

I gave him the number of the pay phone.

"This is terrific," I told him. "You're the best."

"Yeah. The best."

He didn't seem too happy about it.

After I hung up, I looked around. Some of the working girls were already out. Along with the normal street people. Pan-handlers. Derelicts. Wise guys. This wasn't exactly the scenes of the city they shot for Michelob commercials.

I decided to stay by the phone booth. But I was afraid someone else might want to use the phone before Malone called back. So I picked it up again, pressed down on the receiver so it could still ring and stood there pretending to talk to someone. That's a trick I learned from watching "The

Rockford Files'' on TV. After a few minutes though, I began to feel foolish. No one else seemed interested in using the phone. The hell with it, I said, and hung up again.

I kept my eyes open for anyone who seemed to be China. Nothing. No one looked Asian. After a while, I started to get bored. And hungry.

There was a vendor on the other side of Lexington selling hot salted pretzels. I figured I could walk across the street, get a pretzel, and still be able to race back to the phone in case Malone called. It would help pass the time. Besides, they say walking is great exercise. Maybe after I'd eaten the pretzel, I'd even walk over and get a second one. You can never get too much exercise.

I was on my third pretzel when the phone finally rang.

"McKay here," I said, swallowing down the last of the pretzel.

"Okay, I got it," Malone said. "Tom Sewell made ten long-distance calls in the past three days to a total of five different numbers."

He read me the numbers.

"Did you check out what they're listed to?" I asked.

"What else do I live for?"

"Where?"

"Okay, one is a law office in London, another a lawyer in Los Angeles, there was a call to Senator Wincott's office in Washington, four to the Kerrigan estate in Nantucket, and three to something called the Fairview Institute in Stonehampton, New York."

"What the hell is the Fairview Institute?"

"Beats me. All I know from the area code is that's somewhere outside of Albany. And all the calls were made yesterday and this morning. You think it's important?"

"I don't know. Listen, Rick, thanks a lot. I'll buy you dinner some night, okay?"

"A real sit-down dinner?"

"What do you mean?"

"Well, the last two times we've eaten dinner, you jumped up in the middle of it to go off and chase a story somewhere. I'm

not going through that again. I want your promise that you'll
stay at the table this time for at least an hour."

"Is it okay if I get up once to go to the bathroom?"

"Good-bye, Jenny."

I waited some more, trying to think of a way to kill time until
China showed up. I seem to do a lot of that. Eventually I came
up with an idea. I strolled back across the street to the guy
selling pretzels and bought another one. Actually I made five
trips in all. By then, the pretzel vendor and I were on a
first-name basis. We seemed to be on the verge of a meaningful
relationship.

I went back to the phone booth and dialed a number. Dave
Paxton's.

"Are we still talking?" I asked him drily. I was thirsty from
all the pretzels I'd eaten. I badly needed a soda. But on my last
trip across the street, the pretzel vendor had told me he was out
of cold drinks. Maybe it was time to break off the relationship.

"This is talking, isn't it?"

"You know what I mean."

"Look, Jenny, some of the things I said were out of line. I
was wrong. I'm sorry."

"I can top that," I told him. "I was immature, insensitive,
and a horse's ass."

He laughed. "Apology accepted."

"By the way, I've been thinking about what you said to me.
You're right."

"Hey, we don't have to get into that now—"

"No, I mean it. I *am* too involved in every story. I
sometimes think I'm going through life with blinders on, which
prevents me from seeing what's really important. All I can
see—all I seem to care about—is my name on a story or the red
light on the camera. I've got my priorities all screwed up,
Dave."

"We'll talk about it later," he said.

"Honest, I'm really going to try . . ."

An attractive Asian woman walked by and took a position on
the corner.

"Jesus Christ!" I said.

"What's wrong?"

"I gotta go!"

"Jenny—"

"I'll talk to you later. Promise."

I hung up the phone and walked as casually as I could over to the Asian woman. She was wearing a low-cut sleeveless silk blouse, red leather hot pants, and black platform shoes. Her hair was done up in a kind of beehive and she was wearing too much makeup. A cigarette dangled from her lips as she stood with one foot on the sidewalk and one foot on the curb, trying to attract the attention of passing motorists and passersby. She wasn't quite wearing a sign around her neck advertising what she was, but then she didn't need to.

"Are you China?" I asked, walking up behind her.

She whirled around quickly. Up close, she wasn't that pretty. Her skin had a sallow, unhealthy complexion. And her eyes were dull, as if she'd had too much to drink or too much of something else.

"Who wants to know?"

"I do. My name's Jenny. Jenny McKay."

She eyed me suspiciously.

"You a cop?"

I shook my head.

"Do-gooder?"

"Huh?"

"You know—social worker, welfare, church lady . . ."

"I'm a TV reporter with Channel Six News." I took out a card and handed it to her.

She looked at the card, sniffed, and ripped it up. It fell in little pieces to the pavement.

"Same thing as a cop. Only I don't have to talk to you. Get off my corner, TV lady. You're cuttin' into my business."

I stood there, not moving.

"I'll make it worth your time," I said.

China took the cigarette from her mouth, flicked it onto the sidewalk, and ground it out under the heel of her platform shoes. "How worthwhile?"

I thought about it for a minute. "What's your going rate?"

"Forty dollars for thirty minutes. Up front."

"It's a deal."

I reached into my purse, fumbled through my wallet, and found fifty-two dollars. I took out forty of it and handed it to China.

"I've got to give this to Hector first," she said.

"Who's Hector?"

She nodded toward an old Pontiac sitting by a fire hydrant about a half a block up Lexington on the other side of the street. A tall Puerto Rican man in a T-shirt and khaki pants was leaning against the car, casually cleaning his fingernails and staring at us.

"Hector's your pimp," I said.

"Right. He's probably wondering right now why I'm spending so much time talking to you."

China took the money, click-clacked on her high heels over to where Hector was waiting, and handed him the money. He slipped it casually into the pocket of the khakis and she came back to where I was standing.

"Okay, we're legal," she said.

Behind us a wino threw up against a wall, then collapsed slowly onto the sidewalk and fell asleep. An empty bottle lay next to him. People passing by just walked around him and kept going as if nothing had happened.

New York, New York, it's a wonderful town.

"Can we go somewhere else to talk?" I asked.

"Follow me."

We walked into a dilapidated old building, the East Side Hotel, off Lexington. China slipped something to a fat guy eating a sandwich at the front desk, then led me up a rickety set of stairs. We went up three flights, then into a room on the right side of the hall.

"By the way," I huffed, out of breath from the climb, "what did you say to Hector back there about what we were doing?"

"I just told him you were a trick."

I arched my eyebrow. "You don't think he noticed I was a woman?"

She shrugged. "I told him you were a lesbian. He don't care. The money's the same."

The room was about the size of a broom closet. There was a bed in the middle, with a plastic sheet covering it, and a wooden folding chair sitting alongside. A naked light fixture hung by a wire from the center of the ceiling, which gave just enough light to see the paint peeling from the walls and the plaster cracking.

China plopped down on the bed and pointed to the chair for me. I was grateful for that.

"Okay, your meter's running. What do you want to know?" I handed her the picture Kathy had given me.

"You ever see him?" I asked.

She looked down at the photo and shrugged. "Maybe. Maybe not."

"What does that mean?"

"It means it's going to cost you more than forty bucks to find out."

I sighed. "I'm really getting tired of playing games. How about if I just bring the cops in, along with maybe the health department and the building inspectors, too? I think they'd find about one thousand violations before they walked through the lobby of this place."

China didn't say anything.

"Look, I need your help," I told her. "I'm trying to find out what happened to someone. Someone's father. You see there's this girl—"

"Yeah, the one with all the money."

"Then you *are* the one she talked to."

"Sure. Maybe a week ago."

I handed her the picture again.

"You told her you thought you'd seen this man. Is that true, China?"

She nodded.

"Where?"

"Here, there, everywhere," China said, gesturing out the window toward the street below.

I bit my lip. I didn't want to lose my temper and blow it.

"Do you know his name?" I asked.

"Nope. I just called him 'Senator.'"

"Why?"

"Because that's what he called himself. Said he used to be one."

I stared at her.

"Don't look so surprised," China said. "Hell, a lot of people out there used to be important people. Heads of corporations, movie stars, Napoleon Bonaparte. Just ask them."

"But you didn't really think he was once a senator?"

She chuckled. "Sure I did. Just like I was once the Queen of Siam."

China took out another cigarette, lit it, and took a drag. The smoke made the closeness of the room even more unbearable. I wanted to open the window wider, but I decided I didn't want to touch anything.

"I want you to help me find him, China."

"Can't do that," she said.

"If it's the money, I'll—"

"He's gone. They took him."

"Who?"

"Two guys in a car. They came cruising the street for a while looking for something. Finally they grabbed him, put him in the backseat, and drove away. Haven't seen him since."

And she doesn't expect to see him again, I thought. She didn't say that, but it's what she means.

"This was right on the street?"

"Uh-huh."

"When?"

"I don't know. A day ago. Two days. Who remembers?"

"Didn't anyone get the cops?"

"Not in this neighborhood, honey. In this neighborhood, people don't get the cops. The cops get us."

Down the hall the stairs creaked and a door slammed. Probably another sale being rung up. From another room I could hear someone in the throes of pleasure. Or was it agony? I wasn't sure.

"The car," I asked, "do you remember anything about it?"

"It was black."

"Could it have been a Caddy?"

"Yeah, maybe. Why, do you know it?"

"I think so."

Al and Mickey. The two guys who grabbed me outside the studio. Mob guys.

China looked down at her watch. "You're time's up, TV lady. Hector's going to start getting restless any minute now."

"It's probably none of my business, but why do you care about what Hector thinks?"

"Hey, I was really down and out on drugs when he found me. If he bounces me . . ."

I wanted to ask her more about where she went if Hector got rid of her. About what was further down than this? But I didn't. I just said good-bye, then walked down the steps and into the fresh air outside.

It felt good after the oppressive stuffiness of that hotel room. I stood there for a second, taking in deep breaths. The pretzel man was gone now, but that was okay. I wasn't hungry anymore. Then I looked down the street in the other direction. Hector was still there leaning on the Pontiac, watching me with a knowing leer on his face.

I turned in the other direction, headed toward Third Avenue, and got the hell out of that neighborhood.

27

Ratings
Don't Lie

Sanders was waiting for me back at the office with a big smile on his face.

"I've got good news, and I've got better news," he said.

"The joke is supposed to go, 'I've got good news, and I've got bad news.'"

"Trust me, Jenny."

"So what is it?"

"Go see for yourself in Gergen's office."

I stuck my head inside.

"Hi, Joe, how's it going?"

Gergen looked up from his desk. His face was pasty and sweaty. His eyes looked tired. Some of the sweat had trickled down and made the collar of his shirt damp.

"How does it look like it's going?" he growled.

"Uh—fine."

"You always were a lousy liar, McKay," he said. "C'mon in."

I sat down at the chair in front of his desk.

"Maybe you need to take some more time off . . ." I started to say.

"I'm quitting."

"Huh?"

"I told Carstairs and Cafferty this morning. I'll finish up this week—clean out my desk, pick up my gold watch, the whole bit. Then I start four weeks of vacation, followed by official retirement."

"Damn." I swallowed hard. "I never really thought you . . ."

"Neither did I," he said.

"Why? Your health?"

"No, I want to race in the Indianapolis 500 next year. Of course, it's my health."

I nodded.

"What do the doctors say?"

"They say I have two options: One, keep working this job and have a real heart attack and die; or two, take it easy, change my life-style, and I can probably have a number of happy years of living ahead of me. I opted for living."

"That's great, Joe." I paused. "Only do you think . . . ?"

"Do I think I can do it? Do I think I can go the rest of my life without getting excited over every fire and murder I hear about? Do you think I can sit quietly as an observer the next time some president or head of state gets assassinated? Or a 747 crashes? Or a cop gets shot?"

His voice trailed off. I thought about my conversation with Paxton. "Yeah, can you?" I asked.

"I don't know," he smiled. "But I guess we'll find out, won't we?"

Gergen picked up some papers and tossed them over to me. "Here's what you came in for."

I looked down at them. It was a report from a polling service on our ratings for the past few weeks. A kind of ratings before the ratings.

"Turn to page five," he said. "You'll like it."

I did. It said that the sample ratings for "South Street Confidential" were better than any other part of the show. That the demographics were good. That my Q rating was higher than it's ever been.

"That might just have saved your job," Gergen observed.

"Maybe I should ask for a raise."

"Don't get carried away."

"Why not?"

"Because," he said, "Carstairs and Cafferty don't like you."

"Oh."

I remembered what Sanders had said. Good news and even better news.

"Is there anything else I should know about?" I asked.

He flipped through the sheets to page ten. I read it quickly. It said Cassie White's ratings had shown the least growth of any of the Channel Six news team. It said she only put up good numbers when she did something spectacular, such as the bank hostage job or jumping off the Channel Six roof. It suggested she didn't wear well with an audience over a long period of time. What they call a hot performer instead of a cool one. A hot performer blazes brightly, then burns out. A cool one is good for the long haul.

"Has Cassie seen this yet?"

Gergen nodded. "This morning."

"How'd she take it?"

"Badly."

"There is a God," I smiled.

I filled him in on my conversation with China, then went back to my desk to try the number of Fairview Institute. A woman answered, saying it was a Dr. Blakely's office.

"Is this Fairview?" I asked.

"Yes."

"Fairview Institute?"

"That's right."

"What do you do there?"

"Pardon me?"

"What do you institute? I'm just curious."

"Ma'am," she said a bit impatiently, "we are a federally certified medical support facility."

"Medical? You're a hospital?"

"Yes, ma'am."

"What kind of hospital? Heart? Eye? Dog and cat?"

"We provide in-house psychological counseling and treatment for psychiatric disorders of all types."

"A mental hospital?"

"Yes."

A mental hospital! Why not?

"Is there something I can help you with, ma'am?"

"No," I said excitedly. "You've been very helpful already. And, hey, you're doing a great job."

I hung up and looked around for Sanders and Jacobson. Jacobson was working on another crossword puzzle. Sanders was trying to convince a young female production assistant that he knew Eddie Murphy.

"Eddie Murphy really hangs out at your apartment in Queens?" she was saying.

"Sure."

"I don't believe you."

"Would you believe Arsenio Hall does?"

I walked over to them.

"Hey, you guys, we're going to take a trip," I said.

Jacobson put down the puzzle. "Where to?"

"Stonehampton, New York."

"Stonehampton? What the hell's in Stonehampton?"

"That," I said, "is the $64,000 question."

I walked to the ladies' room.

While I was fixing my hair at the mirror, I heard noises coming from one of the stalls. As if someone was sick. And crying. And pounding on the side of the stall. I walked over and knocked on the door.

"Are you okay in there?" I asked.

"Go away!"

I recognized the voice.

"Cassie?"

I pushed on the door slightly. It opened. Cassie White was in there all right, but it wasn't the Cassie I knew. Her hair was a mess, her eyes red, her face streaked with tears, and she seemed to be almost hyperventilating. Then I looked down at her hands and saw the knuckles were raw and bloody. She'd apparently been pounding on the walls in frustration.

"What's wrong?" I asked.

"That."

She pointed to some tattered pieces of paper on the floor that she'd tried to flush down the toilet. I picked one up. It was the ratings report I'd read a few minutes earlier.

"They don't like me," she sobbed.

"Hey, c'mon, it's just a ratings sheet."

"No one likes me."

I didn't know what to say.

"I know what I have to do though. I have to try harder. And if that doesn't work, I'll just try even harder. I'll make them like me. I'll make them . . ."

Her whole body was trembling now. I was afraid she was having a nervous breakdown. I didn't know what to do, so I just acted instinctively. I put my arm around her and hugged her.

"It's going to be all right, Cassie," I said.

She sobbed on my shoulder for a while.

"You don't like me either, do you?" she said finally.

I started to answer, but she cut me off.

"It's okay. Most people don't. I guess I just come on too strong and rub people the wrong way." She was talking more normally now. "I don't mean to be like that. But it generally seems to work out that way."

"Look," I told her, "it's not a one-way street. I'm not always the most lovable person either. It takes two to make a feud."

"Yeah. Anyway, Jenny, what I'm trying to say is . . . well . . . look, if you want . . . I mean . . ."

She wiped some of the tears from her face.

"Do you think maybe we could be friends?" she asked in a nervous voice.

I stared at her.

"I really need a friend," she said.

I smiled. "Well, stranger things have happened."

She smiled, too.

"How about we get together for coffee or something tomorrow and talk?" I suggested.

Cassie nodded. "I think I'd like that."

A few minutes later she'd gotten herself together and looked like the Cassie of old. Every hair in place. Skin without a mark on it. She looked at me, smiled one more time, then headed back to the newsroom.

Dammit, I thought to myself after she was gone, I hate it when I'm wrong about someone.

28

Into the Cuckoo's Nest

Fairview Institute turned out to be located about twenty-five miles outside Albany. We pulled up at the gate the next morning. It was a big, white antiseptic-looking building, surrounded by rolling grounds and a big iron fence. Sanders looked at the fence and frowned.

"So how do we get in?"

"Easy," I said, and rang the bell on the gate.

"Just like that."

"Sure. Security at a place like this is aimed at keeping the people inside from sneaking out. They're not worried about people from the outside sneaking in. No one wants to get *into* a mental hospital."

"Except us."

"Yeah, that's why we've got surprise on our side."

Sure enough, we were buzzed in. I told Sanders and Jacobson to wait for me in the rental car with the cameras. Then I went to Dr. Blakely's office. He was the director of the hospital. A middle-aged, slightly overweight man with a harried expression on his face.

"Miss—Miss Brannigan, is that it?" he asked.

"That's right. Jane Brannigan."

"Do I know you?"

"No. I'm an assistant to Tom Sewell, working with the Kerrigan family. You know Mr. Sewell, don't you?"

"Oh, of course."

Bingo.

"He wanted me to stop by and make sure everything was going according to plan here."

Blakely nodded.

"No problems at all?"

"No, everything's fine now. Tell him that."

I was going to have to wing it and hope I hit the right target.

"Where is he now?"

"Resting. Do you want me to take you to see him?"

"No, I've got to catch a flight back to New York." I checked my watch. "You're not letting him out onto the grounds, are you?"

"No, no. We learned our lesson. He won't escape again. He's confined in Section A-ten this time. That's our most secure block. He's been there since the two—the two gentlemen brought him back the other night."

"Good," I said. "Section A-ten. That's real good."

Five minutes later Sanders, Jacobson, and I carefully made our way through the hospital. No one stopped us. No one asked us any questions. Like I said, no one ever thinks anyone's going to break into a mental hospital.

It took us another ten minutes to find Section A-10. It was a small cubicle of a room with a wire-mesh screen on the door so you could see in. The room had white walls, an iron bed, a simple straight-back chair, and a window looking out over the grounds and some mountains in the distance. There were heavy bars on the window. A constant reminder to the patient of the freedom he can't have, I thought. There was someone in the room, but he wasn't on the bed or the chair. He was sitting cross-legged on the floor and staring out the window.

I took out Kathy's picture and looked at it one more time. Then I looked at the man in front of me. Identical.

"Michael?" I said in a loud voice.

No answer.

"Are you Michael Kerrigan?"

Still nothing.

"I understand they call you the senator. . . ."

"Yeah, I'm a senator," he said suddenly, springing to life. He walked over to the wire mesh door and pressed his face against it. "Senator Mike Kerrigan of New York, glad to meet you. I'm not sure of my White House plans yet, but I'm not ruling anything out. I've been to the White House, you know. My father and I drop by . . ."

He was talking nonstop. Hyperactively. I signaled to Sanders and Jacobson to make sure they got all this, but I didn't have to bother. The camera was already rolling.

"Now I may go to the Soviet Union next month to negotiate a nuclear arms treaty," he was saying. "Then I have to deal with Vietnam and Berlin and the space race. It's so much responsibility. But like I always say: 'Ask not what your country can do for you, ask what you can do for your country.' I like that, don't you? In fact, I may use it for my campaign slogan when I run for the White House. But I better ask my father first . . ."

"Let me get this straight," Sanders said, pointing to the chattering man. "This is Michael Kerrigan?"

I nodded.

"He's alive?"

"Seems to be."

"He's also nutty as a fruitcake."

"Yeah."

After getting more footage through the wire grating, Sanders and Jacobson took the camera and other equipment back to the car. I stayed there for a little longer, hoping to get something—anything—out of Michael Kerrigan that made sense. I was just about ready to give up when I heard someone come up behind me.

"Who are you?" a voice asked.

I whirled around.

A doctor was standing there. A woman doctor. She was holding a clipboard and staring at me with a concerned look on her face. There was a name tag on her white coat that identified her as a Dr. Delgado.

"Hi," I said, sticking out my hand and trying to act as casually as I could, "I'm Jane Brannigan."

She wasn't buying it. She stared at my outstretched hand.

"I don't mean your name," she said. "I mean *who* are you? What are you doing here?"

"Oh that . . ."

I reached into my purse and pulled out a piece of paper. It was a piece of memo paper with Dr. Blakely's letterhead on top. I'd swiped it while I was in his office just in case something like this happened. On the way over here, I'd scribbled a message on it in nearly illegible handwriting. Now I handed it to her.

Dr. Delgado looked at the note and frowned.

"What's this?" she asked.

"A letter from Dr. Blakely identifying me as a representative of the Kerrigan family. It gives his approval for me to see the patient."

Michael Kerrigan was screaming something from behind the wire door now about Communists at our doorstep and firing General Westmoreland. I tried to ignore him.

"How can I be sure this is really from Dr. Blakely?" she asked.

"You don't know his writing?"

She shook her head.

"But you know his voice."

"Of course."

"So let's call him."

We walked to her office at the end of the hall. There was a phone on her desk. I dialed Dr. Blakely's extension.

"Hi," I told him when he came on the line, "Jane Brannigan again. Listen, I changed my mind and stopped by Section A-ten after all to see the patient. So I can give the Kerrigan family a complete report. Is that all right?"

"Sure," he said. "I'll come down and let you in."

"That's not necessary. I'm with a Dr. Delgado. Just clear me with her."

"Put her on," he said.

After she hung up the phone, Dr. Delgado was a lot more expansive.

"Sorry about that," she said, "but we've got to be really careful. Especially in this case. We don't want another slipup."

"When did he escape again?"

"About six months ago," she said.

"And he's been back only a day or so?"

She nodded.

"Tell me about him. Medically, I mean."

She shrugged. "What's to tell? He's severely retarded."

"Can he function at all?"

"Not really. Not anymore. What you see is what you get. He lives almost entirely in a fantasy world. Most of his points of reference are from prior to 1973 when he was first institution-alized."

How about before 1973, I wondered? How did he manage to get elected to Congress?

"Has he been like this all his life?" I heard myself ask.

I was afraid I was asking too many questions. But I didn't care. I needed the information.

"Many times in cases like this, the patient's condition doesn't really become clear for a number of years," Dr. Delgado explained. "As a child, it just appears that the person is a bit slow in learning things. In this particular case, even as a young adult he could hold conversations, comprehend things—in short, function as a human being in a limited sort of way. Many times this continues throughout the course of the patient's life and he doesn't even have to be institutionalized."

"But that's not what happened here," I said.

"No, it isn't. When a person in this condition is forced into situations beyond his capabilities—well, his condition rapidly deteriorates. He becomes confused, hyperactive, and—at times—violent because of frustration."

I thought about Thomas Kerrigan pushing his son for greatness. To Harvard. To Congress. Even to the White House. It must have just been too much for him. So at some point he simply stopped functioning and retreated into his fantasy world.

"Can he ever be cured?" I asked Dr. Delgado.

She shrugged. "Miracles do happen."

"But you don't think so."

"No, but I don't think I'll win the lottery tomorrow either. The odds are about the same."

I stood up.

"Well, thanks for your time. I'll make sure the Kerrigan family is aware of your close attention to this—ah, delicate—matter."

"Thank you."

"Who besides you and Dr. Blakely know about this?" I asked.

"No one," she said. "To everyone else here he's just a John Doe with delusions of past grandeur."

"That's fine," I said. I played a hunch. "By the way, is everything in order with the checks to both of you? Are they still coming on time?"

"No problem. Every month. Like clockwork."

"Good, Dr. Delgado," I smiled. "Very good."

Five minutes later Sanders and Jacobson and I were back in the car together and headed to New York.

"What now?" Sanders asked. "We putting this on the air?"

"Not yet," I told him. "I want to talk to one more person first."

"Who?"

"Audrey Wincott."

29
True
Confessions

The same doorman was on duty at the Hilldale House.

At first he tried to give me a hard time again. But I was adamant. I was tenacious. I was determined. I'd also called ahead and arranged my visit with Kathy Kerrigan. So eventually he just waved me toward the elevator.

"Does that help you with the girls?" I asked.

"What?"

I pointed to his doorman's uniform. "The Salvation Army getup you're wearing."

"What are you talking about?"

"Well, they say women always go for a man in uniform. That, plus your sunny personality . . ."

"Get the hell out of here," he yelled.

Upstairs Kathy Kerrigan let me in.

She was wearing a pale blue summer skirt, a short-sleeved white blouse with blue trim, and open-toed sandals. It was the first time I'd seen her in anything other than the baggy T-shirt and jeans she had on when I met her in the park. Her hair was brushed away from her forehead and tied neatly in the back.

She looked pretty, except for her eyes. There was no spark in them, no life at all.

"My mother's in the living room," Kathy said. "If you hurry, maybe she'll still be conscious."

"She's drinking."

"Ever since I came home. More than ever."

"How about your stepfather?"

"In Washington. Where he always is."

"Good." I didn't want another confrontation with him right now.

Audrey Wincott was sitting on the velvet couch. There was a glass in her hand and a container of bourbon on the coffee table in front of her. She was humming a song that sounded a bit like "Yesterday." Or maybe "Ninety-nine Bottles of Beer." Or both.

I sat down across from her.

"Hi. Remember me."

She squinted her eyes in my direction. "You. You're that TV lady." She giggled. "The one everyone got mad at me for talking to. Well, you won't get anything out of me this time. My lips are sealed."

She made a zipping motion across her lips.

I turned to Kathy. "Can you get us some coffee?" I asked. "Sure."

She got up and left. I leaned closer to Mrs. Wincott.

"I've seen your husband," I said softly.

"You've been to Washington?"

I shook my head. "No, I mean your first husband. Michael Kerrigan."

She looked at me with a confused expression on her face. Then down at her glass, which was empty. She leaned forward to reach for the container on the table. I put my hand on her wrist and stopped her.

"He's alive, Mrs. Wincott."

She sat there frozen for a second. Even through the booze, I think she heard me.

"No, he's not," she said. "He died a long time ago."

"I'm afraid not."

"You've been listening to my daughter too much. My

daughter makes things up." She giggled. "Ask my husband. Ask Tom Sewell."

"I've been to Fairview," I told her.

"Oh," she said quietly.

Kathy came back with the coffee. Mrs. Wincott made another try for the drink, but I picked up the bourbon bottle and handed it to Kathy.

"There's plenty more where that came from," Mrs. Wincott chortled.

"I'm sure." I looked at Kathy. "Do you think you could go out somewhere and leave us alone for a while?"

I didn't want her to know the truth about her father. Not yet. Not like this.

"Well, I . . ."

"If you don't trust me now, it's a little late, isn't it?" I said.

She nodded. "Sure, I can go out. I've got some things to do anyway."

When she was gone, I turned back to Mrs. Wincott.

"Drink some of the coffee," I said.

She took a sip, then made a face. But we kept at it. After a while she wasn't so drunk. She wasn't sober either, but she was better than before.

"So you know all about Michael, huh? Imagine that."

"You want to tell me about it?"

"What's to tell? You saw him."

"What's wrong with him?"

She made a circular motion with her index finger next to her head.

"I know he's crazy," I said, "but what happened?"

Audrey Wincott sighed. The coffee was having a real effect now. "Michael's mother died at childbirth. She'd had a lot of trouble during the pregnancy and then I guess she just . . ."

I nodded. I remembered reading about it in one of the clips.

"Anyway, Michael survived the birth. But he was never quite right. The doctors think he was deprived of oxygen for too long a period during the birth. And so he was . . . he was . . ." She looked longingly down at the empty bourbon glass.

"Retarded?" I said.

"Yes."

"Did he seem normal when he was younger? I mean how noticeable was it?"

"Oh, Michael could function—sort of—in those days. He was quite good-looking and at times charming with women, for instance. That's how he was when I met him. I mean he wasn't a Rhodes scholar, but he had the Kerrigan name. And all that money. And enough intelligence to get elected to Congress." She smiled. "Of course, it doesn't take that much, you know.

"Anyway," she continued, "they were really careful with him during the campaign. Everything he said was scripted out in advance. They limited his appearances—just let the crowds see him but not really talk to him. No long interviews or debates. And it worked. He got elected on the Kerrigan name and money."

"They sold him," I said. I thought about something Joseph Kennedy once said about JFK's first election to Congress. "They sold him like soap flakes."

"Something like that."

"But then it all fell apart? Why?"

"You see . . . you see Michael had bad spells, too," she said. She bit down on her lower lip. "Periods when he wasn't so charming. When he couldn't function. When he became . . . well, he became violent. As he got older, these bad spells came more frequently and lasted longer. Until—"

"Until he couldn't function at all anymore."

She nodded.

"He had to be put away. For his own good." She looked up to me as if she were seeking approval for what they'd done. "You've seen him, you know that."

"Why all the mystery?" I asked. "Why the faked story about his death?"

"You'd never understand."

"Try me."

She pointed to a picture on the mantel. It was of King Kerrigan. Standing on the coastline with Michael at his side.

"Michael's father just couldn't accept it. I mean the doctors kept telling him about Michael, they'd been telling him all of Michael's life about his limited intelligence. But the old man wouldn't listen. He said Michael was his heir, his destiny, a future president of the United States—and that was it. It's almost as if he thought his money and his power and his influence could change what God had done.''

I looked at the picture again. Father and son. Perfect serenity, or so it seemed. But all the time hiding this terrible secret from the world.

''Tell me about the Brooke School,'' I said.

She looked startled.

''How do you know about that?''

''I know everything,'' I lied.

''He raped a girl there. A thirteen-year-old student. His father paid off the parents and the head of the school to cover it up.''

''And all his top honors there?''

''His father again. Michael could barely comprehend anything he read. But the old man wouldn't accept that—so he made everything conform to his image of his son.''

''The same with Harvard? And the heroism in Vietnam?''

''Uh-huh. You can do a lot of things with money.''

''So he kept getting worse,'' I said.

''That's right. Little by little, day by day. By the time he got to Congress, he was in pretty bad shape. He would constantly erupt into tantrums, rages—it was frightening. He'd smash things in the house, in his office. A few times he came after me. And once . . . once he tried to hit Kathy. He was kicking and pummeling her until . . . until Tom Sewell and some of the others managed to pull him off her.

''I tried to talk to his father about it. Everyone did. But the old man still wouldn't listen. It was as if he found it shameful, embarrassing to himself. As if he had failed somehow as a father. And a Kerrigan never failed. So he just shut it out and pushed on as if nothing were wrong.''

Mrs. Wincott sighed. ''It was obvious something was going to have to happen. And it did. That's when Carla came along.''

''Carla? Is that Vincent Delvecchio's wife?''

Mrs. Wincott nodded. ''She claimed Michael raped her. He says she came on to him. Not that it mattered to Delvecchio. His honor was at stake. So his wife had to die. And Michael . . .

well, Delvecchio wanted to kill him, too. But the old man worked out this deal. You see the two of them had done a lot of business together, made a lot of money. And there was this big Congressional investigation going on into their dealings. Tom Kerrigan had bought off the chairman of the committee and gotten Michael on the panel, too. The two of them—he and Delvecchio—needed each other. For protection. If one went down, he'd pull the other one down with him.

"So they worked out a deal. The old man told Delvecchio Michael was sick and needed to be committed to an institution. It would be the same as killing him, he said. He would disappear forever. Delvecchio agreed, as long as Michael remained there for the rest of his life."

Of course, I thought. That's why the mob was so interested when I broke the story about Kathy asking questions about him. And why they picked him up off the street after I went on the air with the homeless person angle.

"The only problem," Mrs. Wincott said, "was that a Kerrigan could never admit that his son was in a mental institution. So his father made up this story about him dying at sea and we all stuck to it."

"For all these years?"

"Sure. After a while it became easy. I mean he really was the same as being dead. And life went on. I got married again. Kathy grew up. And we all forgot about Michael. Or almost . . ."

She looked down at the coffee cup in her hand and then at the empty bourbon glass on the table. "I need a drink," she announced.

"Later," I said. "This won't take much longer. When did he get out?"

"Six months ago," she sighed. "Michael just got up one morning, left his room for a walk, and never came back again. No one knew what to do. I mean we couldn't get the police involved because he was supposed to be dead. . . ."

"And then things really got complicated. Kathy caught a glimpse of him on TV."

"Yes. It's kind of funny really, when you think about it. I mean we'd built him up so much over the years—her grandfather, me, Tom Sewell—that Kathy became obsessed with him. She really did think of him as this great man. Me, Jonathan—none of us measured up to her image of her father. So when she thought he was still alive . . ."

"She went looking for him."

"Yeah. Then everyone got excited. You. The mob. Tom Sewell." She shook her head. "What a mess. What do I do now?"

I stood up.

"You can start by telling your daughter the truth when she comes back," I said.

"I—I don't know . . . I mean how can I?"

"The truth is always the best way," I said.

She stared down again at the empty bourbon glass. As if she could find the answer there.

"Your daughter needs a mother, Mrs. Wincott," I said. "It's time for you to start being one. You owe her that much."

"I—I—I . . ."

"Get some professional help for yourself. Deal with your drinking. Somebody's going to have to put the pieces of this family back together when this is over."

"But when the truth comes out, it'll all be over. My husband's chances for the White House. The Kerrigan family name . . ."

"I don't give a damn about your husband's political career," I said. "I don't give a damn about about the Kerrigan family image. I do care about Kathy. And I think you do, too. That's why you talked to me that first day."

"But . . . but my daughter hates me."

"I don't think so."

"She'll hate me even more when she hears all this."

"Give her a chance, Mrs. Wincott."

She looked up at me. Her eyes were red. "A chance?"

"Give her a chance to love you."

I rode the elevator down to the lobby, said good-bye to the doorman for the last time, and called Gergen from a pay phone on the street.

"Stop the presses!" I said. "I've got the lead story."

"You stop the presses at a newspaper, not a TV station, Jenny. We use videotape, remember?"

"Okay, then stop the videotape. This is really hot, Joe."

"I've already got a hot story."

"What?"

"Two murder suspects grabbed a guard at the courthouse in downtown Manhattan. Took his gun and are holding him hostage. They're holding off an army of cops."

"Okay, but—"

"Wait, there's more. The prisoners asked for a media representative to come inside and listen to their demands. Cassie White volunteered. She's inside with them now."

"Jesus."

"Yeah."

"I thought you told her not to do that kind of stuff."

"I did. She doesn't listen. So you still think you've got something hotter than that?"

"Hold on to your hat," I said.

I told him the whole thing. At first, he didn't believe me. But when I told him about the film of Michael Kerrigan at the institution and my interview with Audrey Wincott, he was ecstatic.

"That's not just a lead story," he said. "That's a fuckin' career maker."

"I know."

"Grab a cab and get in here as fast as you can."

The cab ride took me through the downtown area, near Foley Square, where all the courthouses are. I heard sirens in the distance and saw police cars speeding by.

The hostage job, I thought. Poor Cassie. Her big exclusive was going to be overshadowed by me today. A few days ago, I would have been delighted by that. Now I felt for her.

When I got to the station, I made sure the videotape from Fairview was ready to go on the air, wrote up my copy, then got made up for the show. At 5:55, five minutes before air time, I walked into the studio.

It was a madhouse.

"We're going to do Jenny first," Gergen was saying. "It's

gonna be big. Real big. Channel Six world exclusive—the whole bit. Let's pull out all the stops.''

Everyone nodded.

"Then we're going to a live feed from Cassie White inside the courthouse.''

"Has anyone heard from Cassie?'' Carstairs asked.

"Not recently.''

"What the hell is recently?''

"Maybe forty minutes ago. . . .''

"Jesus Christ,'' Gergen screamed. "What's she doing?''

"She is a little busy,'' I pointed out. "She's in the middle of a hostage drama. It is a real exclusive.''

"Well, it's not going to do us a damn bit of good if we can't get it on the air,'' Gergen snapped.

"We're going to need a fill. A holding story to go with until Cassie is ready.''

The telephone rang. It was the hot line—the one crews on the street use to call on big breaking stories.

"That's her! I know it!'' Gergen shouted.

He grabbed for the phone.

"Yeah, Gergen here. Go.''

He listened for a second. There was a strange look on his face.

"Say that again?''

We all waited.

"You're sure about that?''

He put down the receiver silently. Then he sat down.

"Was that Cassie?'' Carstairs asked.

He shook his head.

"Where is Cassie?''

No reply.

"Joe, what happened?''

The clock now read 5:57. Three minutes to go.

"There was a shootout at the court,'' Gergen said softly.

"Is Cassie all right? I mean was that her on the phone?''

He shook his head.

"Cassie's dead,'' he said.

30

It's 6:00 P.M., Here's What's Happening

It was 5:58.

Two minutes until air time. No one seemed to care. We all sat there without moving, trying to take in what we'd just heard. This can't be true, I thought. Death isn't real. It's just something we talk about every night that happens to other people so we can put on a news show. But it can't happen to us. We're the news.

I looked up at the clock again. Now it was 5:59.

"What do we do?" I said to Carstairs and Gergen.

Carstairs looked confused. His lip trembled and there was a twitch under his right eye. He didn't answer me.

Gergen took over.

"Conroy," he said, turning to the anchor, "it's up to you."

"Me?"

"We'll go to you first, and you'll just do the story of Cassie's death. Do it like any other story. It's news. We cover news. That's all we can do."

"But—but," he said, pointing to the teleprompter, "that copy isn't any good anymore, is it?"

"Of course not," Gergen told him.

"Will there be new copy?" he asked hopefully.

Gergen shook his head. "There's no time for that. You'll just have to wing it."

"W—w—wing it?"

"Ad lib. Do it off the top of your head. Say what you feel, Conroy."

"Maybe if somebody wrote something up real fast—"

It was six o'clock now. The theme music came on.

"There's no time," Gergen yelled. "Now get out there."

Conroy took his place in the anchor's chair as the announcer's voice boomed:

It's the News at Six on Six—with the WTBK team of newsbreakers.

Conroy Jackson at the anchor desk, Bill Hanrahan on sports, Larry Travers with the weather, and Jenny McKay covering the celebrity scene.

And now—here's Conroy with the news:

We sat there and waited to see what Conroy would say.

And waited.

And waited.

"Jesus Christ, he's freezing!" Gergen said.

Sure enough, Conroy Jackson sat immobile as a statue, staring speechlessly at the camera.

The director looked around frantically at Carstairs. "What do we do?"

Carstairs seemed frozen himself.

"Bob? Do something!"

"I don't know . . . I mean I never—"

Gergen suddenly jumped in.

"Go to black!" he yelled.

"What?"

"Get us off the air now!"

"We can't go off the air in the middle of a newscast," the production guy said.

"Do it!" Gergen screamed. "Just take us to black. Now."

The guy looked dubious. He looked to Carstairs for another opinion, but Carstairs still wasn't saying anything. Finally he just shrugged and gave the order to go to black. The monitor in the studio suddenly went dark.

"Okay, we're off the air. Now what?"

Gergen turned to me.

"Jenny, get out there."

"Me?"

"Yeah. You can do it. Remember Joseph Leone?"

I nodded. Joseph Leone was a New York City crime boss who was gunned down one day in the middle of a Columbus Day rally. I was standing about five feet away from him when it happened. The paper I was working for had afternoon editions, and we only had ten minutes to make the Late Extra. So I dictated the whole thing off the top of my head, as I stood there with cops and medical people frantically converging on the wounded mobster a few feet away.

"Just do the same thing," Gergen was saying. "Tell the story. Straight. Dramatically. The way you feel it. Forget about the camera. You're just telling one person about something you saw. Got it?"

I nodded. "I think so."

"Okay," he said. "Jenny, this is the last decision I may ever make in this business. It would be nice if you could make me look good."

I walked slowly onto the news set, sat down, and pinned a microphone to the lapel of my WTBK blazer. Conroy Jackson looked at me, but it didn't seem to register. I wondered if he even understood we were off the air.

"Everyone ready?" the director yelled.

I nodded.

"Okay—we're going back on the air."

The monitors came back on.

ANNOUNCER: WTBK has experienced some technical difficulties. We apologize for the delay. And now—here's Jenny McKay with the news.

I looked at the camera. The red light was on. Show time.

McKAY: Good evening, ladies and gentlemen, here's what's happening.

The camera's eye stared back at me. There were probably a million people out there watching me. But I tried not to think about that. Just tell the story.

McKAY: Cassie White, this station's newswoman and co-anchor, was killed this evening.

It happened only minutes ago during a hostage standoff at the Criminal Courthouse in lower Manhattan.

Details are sketchy, but here's what is known at the moment.

The camera cut to a picture of the hostage scene.

McKAY: At 1:40 this afternoon two convicts being brought to the facility on Centre Street overpowered a guard and took his gun.

They then made a series of demands—asking for such things as food, money, a police escort out of the area, and a plane to take them to a Third World country.

The standoff continued all afternoon until shortly before 5:00 P.M., when they asked to present their demands to a member of the media.

Cassie White volunteered for that assignment.

A production assistant handed me a piece of paper. I scanned it quickly, then looked up again at the camera.

McKAY: We now have some more details on what happened this evening in downtown Manhattan.

As the negotiations were proceeding through the afternoon, observers say the two convicts became more tense and edgy. They began making threats. The police hostage negotiating team tried to defuse the situation as best it could, but . . .

My eyes were becoming moist. I wiped them quickly with my hand.

McKAY: It appears that a little after five o'clock a truck on Centre Street made a loud backfiring noise. Police now believe this is what panicked the gunmen. They believed they were being shot at, and began shooting themselves. Police returned the fire, wounding one and killing the other.

Cassie White died during that cross fire.

It's unclear whether she was hit by a police bullet or by one from the gunmen.

The guard who was being held hostage escaped unharmed.

Another piece of paper was handed to me. It was a bio on Cassie White, from the WTBK personnel department.

McKAY: Cassie White had been a newswoman at this station for a little more than ten months.

During this time she covered such stories as . . .

While I talked a picture of Cassie appeared on the screen. When I was finished with her biography, I looked into the camera again. Just say what you feel, Gergen said.

McKAY: I'd like to add a personal note here.

Today I had what I thought was a really hot story. I figured it would lead off this newscast, and I was happy about that. But I was wrong. You can never predict the news. Things happen all the time. Some of them are good, some bad. That's what occurred here today. So my story—no matter how sensational—wasn't the biggest news story in town.

Cassie White is.

I paused. My eyes were getting moist again.

McKAY: Wherever Cassie is, I think she'd like that.

I was starting to cry now. I could feel tears trickling down my face.

McKAY: For a long time I didn't know Cassie very well. I mean we worked together. We covered the news together. But I didn't really know Cassie as a person.

That changed before she died, and I'm glad.

More tears. I wondered if I could make it through this.

McKAY: Cassie White was my friend. I'll miss her.

I looked around the studio. Everyone was staring at me with frozen expressions on their faces. No one moved. No one said anything. Then some of them started crying, too.

McKAY: We'll all miss her.

There was a long pause, and then Gergen signaled me to go to a break.

McKAY: We'll be back—with the rest of the news—after these words. . . .

The screen went to a commercial. On the studio monitor a woman was demonstrating why one brand of paper towel was stronger than another. "Try the test at home yourself . . ." she was saying. I lay my head down on the desk. Gergen came over and put his arm around me.

"Sorry, Joe," I said, wiping my eyes. "I never cried on camera before."

"You were terrific," he said softly.

Other people then began coming over and shaking my hand, patting me on the back, and telling me how moving it was. Hanrahan. Travers. Sanders. Even Carstairs.

But the biggest surprise was Artie Jacobson.

He'd been sitting off in a corner of the studio, doing his crossword puzzle as usual. Now he put the paper down and walked over.

"Hey, McKay."

"Yeah, Artie?"

He took my hand and shook it.

"That was a helluva job," he said. "Really incredible. Best thing I've ever seen in all my years in the business."

Then he went back to his seat, picked up his newspaper again, and went back to the crossword puzzle.

Now that's high praise indeed.

Then the last commercial ended. A woman wearing designer jeans faded from the screen and the camera came back to me. The red light was on again. The show must go on.

McKAY: In other news tonight, there's been a stunning development in the ongoing saga of the Kerrigan family. Channel Six has learned exclusively that Michael Kerrigan, the ex-congressman long believed killed in a boating accident, is really . . .

Update

I sat down the other day and made a list of one hundred things I'd like to accomplish in the next thirty-five or so years of my life.

The idea came from a story I read about Lou Holtz, the Notre Dame football coach. He did it once when he'd just been fired from a job. He thought it would give some vision to his life, some structure, some goals to shoot for. At last count, he'd accomplished fifty-seven of the one hundred items—including appearing on the Johnny Carson show and having dinner at the White House.

Most of my goals were a little more modest. Make it down to 110 pounds. Buy all my Christmas presents before December 24 just once. Learn how to ski.

Some were admittedly in the fantasy category. Win (A) a news Emmy or (B) a Pulitzer, either one would do. Win a million dollars in the lottery. Have sex with Bruce Springsteen and Tom Cruise at the same time. You know, that sort of thing.

And then there were some things on the list that even surprised me. Get married. Live in a real house with a yard and garden. And—hold on to your hats for this one—have a baby.

Yeah, that's right. Me. Thinking about being a mother. Pretty awesome thought, huh? I mean I don't know for sure if that's what I want. But on the other hand I'm not sure I don't want it either. Clear enough? Well, probably not. About the only thing that is clear about it is I don't have thirty-five years to accomplish that one. Not with the old biological clock ticking away inside.

That's the worst thing about turning forty. I mean it doesn't stop here. In five years I'll be forty-five. In ten years fifty.

Fifty.

The big fifty.

The half-century mark.

Only a short decade away from sixty.

Now *that's* going to be a real crisis.

Carstairs called me in the other day to discuss my future.

"Andrew Cafferty and I have talked, and we've come to a decision," he said. "We want you to stay with us, Jenny. We want to give you a new contract."

I was sort of expecting that after everything that happened.

"But in a new role."

"Huh?"

"We want you to be the anchor of the show."

I wasn't expecting that.

"You showed us something in the past few days, Jenny. Something I hadn't seen in you before. You connected with the audience. I think you've got a big future in this business. What do you say?"

"I'm not sure."

"There's a lot more money for being an anchor. I think I can swing a six-figure salary."

"It's not that," I said quietly.

"What then?"

"I don't know . . ." I hesitated. "I'm just not sure I want to do this anymore. I used to think that covering the news was the most important thing in the world. Now I'm not so certain. I've just seen two people give up their lives for it—Cassie's dead and Joe Gergen's too sick to keep going anymore. It makes me think—maybe the news isn't that important. Maybe there's more to life than the view I've been seeing from behind a press badge all these years. I'd like to find out.''

Carstairs made a face. "You're a newswoman, Jenny. You live and breathe it every day. That's what you do. You've always done it and you always will.''

"Maybe," I said.

"Are you saying you don't want the anchor job?''

"I'll think about it," I told him.

Bill Rohr called to tell me the *Washington Post* job was mine if I wanted it.

"It's a real cushy deal," he said. "The life-style section. Long, leisurely features. Personality pieces. Trends. No more chasing around the street after fire trucks.''

"Sounds good.''

"Washington's a nice place, too. A lot more livable than New York.''

"New York's not that bad," I said.

"C'mon, get serious. Anyway, what do you say? You want the job?''

"Let me think about it.''

Dave Paxton said he wants to marry me.

"I'm leaving Senator Wincott," he told me as we lay in bed after making love. He smiled. "Thanks to you, there's not much future there.

"I've got an offer to be chief of staff for Senator Endicott from California. He's a real comer in Washington and it's more money. So I figure it's time to get my life back in order, settle down with the right woman (he squeezed my hand), and feel like a family man again.''

"Family?''

"Look, Jenny, I'm not going to force you to have a baby if you don't want one. If the family is just you and me, that's okay too.''

I thought about my list. "I might want a baby.''

"No kidding? Hey, that would be great! Now the only problem is our two careers. Once we get married, you'd have to move to Washington for us to be together.''

I mentioned my job offer from the *Washington Post*.

"All right!" he said. He punched the air in celebration with his fist. "That's terrific!"

"On the other hand, I could stay here and be the anchor on the Channel Six news."

Now he frowned. "You in New York and me in Washington. It's tough to make a marriage like that work."

"Connie Chung and Maury Povich did it," I said.

"I want a real life, Jenny. A house. A garden. Someone else there to share it with when I come home at night."

"Me too."

"So take the *Washington Post* job. That's the sensible thing to do."

It did make sense. Perfect sense. Only . . .

"I'm not sure if I'm ready for marriage yet," I said.

"Not ready? Jenny, people get married in their teens. You're forty years old for God's sake."

"You're only as old as you feel," I told him.

"What the hell does that mean?"

"I don't know," I admitted.

"Jenny, do you want to get married or not?"

"I've got to think about it," I said.

I do my best thinking while watching late-night TV with a big bowl of buttered popcorn in front of me. That's what I was doing when there was a knock on my door. Hobo barked at the sound. But he stopped when he saw who it was. Kathy Kerrigan.

"Hi. I just went out for a walk and wound up in your neighborhood. It's not too late, is it?"

I looked at my watch. It was past midnight. Just out walking and happened to be in the neighborhood? Well, okay.

"No problem. C'mon in."

We went into the living room and sat down. Hobo, who had declared her a friend, leaped into her lap and rolled over on his back.

"I didn't just happen to go out for a walk and wind up here," she said.

"I figured that. Especially since you live about sixty blocks away."

"I need to work out some stuff."

"How're things at home?"

"Not terrible. My stepfather and I had this long talk. I think his political career is over, but it seems to have made him a more real person. Maybe I've never given him a chance. And my mom—well, she's started going for counseling. I mean, she's really trying, for the first time."

"That's good," I said. "How about Brad what's-his-name? Your fiancé."

"I told him I didn't want to marry him."

"Probably a good decision."

"The engagement was a mistake all along. I know that now. It was an easy way out. You can't get married until you figure out for yourself what you want out of life."

"Amen," I said.

I thought about Dave Paxton. She could have been talking about me, too.

"I went to see my father today for the first time," she said. "Up at Fairview."

"What happened?"

"Nothing."

She looked down at Hobo and stopped scratching him. His tail thumped furiously on her lap. She started up again.

"He didn't know me," she said. "I could have been from the moon for all he knew."

I nodded. "Look, I know how that must hurt."

She shrugged. "It's okay."

"You don't have to hide it if you—"

"Honest, I was ready for it." She paused. "Listen, do you think I could stay here tonight?"

"Here?"

"Yeah, I just don't have it in me to go home."

"Sure. If that's what you want."

We talked for a while more, maybe an hour or so, and then she went into my bedroom to go to sleep. I fixed up the couch for myself, nibbled on some more popcorn, and watched TV. A Perry Mason rerun was on. I fell asleep just before he got the real murderer to confess.

It was later, I don't know how much later, when something woke me. I got up with a start and listened. It was crying.

Coming from the bedroom. I went in and sat down on the bed beside Kathy.

She was weeping uncontrollably.

"It was so horrible," she sobbed.

"I understand . . ."

"He didn't know me at all. I'm his daughter and he doesn't know it."

I learned forward and held her hand.

"I feel so stupid," she said. "All those years I spent grieving for him. All the time I spent looking for him." She slammed her free hand into the pillow. "And he fuckin' doesn't even know who I am."

She cried for a while longer, then finally fell back into a fitful sleep. But about thirty minutes later, she woke up and started crying again. It went on that way for the rest of the night.

I stayed there beside her—holding her hand—until dawn broke and the first rays of sunlight began streaming in through the bedroom window.

I was standing in front of the WTBK building when the urge came over me again.

One more try for the old Mary Tyler Moore bit. My hat was in my right hand. I heaved it skyward.

"You're gonna make it after all," I sang.

This time the ascent was straighter. So was the descent. I staggered around under it and it landed right in my hand and I brought it up in one big sweeping motion and . . . and at the last second it slipped off the side of my head.

From behind me I heard more laughter. It was the same security guard as before.

"Too bad," he said.

"Why?"

"You missed it again."

I smiled and gave him a wink.

"Yeah," I told him, "but I'm getting closer."

The radio in the mobile van came alive and crackled a message.

''We've got a jumper on the Fifty-ninth Street Bridge,'' Carstairs said. ''Emergency Service Units are converging on the scene right now. Where're you at, Jenny?''

We were at 42nd and Park. On our way to a press conference at Sak's with Liz Taylor for a new perfume she was marketing.

''Can you take a look at the jumper?'' Carstairs was asking. I checked the time: 11:30. Liz was supposed to show at noon.

''Yeah, we'll take it,'' I said into the microphone.

I turned to Sanders who was driving.

''Fifty-ninth Street Bridge. Jumper.''

''All right!'' he said. Sanders hated the Liz Taylor assignment.

''I told Carstairs we can do it,'' I said. ''Can we?''

''I've got my pedal to the metal, baby. Watch our smoke.''

We raced uptown through the city streets. Weaving in and out of cars, taxis, and buses at sixty mph. Manhattan buildings flew by like fenceposts outside our window. At 50th Street we picked up a police escort. A blue-and-white with flashing sirens headed to the scene. Sanders maneuvered right behind him and followed him the rest of the way to 59th Street.

I jumped out of the van and began running for the bridge. My press card dangled around my neck. Sanders and Jacobson were right behind me with the camera.

The police had set up barricades to keep back the crowds. A cop standing there tried to stop me.

''Jenny McKay, Channel Six News,'' I yelled.

He waved me through.

I felt the adrenaline flowing through me now. The way it always did on a story. It was almost like a drug. Or like sex. Or like a great meal.

And that's when I knew.

I knew what I was going to do.

I looked around and took it all in. The sirens. The flashing lights. The people straining forward to get a better look at what was happening.

''Hey, isn't that Jenny McKay?'' someone in the crowd yelled. ''She's on the news.''

God help me, I still love it.